"Dinner with Me."

Whatever reservations that were left in Jillian's mind were banished by the warmth in his eyes. If he wanted more than her company, she decided, she would deal with that as it happened. As the plane jounced onto the runway, she grinned at him. "Count, I'd love to have dinner with you."

He took her hand in his and carried it to his lips. "Dinner with me," he echoed her, "dinner with me."

There was a secret meaning in the soft words that followed, almost lost in the shrieking of the engines.

"I will hold you to that, Jillian Walker. Believe this."

THE SAINT-GERMAIN CHRONICLES

Chelsea Quinn Yarbro

A TIMESCAPE BOOK
PUBLISHED BY POCKET BOOKS NEW YORK

Another *Original* publication of TIMESCAPE BOOKS

A Timescape Book published by
POCKET BOOKS, a Simon & Schuster division of
GULF & WESTERN CORPORATION
1230 Avenue of the Americas, New York, N.Y. 10020

ISBN: 0-671-45903-1

First Timescape Books printing May, 1983

10 9 8 7 6 5 4 3 2 1

Printed in the U.S.A.

Acknowledgments

"Art Songs," Copyright © 1981 by Chelsea Quinn Yarbro. From the 7th World Fantasy Convention program book, Jack Rems and Jeffrey Frane, editors, California.

"Cabin 33," Copyright © 1980 by Chelsea Quinn Yarbro. From SHADOWS 3, Charles L. Grant, editor, Doubleday.

"Renewal," Copyright © 1982 by Chelsea Quinn Yarbro. From SHADOWS 5, Charles L. Grant, editor, Doubleday.

"Seat Partner," Copyright © 1979 by Chelsea Quinn Yarbro. From NIGHTMARES, Charles L. Grant, editor, Playboy Press.

"The Spider Glass," Copyright © 1981 by Chelsea Quinn Yarbro. From SHADOWS 4, Charles L. Grant, editor, Doubleday.

Contents

Text of a letter from le Comte de Saint-Germain to Madelaine de Montalia.

Sassevert Parc
Lausanne, Suisse
3 November, 1889

Monbussy
Nr. Chalons-sur-Marne
France

My dearest Madelaine;

*I read your name and my mind is filled with you,
my heart. I am sorry not to be with you on this day—
on all days. But the earrings that come with this letter
will remind you of my love and for a time that will
have to serve.*

*You tell me that you are distressed that Paul has
decided to marry that Swedish woman. And you want
to be revenged on them for the hurt they have given
you. No, oh, no, Madelaine. It is not good to feel this
way, believe me. Profit from my mistakes, and forgive
them. Not everyone can sustain love as we can. They
have so little time, and we have so much. You once
railed at the shortness of the years, before you came
to my life. What is a decade to you, now? Or a century? And what is it to them. Recall, my heart, that
most of those who love us do so because they cannot
love as they wish to and we offer them empathy and
our special consolation. I do not say this cynically:
remember that it took me almost four thousand years
to find you, and even now we cannot love as we
would want. Leave Paul to his Swedish woman and
let him believe that vampires are myths to frighten
children and those who read Hoffmann and Polidori.*

*Yes, I think it would be wise for you to leave Mon-
bussy for a time. The expedition to Babylon should
intrigue you. You are right to deplore most of the*

11

practices of those digging up artifacts. They are anxious to bring up wonders and in the process destroy greater treasures. Time is your great asset, as you will learn. When you return to France, you may become your own niece or granddaughter or any other appropriate fiction.

It is time for me to travel as well; I have been here almost fifteen years. My country house in England will provide me an interlude of quiet, but I do not think it would be wise to remain there long. Paris, Lausanne, Madrid, all of them are too familiar to me. So perhaps I will go to Stockholm, or Warsaw or St. Petersburg. Wherever I am, I will send you word where you will reach me. If ever you require my aid, or my company, you have only to tell me and I will come to you.

You must not lose your courage. Love that can embrace our secret and our nature is rare, but it illuminates all of life. For it is life, Madelaine, in spite of our deaths. Believe this, for I assure you, I promise you, it is true, as it is true that I love you, will always love you.

Saint-Germain
his seal, the eclipse

THE SPIDER GLASS

An Edwardian Story

"THERE is a curious tale behind this mirror, actually. I'm pleased you noticed it," their host said to the select and exclusively masculine company that had gathered in the Oak Parlor at Briarcopse after dinner. He reached for the port to refill his glass and rather grandly offer it around. "Surely you'll have some. It was laid down the year I was born—splendid stuff. My father was quite the expert in these matters, I assure you."

Five of his guests accepted with alacrity; the sixth declined with a polite, Continental bow, and the Earl put the decanter back on the silver tray set out on the gleaming mahogany table. "Don't stand on ceremony, any of you," he said with a negligent wave of his long, thin hand. He then settled back in his chair, a high-backed, scallop-topped relic of the reign of Queen Anne and propped his heels on the heavy Tudor settle before the fire. Slowly he lit his cigar, savoring its aroma as well as the anticipation of his guests.

"For the lord Harry, Whittenfield . . ." the rotund gentleman with the brindled mutton-chop whiskers protested, though his indignation was marred by an indulgent smirk.

Their host, Charles Whittenfield, ninth Earl of Copsehowe, blew out a cloud of fragrant, rum-soaked tobacco smoke, and stared at the small dull mirror in its frame of tooled Baroque silver. "It *is* a curious tale," he said again, as much to himself as any of the company. Then recalling

13

his guests, he directed his gaze at his wiry, middle-aged cousin who was in the act of warming his brandy over one of the candles. "Dominick, you remember my mother's aunt Serena, don't you?"

"I remember all the women on that side of the family," Dominick said promptly. "The most amazing passel of females. My mother refuses to mention half of them—she feels they aren't respectable. Well, of course they're not. Respectable women are boring."

"Yes, I'm always amazed by them. And why they all chose to marry such sticks-in-the-mud as they did, I will never understand. Still, they make the family lively, which is more than I can say for the males. Not a privateer or adventurer among them. Nothing but solid, land-loving, rich, placid countrymen, with a yen for wild girls." He sighed. "Anyway, Dominick, great-aunt Serena . . ."

Dominick nodded with vigorous distaste that concealed a curious pride. "Most misnamed female I ever encountered. That whole side of the family, as Charles says . . . they marry the most unlikely women. Serena came from Huguenot stock, back in the middle of the seventeenth century, I think." He added this last as if the Huguenot influence explained matters.

"Ah, yes, great-aunt Serena was quite a handful," the host laughed quietly. "The last time I saw her—it was years ago, of course—she was careering about the Cotswolds on both sides of her horse. The whole countryside was scandalized. They barred her from the Hunt, naturally, which amused her a great deal. She could outride most of them, anyway, and said that the sport was becoming tame."

"Whittenfield . . ." the rotund man said warningly.

"Oh, yes, about the glass." He sipped his port thoughtfully. "The glass comes from Serena's family, the English side. It's an heirloom, of course. They say that the Huguenot who married into the family took the woman because no one else would have her. Scandal again." Again he paused to take wine, and drained his glass before continuing. "The mirror is said to be Venetian, about three hundred forty-or-fifty years old. The frame was added later, and when Marsden appraised it, he said he believed it to be Austrian work."

"Hungarian, actually," murmured the sixth guest, though no one heard him speak.

"Yes, well." Whittenfield judiciously filled his glass once

14

more. "Really wonderful," he breathed as he savored the port.

"Charles, you should have been an actor—you're wasted on the peerage," Dominick said as he took a seat near the fire.

"Oh, very well. I'll get on with it," Whittenfield said, capitulating. "I've told you the glass is Venetian and that it is something over three hundred years old. The latest date Marsden ventured was 1570, but that, as I say, is problematical. In any case, you may be certain that it was around in 1610, which is the critical year, so far as the story is concerned. Yes, 1610." He sank back in his chair, braced his heels once more on the Tudor settle, and began, at last, in earnest.

"Doubtless you're aware that Europe was a great deal more chaotic then than it is now . . ."

"That's not saying much," the rotund man interjected.

"Twilford, for God's sake, don't give him an excuse to digress again," Dominick whispered furiously.

"*As* I was saying," Charles went on, "Europe was doing very badly in 1610. That was the year that Henri IV of France was assassinated and his nine-year-old son succeeded him, and you know what Louis XIII turned out like! James was making an ass of himself by prolonging Parliament and by locking up Arabella Stuart for marrying William Seymour. One of the Tsars was deposed, but I can never keep them straight, and I believe a Prussian prince was offered the job . . ."

"Polish," the sixth guest corrected him politely. "Vasili Shuisky was deposed in favor of Vladislav, Sigismund III's son."

"Very likely," Whittenfield agreed. "Spain and Holland were having a not-very-successful go at a truce. The German Protestant States were being harried by their neighbors . . . That will give you some idea. Well, it happened that my great-aunt Serena's nine times great-grandmother was living . . ."

"Charles," Twilford protested, "you can't be serious. Nine times great-grandmother!"

"Of course I am," Whittenfield said, astounded at being questioned. "Serena was born in 1817. Her mother, Eugeinia, was born in 1792. *Her* mother, Sophia, was born in 1774. Sophia's mother Elizabeth was born in 1742. Her mother, Cassandra, was born in 1726. Cassandra's mother was Amelia Joanna, and she was born in 1704 or 05,

15

there's some doubt about the actual date. There was flooding and fever that winter and they were not very careful with recording births. Amelia Joanna's mother, Margaret, was born in 1688. *Her* mother, Sophronia, was born in 1664 . . ."

"Just in time for the Plague and the Fire," Dominick put in.

"Yes, and only three of the family survived it: Sophronia, her mother, Hannah, and one son, William. Terrible names they gave females in those days. Anyway, William had four wives and eighteen children in his lifetime and Sophronia had six children and even Hannah remarried and had three more. Hannah's mother was Lucretia and she was born in 1629. Her mother, Cesily, was born in 1607, and it was *her* mother, Sabrina, that the story concerns. So you see, nine times great-grandmother of my great-aunt Serena." He gave a grin that managed to be smug and sheepish at once. "That Lucretia, now, she was a sad one—married off at thirteen to an old reprobate in his fifties who kept two mistresses in separate wings at his principal seat as well as having who knows how many doxies over the years. Lucretia turned nasty in her later life, they say, and there was an investigation over the death of her tirewoman, who apparently was beaten to death under mysterious circumstances. The judge in the case was Sir Egmont Hardie, and he . . ."

"Charles!" thundered his cousin.

Whittenfield coughed and turned his eyes toward the ceiling. "About Sabrina. Let me see. She was twenty in 1610, married to Captain Sir James Grossiter. Cesily was three and her boy, Herbert, was one. It is a little hard to tell about these things after so long, but apparently certain difficulties had arisen between Sabrina and her husband. Sir James had quarreled with his father when he had got into trouble with his commanding general, and had run off to the Continent, which was a damned silly thing to do, considering the times. He tried a little soldiering, which was the only thing he knew, and then got caught for some petty offense and was flung into gaol, leaving his wife with two children to feed and no one to help her, and in a foreign country, to boot."

"Well, she's not the first woman to earn her bread on her back, but I shouldn't think you'd bring it up . . ." one of the guests was heard to remark.

Whittenfield shook his head. "Most men prefer whores

16

who can speak to them, which Sabrina could not. And her children were inconvenient for such a profession. She knew some French and had been taught a few Italian songs as a child, but for the most part she was as good as mute." He drained his glass again. "She was greatly distraught, as you might suspect, and did not know which way to turn."

"That's a female for you," the same guest said, and the sixth guest turned to him.

"What makes you believe that a man in those circumstances would fare any better?" The sixth guest clearly did not expect an answer, and the man who had spoken glared at him.

Charles went on as if he had not heard. "She sold all that she and Sir James possessed, which was not much, and then she began to sell their clothes so that they had only what they wore on their backs, and that quickly became rags. However she was able to afford a few bits of food and to hire mean lodgings in a backstreet of Antwerp. By doing scullery work at a nearby inn, she got scraps to eat and enough to buy cabbages to boil for her babes. But it was inevitable that there come a time when she would not have enough money even for these inadequate things, and her children would have no shelter or food."

"What on earth has that to do with the glass?" Twilford asked, blustering to conceal his perplexity.

"I'm coming to that," Charles Whittenfield said with a great show of patience. "If you'll let me do it in my own way."

"Well, I don't see how we can stop you," muttered an older man sitting in the corner hunched over his pipe.

"Everard, please," Dominick put in imperiously.

The older man gave Dominick a contemptuous glare. "No manners these days. None at all."

"Pray go on," said the sixth guest in slightly accented English. It might have been because he was the only one not drinking that his clothes were the neatest and most elegant of any man's in the room.

"I intend to," Whittenfield said to his guests. "As I've intimated, my many-times-great-aunt Sabrina was stranded in Antwerp because Sir James was in prison and she was destitute. She had been cast out by her family when she had elected to follow her husband to the Continent, so she could not turn to them for relief, not that she was the sort who would have, in any case. Of course, Sir James' family had washed their hands of him some years before and

17

would have nothing to do with him or any of his. Sabrina could play the virginals and had a fair knowledge of botany, as many well-bred women did in those days, but those were the limits of her skills. Yet she must have had courage for all of that, because she did not despair, or if she did, she conquered it. She was determined to keep her children with her, as the alternative was giving them to the care of nuns, and being a good English churchwoman, she could not bear to surrender her unprotected babes to Roman Catholics." He recrossed his legs. "My uncle George married a Roman Catholic, you know. There was the most frightful uproar and dire predictions, but Clara has shown herself to be a most reasonable woman and a truly excellent wife. No trouble there, I assure you. So all those warnings came to naught."

"The glass, Charles, the glass," Twilford insisted.

"I'm coming to that," the young peer protested with mock dismay. "You've no patience—positively you haven't a jot." He held out his glass for refilling as Everard helped himself to the port. "So," he resumed after an appreciative moment, "I trust I've made her predicament clear to you. Her husband was in prison, she had no one to turn to, her children as well as herself were in real danger of starvation, she was living in the poorest part of the city in a low-ceilinged garret in a house that should have been pulled down before the Plantaganets fell. There was no reason for her to hope for anything but an early grave in Potter's Field."

"Yes, yes, yes," Dominick interrupted. "Very touching plight. But as her daughter had a daughter we must assume that all was not lost, at least not then." He splashed a bit more brandy into his snifter and lit up another cigar.

"Well, Charles, what happened?" Everard demanded. "Did she catch the eye of an Earl traveling for pleasure, or did some other person come to her aid?"

"Not quite that," Whittenfield conceded. "Not a traveling Earl in any case, but a traveling Count."

"Same thing," Dominick scoffed.

"He was, as you perceive from the title, a foreigner," Charles persisted. "He had arrived in Antwerp from Ghent some time before and had purchased one of the buildings not far from where Sabrina lived in terrible squalor."

"And he gave her the mirror for primping," Everard finished. "There's nothing very mysterious about that."

"Now, that's the odd part of it," Whittenfield said lean-

18

ing forward as he spoke. "He didn't give it to her, she bought it for herself." He did not wait for his listeners to exclaim at this, but went on at once. "But that comes later in the story. Let me tell it as it must be told." He puffed his cigar once and set it aside again. "She became acquainted with this foreigner through an act of theft."

"What could anyone steal from her?" Twilford asked of the air.

"You don't understand—it was Sabrina who was the thief."

The reaction ranged from guffaws to shock; the sixth guest gave a small, wry smile and said nothing.

"Yes, she had decided to steal money so that she and her children could eat that night. You must understand that she had not stolen before and she knew that the penalties for it were quite harsh, but she had come to believe that she had no other choice. It was late in the afternoon when she saw this foreigner come to his house, and she determined to wait for him and accost him as he came out. She thought that since the man was not a native of the place, he might be reluctant to complain to the authorities, and of course, since he was foreign, he was regarded with a degree of dislike throughout the neighborhood."

Everard shook his head. "Sounds like a rackety thing to do."

"It was better than starving," said the sixth guest.

The other man with the pipe coughed and made a gruff protest. "But what is the point of all this, Whittenfield? Get on with it, man."

"Lord Graveston, you are trying to rush me," Whittenfield said with the slightest hint of a slur in his pronunciation. "That won't do. You'll have to listen, the same as the rest."

"Then stop this infernal dallying about," Lord Graveston said with considerable asperity. "At this rate, it will be time for breakfast before you're half done with your story, and we'll never know what the point of it is."

Whittenfield shrugged. "I don't see the virtue in haste when one is recounting the travail of a family member, but if you insist, then I will do my humble best . . ."

"For all the saints in hell, Charles . . ." Dominick expostulated.

"Very well," Whittenfield sighed lavishly. "Since you insist. As I told you, Sabrina conspired to set upon this foreigner and rob him so that she would have money for

19

food and lodging for her and her children. She went down the street at night, filled with terror but determined now on her course. There were beggars sleeping in doorways, and a few poxy whores plied their trade in this quarter, but most of the denizens of the night left her alone. She was an Englishwoman, don't you see, and isolated from them. It was a cold, raw night and her shawl did not keep her warm. Think of her predicament, gentlemen—is it surprising that she nearly turned back half a dozen times?"

"What's surprising is that she attempted it at all," Dominick said quietly. "Not that I approve of thieving, but in this case . . ."

"Precisely my point," Whittenfield burst out, the contents of his glass sloshing dangerously. "Most women would have not been able to do a damned thing, at least not any of the women I know. Sabrina, though, was most—unfeminine."

"Hardly that," murmured the sixth guest.

"She reached the house of the foreigner and slipped into the doorway of the shuttered baker's shop across the street, and set herself to wait for her prey to appear."

"How do you know that?" one of the guests interrupted. "How do you know that her shawl wasn't warm, or that there was a baker's shop where she could wait for the man?"

"I know," Whittenfield said with a faintly superior air, "because she kept a diary, and I've read it. She devoted a great many pages to this unfortunate time in her life. Her description of the rooms where she lived with her children almost make me itch, so deeply does she dwell on the filth and the vermin that lived there." He shuddered as proof of his revulsion.

"Well, you've got to expect that poor housing isn't going to be pleasant," Twilford observed, appealing to the others with a wave of his hand. "Some of the tenant farmers I've visited—appalling, that's what it is."

"Now who's digressing?" Whittenfield asked.

"Charles is right," Dominick admitted. "Let it keep, Twilford."

"Well, I only wanted to let you know that I had some comprehension of what . . ." Twilford began but was cut off.

"We can all agree that we're shocked by the reduced circumstances of your whatever-many-times-great-aunt," Lord Graveston said portentously. "Get on with it."

Whittenfield glared around the room to be certain that all his guests had given him their attention. All but one had. His sixth guest was staring at the spider glass with a bemused smile on his attractive, foreign face. Whittenfield cleared his throat and was rewarded by the sixth guest's reluctant attention.

"Pray forgive me," he said politely. "That glass . . ."

"Precisely," Whittenfield said. "That is why it has remained intact for so long, I am convinced. In any case, I was telling you about how Sabrina Grossiter came to try to rob this foreigner in Antwerp. She took up her post outside the baker's shop, hidden in the shadows, and waited for many long hours. She had thought that the foreigner used the house for romantic assignations, but that did not seem to be the case, for no woman came to the house, or man either, for that matter. Well after midnight a middle-aged man in servant's livery left the building, but the foreigner remained. It was cold, very cold and Sabrina's hands and feet were numb by the time she saw the lights in the upper windows go out. She hoped that the foreigner was going to leave so that she could at last try to take his purse. There was no one else on the street: even the beggars had found whatever shelter they could."

"Sounds a foolish thing to do, wait up half the night for a man to walk out of his house. Not very sensible of her." Twilford looked to the others to support him.

"All the women in our family are like that," Dominick said, at once proud and disgusted.

"She was desperate," the sixth guest said.

"In her journal," Whittenfield went on more sharply, "she remarks that it must have been an hour until dawn when the man came out. She did not remark him at first, because he was dressed all in black, and at night, in the shadow of the buildings, he was little more than another shadow."

"He was a knowing one," Lord Graveston said to the air. "Should stay away from such men, if I were her."

"But she didn't," Whittenfield put in, downing the last of his wine before going on. "She couldn't, you see. She says herself that hunger and worry had driven her slightly mad. She believed that there was no other course, but when she saw the man start away from the building, she all but failed. It was only the click of his heels on the pavement that alerted her to his departure. It may be that she dozed, though her journal insists that she did not. However it was,

21

she did not have quite the element of surprise she wished for and took after him, stumbling in the dark so that the foreigner turned and reached out a hand to her to keep her from falling."

"Did she abandon the idea of robbing him then?" Lord Graveston asked as he filled his pipe a second time.

"No," Whittenfield said with half a smile. "She thought this might be to her advantage, so she leaned up against the man and reached out for his belt. You know how they wore them then, over the padded doublet and a trifle below the waist in front? She thought she might be able to release the buckle and pull the whole belt away. Most men carried their purses on their belts in those times, and if she got the belt she would also have the purse."

"A clever woman," said Peter Hamworthy, who had been listening in silence. "Surprising she had so much gumption."

Whittenfield glanced over at the speaker. "Gracious, Peter, I thought you were asleep," he said with sarcastic sweetness.

"Not quite, merely dozing a bit," Hamworthy responded affably. "I'm finding your tale, though circuitous, interesting."

"You relieve me," Whittenfield said, then went on. "I've told you that it was a cold night, a very cold night, and that Sabrina's hands and feet were chilled. This probably accounted, at least in part, for her ineptness. She had not stolen before, and with her hands nearly blue with cold, she had little control of her fingers, which fumbled on the buckle. The foreigner seized her hands in his and held her securely."

"And then he called the Watch, and she was taken along to join her husband in gaol. And that still doesn't explain about the glass," Twilford said, exasperated.

"But he didn't summon the Watch," Whittenfield said slyly. "He held her hands and stared hard at her, and though it was deepest night, Sabrina said in her journal that she had the uneasy feeling that he could see her plainly. He demanded to know what she was about, in Dutch, of course."

"Of course," Dominick said as he refilled his glass and poured more port for his cousin.

"She does mention that he had an accent she could not place, but that is to be expected, since she had no more than a few words of the language herself. She tried to explain

22

that she had only fallen, but he did not believe her. He also realized that her native tongue was not Dutch, for he addressed her in French and German and then English, of which, Sabrina insists, he had fluent command." Whittenfield drank half of his port with the air of a man making a sacrifice.

"Go *on,* Charles!" Twilford bellowed.

"In good time; I must not abuse this wine." He drank again, less deeply, and set the glass down on the rolled arm of his chair where it balanced precariously. "So this foreigner discovered that she was English and upon learning that, asked to be told how she came to be in a backstreet in Antwerp. At first Sabrina refused to answer him, saying that it was her concern. He protested that since she had attempted to rob him, he was entitled to some explanation before he called in the authorities. It was that threat that caused her to tell him what had befallen her. At least that is what her journal says on the next day, though there are later entries that hint at other factors."

"What other factors?" Hamworthy spoke up. "Don't be mysterious, Charles. What factors are you talking about?"

Whittenfield lifted his wine and stared into its garnet-colored depths. His expression was slightly bemused. "Other factors—well, it's hard to know how much to believe, but this man was not what Sabrina had expected. She remarks, several days later, upon his kindness, which she first perceived that night. Apparently she held nothing back and out of caprice or compassion, he made a bargain with her."

"I can imagine the bargain," Twilford said, his tremendous sidewhiskers bristling like the jowls of a tomcat.

"No, you can't," Whittenfield corrected him mildly. "You know what most women, and men too, for that matter, would expect at such times. Yet that was not Sabrina's experience. She says in her journal that she wondered at first if he was one of those whose love is inverted, but it turned out otherwise. She made a bargain with this foreigner, as I say. She agreed to live in the house he had bought, to keep it for him. He did not object to her children and gave her permission to care for them as she felt best. He did not require them to serve him. . . ."

"Well, they were what, one and three? Hardly old enough to wait upon anyone, foreigner or not," Dominick pointed out.

"There was the matter of bonds," the sixth guest said quietly.

"Precisely," Whittenfield agreed. "And this foreigner did not require that Cesily and Herbert be bonded to him, which was something of a wonder in those times. Sabrina mentions in her journal that her employer's manservant told her that he had been a bondsman when his master first found him, and that he refused to continue the bond."

"One of those damned humanitarian sorts," Lord Graveston sighed portentously. "The world's full of 'em."

"Doubtless an opinion shared by the children of Whitechapel," the sixth guest commented without smiling.

"Terrible state of affairs, those slums," Dominick said indignantly. "Had to drive through there once—there'd been an accident and it was the only way around. There was the most appalling stench and the buildings looked to be held together by filth alone. The people—a complete want of conduct." Two of the other men nodded their understanding and disapproval. "One drab tired to climb into my carriage, and those who saw her make the attempt said such rude and licentious comments . . . The children were as bad as their seniors."

"This is hardly appropriate after-dinner conversation," Hamworthy opined.

"Very true," Whittenfield said smoothly. "My great-aunt's adventures with a foreigner are much more suitable." He drank down the last of his port and let the glass tip in his fingers. "Unless, of course, you're not interested in what became of her . . ."

"Oh, get on with it," Dominick said, nudging Everard with his elbow so that he would add his support.

Obediently Everard spoke up. "Yes, by all means, Charles, let's have the rest of the story."

"I still don't see how that bedeviled glass comes into it," Twilford muttered, dropping his chin forward.

"It *is* bedeviled, if Sabrina is to be believed," Charles said rather dreamily. "How aptly you put it, Twilford."

Lord Graveston coughed twice in an awesome way.

"Yes. Of course." Charles leaned forward in his chair and filled his glass. "I'll probably regret it in the morning, but for the present, this is precisely what's wanted." After he had settled back again and once more propped his heels on the settle, he resumed his story. "Well, as I said, Sabrina agreed to be the housekeeper to this foreigner in exchange for shelter and meals for herself and her children. She was most uneasy about the arrangement at first, because there was no saying that her benefactor might suddenly decide to change the nature of their arrangements and make demands of her or her children. She was also very much aware that he could dismiss her at any time and she would be in the same sorry state that she was when he made his agreement with her. Yet she had no other choice. She could not return to England, she had no one she knew who would protect her in Antwerp, or indeed any European country, and there seemed to be no other way to get money. The foreigner settled a small amount of money on her to enable her to buy cloth from the mercer so that she could dress herself and her children."

"Sounds like one of those missionary types," Twilford growled. "They're always doing that kind of thing."

"There were, naturally, certain restrictions to her duties," Whittenfield continued, "and they caused her some alarm. There were rooms of the house where she was not allowed to venture, and which were locked day and night. The foreigner often received heavily wrapped parcels from many strange lands. Gradually, Sabrina began to fear that the Count was engaged in nefarious or criminal activities. And she became convinced of it some seven months after she entered his employ. There are three entries in her journal that are at once baffling and thought provoking. She mentions first that the Count often does not go abroad in the day. At first this disturbed her, but she saw him more than once in sunlight and noted that he did cast a shadow, and so her fear that she had fallen into the hands of a malignant spirit was lessened. Oh, you may all laugh if you choose," he said in a wounded tone. "In those times there were many with such fears. It was a superstitious age."

"And this one, of course, is not," the sixth guest said, his fine brows raising in courteous disbelief.

"Oh, those uneducated and unintelligent masses, I daresay, are still in the throes of various dreads, but for those of us who have the wit to learn, well, most of us have cast off the shackles of superstition before we were out of leadstrings." He took a meditative sip of his port. "Still, I suppose we can understand a little how it was that Sabrina felt the dread she did."

"Well, women, you know . . ." Hamworthy said with an indulgent smile. "Wonderful creatures, all of them, but you know what their minds are. Not one in a thousand can think, and the ones that can are always distressingly masculine. The Frenchwoman, the writer with the English name—Sand, isn't it? That's a case in point."

"My great-aunt Serena was another," Whittenfield said, frowning a trifle. "Wasn't a man in the county cared to trade words with her. They respected her, of course, but you couldn't say that they liked her. Nonetheless, most of us loved her when we were children."

"Will you get back to Sabrina?" Dominick asked plaintively.

"Oh, Sabrina; yes. Told you, didn't I, that she was afraid of malign spirits? Of course. And she made up her mind that it was not the case. She thought for a while that her employer must have a mistress somewhere because of the strange hours he kept and the absolute privacy he maintained. There was always the chance that he was working for the Spanish or the French, but she found no evidence of it, and after the first few months she was looking for it. She feared that if the man was working for another government and was discovered, she would suffer as well, and after enduring so much, she did not wish to expose herself to such a hazard. She came to believe that the Count was not, in fact, an agent of any of the enemies of the state. And that intrigued her even more, for there did not seem to be any reasonable explanation for his behavior, if he was not keeping a mistress or doing some other questionable thing. So she set herself the task of finding out more about her employer and his locked rooms."

"Very enterprising," Hamworthy interrupted. "Dangerous, too. I wouldn't like my housekeeper prying into my activities."

"Sabrina also had to deal with the manservant, who was as private and aloof as his master, and whom she suspected of watching her. She describes him as being of middle age or a trifle older, lean, sandy haired and blue eyed, and yet she did not think that he was from Northern Europe as such characteristics might indicate. Once she heard the manservant in conversation with the Count and she thought that they spoke in Latin, though she had not heard the language much. Their accents, if it was indeed that tongue, were strange to her, quite unlike what little scholarly intercourse she had overheard in the past, and not at all like the doggerel of the Roman Church. Yet there were a few words that made her think it was Latin, and for that reason she was more curious than ever. So she set upon a series of vigils, and after many months her patience was rewarded to a degree."

"To a degree," Lord Graveston repeated derisively. "Speak plainly for once in your life, Charles."

"Of course. I am speaking plainly. This story is not easily told, and the wine is playing great hob with my thoughts. You must make allowances for the excellence of my port, Graveston."

"I'll make allowances for anything that gets on with the tale!" was the acerbic answer.

"I'm doing my poor best," Whittenfield said in a slightly truculent manner. "I'm not certain you appreciate the intricacies of Sabrina's life."

"Of course I do. She was serving as housekeeper to a mighty private foreigner in Antwerp and her circumstances were badly reduced. There's nothing incomprehensible in that." Lord Graveston emptied out his pipe and gave Whittenfield a challenging glare through the tufts of his eyebrows.

"And that is not the least of it," Whittenfield insisted.

"Probably not, but you have yet to tell us that part," Dominick put in.

"Which I will do if only you will give me the chance," Whittenfield remonstrated. "Each of you it seems would rather discuss your own adventures. If that's your desire, so be it."

"Oh, Charles, you're being temperamental." Everard had dared to speak again, but he laughed a little so that his host would not think he had been reprimanded.

Whittenfield stared up at the ceiling in sublime abstraction, his eyes faintly glazed. "You know, when I first read her journal, I thought that Sabrina was indulging in fancy, but I have read a few things since then that lead me to believe she was telling the wholly accurate truth about her experiences. That disturbs me, you know. It means that a great many things I used to regard as nonsense may not be that after all."

"What are you talking about, Charles?" Dominick demanded. He had selected another cigar and paused to light it.

"You haven't read the journal, have you?" He did not bother to look at his cousin. "Naturally not. But I have, several times now, and it is a most . . . unnerving document."

"So you persist in telling us," Hamworthy sighed. "Yet you have not particularly justified your claim."

"How little faith you have, Peter," Whittenfield said with an assumption of piety. "If you would bear with me, you will find out why I have said what I have about Sabrina and that glass. *I* wasn't the one who brought the subject up: I have merely offered to enlighten you." He drank again, licking away the crescent it left on his upper lip.

"Then be kind enough to tell us the rest," said the sixth guest.

With this clear invitation before him, Whittenfield hesitated. "I don't know what you will make of it. I haven't sorted it out myself yet, not since I realized she was telling the truth." He smiled uncertainly. "Well, I'll leave it up to you. That's probably best." He took another nervous sip of wine. "She—that is, Sabrina, of course—she continued to watch the Count. She was up many nights, so that it was all she could do to work the next day. During that time she took great care to do her work well. And she made herself as useful as possible to the manservant so that she might stay in his good graces. In her journal she related that he never behaved in any but the most polite way, and yet she felt the same sort of awe for the servant that she did for the master. And she feared to face him directly, except when absolutely necessary. When she had been the Count's housekeeper for a few months, she had enough coins laid aside to enable her to purchase a crucifix—she had sold her old one the year before—and she mentions that the Count commented on it when he saw it, saying that it was merely gold plate. She indignantly reminded him that it was the best she could afford, and that the gold was not important, the faith it represented was. The Count acknowledged her correction, and nothing more was said. Then, two weeks after that, he presented her with a second crucifix of the finest gold, finished in the Florentine style. It was in the family for some time, I recall. Aunt Serena said that her grandmother was used to wear it. That was a great surprise to Sabrina, and she promptly took it off to a Roman priest, for all she did not trust him, and asked him to bless the treasure, just in case. He did as she asked, after he had satisfied himself that though Sabrina was one of the English heathen, yet she knew enough of religion to warrant making the request that she did."

"And did her Count vanish in a puff of smoke next morning?" Dominick ventured sarcastically.

"No. He was unperturbed as ever. From what Sabrina says, he was a man of the utmost urbanity and self-possession. She never heard him raise his voice, never saw any evidence that he abused his manservant, never found any indications of moral excesses. I've been trying for years to puzzle out what she means by moral excesses. Still, whatever they were he didn't do them. Finally one night, while she was keeping her vigil on the stair below one of the locked doors, being fatigued by her housekeeper's tasks during the day, and having spent the better part of most nights watching, she fell asleep, in this case quite literally. She tumbled down the stairs, and in her journal she states that although she does not remember doing so, she must have cried out, for she does recall a door opening and light falling on her from one of the locked rooms."

"Was she much hurt?" Everard asked. "I fell down the stairs once, and ended up with torn ligaments in my shoulder where I'd tried to catch myself. Doctor said I was fortunate not to have broken my skull, but he is forever saying such things."

Whittenfield's brow puckered in annoyance. "She was much bruised and she broke her arm, luckily the right one, for she was left-handed."

"Ah," Twilford said sagely. "That accounts for it."

"The left-handedness?" Whittenfield asked, momentarily diverted. "It may be. There are some odd *gifts* that the left-handed are supposed to have. Come to think of it, Serena was left-handed. There might be something to it."

The sixth guest smiled wryly. "And the ambidextrous?"

"I don't approve of that," Lord Graveston announced. "Isn't natural."

"You don't think so?" the sixth guest asked, but neither expected nor got an answer from the crusty old peer.

"Back to Sabrina," Dominick ordered.

"Yes, back to Sabrina," Whittenfield said, draining his glass again. "Remarkable woman that she was. Where was I?"

"She had fallen down the stairs and broken her arm," one of the guests prompted.

"Oh, yes. And her employer came out of the locked room. Yes. She swooned when she fell, or shortly after, and her next memory was of being carried, though where and by whom she could not tell, for her pain was too intense to allow her much opportunity for thought. She contented herself with closing her eyes and waiting for the worst of her feeling to pass."

"Only thing she could do, probably," Everard said grimly.

"It would seem so. This employer of hers took her into one of the rooms that had been locked, and when she came

29

to her senses, she was on a splendid couch in a small and elegant room. You may imagine her amazement at this, for until that time she had thought that the house, being in one of the poorest parts of the city, had no such finery in it. Yet there were good paintings on the walls, and the furniture was luxuriously upholstered. And this was a time when such luxury was fairly rare, even among the wealthy. This Count was obviously a much more impressive figure than Sabrina had supposed."

"Or perhaps he was a rich tradesman, amusing himself with a pose, and that would explain the remote house and the lack of company," Dominick said cynically.

"I thought that myself, at one time," Whittenfield confessed. "I was sure that she had been hoodwinked by one of the best. But I made a few inquiries and learned that whoever this Count was, he was most certainly genuine nobility."

"How curious," the sixth guest said.

"And it became more curious still," Whittenfield went on, unaware of the sardonic note in the other man's voice. "The Count dosed her with syrup of poppies and then set her arm. She describes the whole event as unreal, and writes that she felt she was floating in a huge warm bath though she could feel the bones grate together. There were so many questions she wanted to ask, but could not bring her thoughts to bear on any of them. Then she once again fainted, and when she woke she was in her own chamber, her arm was expertly splinted and bound with tape, and her head felt that it was filled with enormous pillows."

"And her employer? What of him?" Twilford inquired, caught up now in spite of himself.

"He visited her the next day, very solicitous of her, and anxious to do what he could to speed her recovery." Whittenfield paused for a reaction, and got one from Everard.

"Well, she was his housekeeper. She was of no use to him if she could not work."

"He never told her that," Whittenfield said, gratified that one of his guests had said what he had wanted to hear. "She made note of it in her journal. Finally, after ten days, she got up sufficient courage to say something to the Count, and he reassured her at once that he would prefer she recover completely before returning to her duties. There is an entry then that hints at a more intimate exchange, but the phrases are so vague that it is impossible to tell for sure. Mind, that wasn't a mealy-mouthed age like this one.

If something had passed between them, there would be no reason for her to hide behind metaphors, unless she feared the reproach of her husband later, which I doubt she did. When at last Sir James was released from gaol, he hired on as a mercenary soldier and went east in the pay of the Hapsburgs and nothing is known of his fate. On the other hand, at the end of her three years with her Count, Sabrina came back to England and set herself up in fairly good style. She never remarried but apparently had one or two lovers. Her journal is fairly explicit about them. One was named Richard and had something to do with Norfolk. The other was Henry and was some sort of relative of the Howards. She is very careful not to be too direct about their identities except in how they had to do with her. Doubtless Sir James would have gnashed his teeth to know that his wife ended up doing well for herself. Or he might have liked to live off her money."

"But surely your great-aunt did not become wealthy through the good offices of this Count, did she?" Twilford asked, eyeing his host askance.

"Probably a bequest. Those Continentals are always settling great amounts of money on their faithful servants. I read of a case not long ago where a butler in France got more than the children . . ." Lord Graveston stopped in the middle of his words and stared hard at the sixth guest. "No offense intended."

"Naturally not," the sixth guest said.

"You're a Count, too, they say?" Dominick inquired unnecessarily.

The sixth guest favored him with a wry smile and a slight inclination of his head. "That is one of my titles, yes."

"Smooth spoken devil, aren't you?" Dominick challenged, his eyes growing bright.

"In the manner of my English . . . acquaintances," he replied, adding, "If I have erred, perhaps you will be kind enough to instruct me."

Everard stifled a laugh and Dominick's face reddened.

"Let it alone, Dominick, can't you?" Twilford said before Dominick could think of another insult to launch at the sixth guest.

"Get back to Sabrina, Charles, or you'll have Dominick asking to meet your foreign guest at dawn." Lord Graveston sounded both disgusted and disappointed.

"Yes, I will," Whittenfield said with alacrity. "She had broken her arm and took time to mend, during which time her employer was most solicitous of her health. He saw to it that she was well fed and that her children were cared for so that they did not impose upon their mother. Sabrina was astounded and grateful for this consideration. She had never expected such charity from a stranger. And the more she learned about the Count, the more curious she became. He was without doubt wealthy, and had chosen to live in this poor part of Antwerp so that he would not be put upon by the authorities, she suspected. Yet she doubted that he had broken the law or was engaged in espionage. Eventually she wondered if he were doing vivisections, but never found a body, or any part of one, in the house, though she did once find the manservant with a large piece of raw meat. With every doubt that was quelled, another rose to take its place. She did not dare to approach him directly, for although he had never shown her anything but kindness, Sabrina reveals that she sensed a force or power in him that frightened her."

Twilford shook his head. "Women! Why *will* they endow us with godlike qualities?"

Dominick stifled a yawn.

"It was Sabrina's daughter, Cesily, who first stumbled upon the Count's secret, or one of his secrets," Whittenfield said, and took time to top off his port. He was enjoying the sudden silence that had fallen. Slowly he leaned back, smiling in delight with himself.

"Charles . . ." Dominick warned.

"The secret was one that Sabrina said she should have guessed. How it came about was . . ."

"You'd try the patience of half the saints in the calendar, Whittenfield," Everard said, attempting an amused chuckle with a distinct lack of success.

Whittenfield refused to be rushed. "Cesily came running into her mother's chamber one afternoon with a large glass beaker clutched in her small hands. She said she had come upon it in the hallway near the locked door, but upon close questioning, she admitted that she had found the door unlocked and had decided to explore. You may imagine how aghast Sabrina was to hear this, and she trembled to think how the Count would react to the news that the child had invaded his private rooms. She thought it best to be prepared for the worst, and determined to approach the Count before he came to her. She had a little money set aside, and if the worst came to pass, she was fairly confident that after she had paid for the damage, she would still have enough money left to afford passage to England, though she did not know what she would do once she got there."

"Just like a woman," Everard said, attempting to look world-weary, though his young features did not easily lend themselves to that expression.

"Whittenfield, have you had pipes put in, or must I seek the necessary house in the garden?" Lord Graveston asked unexpectedly.

"You'll find what you need by the pantry door, my Lord," Dominick said, a malicious undertone to his good manners.

"Thanks, puppy," the old man said, getting out of his chair. "Should be back in a little time." He walked stiff-legged to the door and closed it sharply behind him.

"Well . . ." Whittenfield said, rather nonplussed by Lord Graveston's departure, and uncertain now how to pick up the threads of his narrative, "as might be expected . . ." —he covered the awkward moment by pouring himself yet another glass of the excellent port—"it took her some time to convince herself that it was appropriate to interrupt the Count at his work. She did not want to go to that locked door and knock, for fear of his wrath. She also realized that she was not eager to be dismissed. The man was a generous master and had treated her far more kindly than she had thought he would. Yes. You can see her predicament. But if the broken beaker were not acknowledged, then it might go unpleasantly for her and her children. Sabrina was not a foolish woman . . ."

"What woman is not foolish where her children are concerned?" Hamworthy inquired piously. He often remarked that heaven had seen fit to visit seven daughters on him, as others were visited with plague. It was tacitly acknowledged that one of his reasons for attending this gathering was to talk with Everard about a possible alliance with his fourth daughter, Isabel.

"Be that as it may . . ." Whittenfield said more forcefully, glad that the general irritation with Hamworthy for once worked to his benefit. "Indeed, Sabrina feared for what would become of her and her children. There were several possibilities, each one more horrifying than the last. She could be dismissed. That was not desirable, but she could manage, if she acted with caution. If, however, the Count decided to take action against her or—more horribly—her daughter for her actions, then it might go very badly for them. Her thoughts were filled with the tales she had heard

33

of the fate of children in prisons, their abuses and their degradation. At the very contemplation of such a possibility, Sabrina was filled with overwhelming fright. She considered taking her children and leaving under the cover of night, and getting as far from Antwerp as she could. Lamentably, her resources would not allow her to fly a long way, or rapidly. She had to hope that she could persuade the Count that any restitution he demanded, no matter how severe, should be taken from her and not from her children. Imagine what terrors filled her as she went up the stairs—the very stairs down which she had fallen—to knock on that sinister locked door."

"Why did she not simply talk to the manservant, and ask him to explain what had happened?" Twilford suggested.

"Apparently she did consider that, but decided that if she had to face the Count, she would prefer to do it at once, rather than go through the ordeal twice. It's an understandable attitude, don't you think?"

"And this way she would have the strategic element of surprise," the sixth guest said quietly.

"Just so," Whittenfield said emphatically. "You understand me very well, Count." He drank again, inwardly delighted at the increased attention he had been given. "So she knocked at the door. A gentle rap at first, and then a stronger one. You would have thought she was far more brave than she claimed to be, so boldly and directly did she present herself. In her journal, she says that she quaked inwardly, and that there was almost nothing she could do to keep her hands from shaking, yet she did not allow these considerations to hold her back."

"Females, so precipitate," Twilford muttered.

"In a general, that quality would be called audacity, and would earn glory and praise," the sixth guest pointed out.

"Not the same thing at all," Twilford said, much shocked.

"Of course not," answered the sixth guest.

"To return to Sabrina," Whittenfield said sharply. "She knocked on the door and waited. When there was no response, she knocked a second time, hoping all the while that the Count would not be there, or for whatever reason, would not answer. She had begun to worry again—what if this man were hiding men and women in those rooms? What if he had a cache of arms or gunpowder? What if there were other sorts of equipment, things that would not be favored by the officials of Antwerp? Was she required to report what she saw, assuming the Count allowed her to leave the house at all? When she had knocked a third time, she was convinced that the Count was away, and she turned with relief to descend the stairs. And then the door behind her opened and the Count asked her why she had disturbed him. He spoke reasonably, her journal says, telling her that her errand must be of great urgency, for she had never before gone contrary to his orders regarding that door. Sabrina gathered up her faltering courage and told him what her daughter had done, then stood silent, waiting for his wrath to fall on her, for it was not rare for a master to vent his ire with a belt or a stick on servants who did not please him. That's not done much any more, but in this time, Sabrina had every reason to think that she might be beaten for her daughter's offense, and Cesily might be beaten as well. She tried to explain to the Count, then, that Cesily was only a child and had not intended to harm his property, or to trespass in his private rooms. She had got halfway into her tangled arguments when the Count interrupted her to say that he hoped that Cesily was not hurt. Dumbfounded, Sabrina said that she was not. The Count expressed his relief to hear this and assured Sabrina that he was not angry with her or her child, that he was upset to realize they regarded him as such an object of terror. Sabrina demurred, and tried to end this awkward interview, but it was not the Count's intention to allow this. He opened the door wider and asked her if she would care to see what lay beyond. Poor Sabrina! Her curiosity was fired at this offer, for she wanted to enter those room with a desire that was close to passion, but at the same time, she knew that she might be exposing herself to danger. Had it been only herself, she wrote in her journal, she would not have hesitated for a moment, but again, her consideration for her two children weighed heavily with her and for that reason she did not at once accept his offer. After a moment, her curiosity became the stronger force in her, and she went back up the stairs to the open door."

"They'll do it every time. They're as bad as cats," Twilford said, and looked to Hamworthy for support.

"Charles, you're the most infuriating of storytellers," Dominick said as the door opened to re-admit Lord Graveston, who made his way back to his seat without looking at any of the others in the room.

"Doubtless," Whittenfield said, quite pleased with this

encomium. "Let me go on. I think you'll find that much of your doubts will be quieted. For example, I think all of you will be gratified to learn that this mysterious Count was nothing more ominous than an alchemist."

"Of *course!*" Everard said as the others nodded in varying degrees of surprise.

"That was the great secret of the closed rooms. The man had an alchemical laboratory there, as well as a library where he kept some of his more . . . objectionable texts for perusal." He smiled at this revelation and waited to hear what the others might say.

"Alchemist!" Dominick scoffed. "Demented dreamer, more like."

"Do you think so?" the sixth guest asked him.

"Base metal into gold! The Elixir of Life! Who'd believe such trash?" He got up from his chair and went to glare into the fire.

"Who indeed," murmured the sixth guest.

"You're going to tell us that all your aunt's precious Count was doing was pottering around among the retorts trying to make his own gold?" Hamworthy demanded. "Of all the shoddy . . ."

"Yes, Sabrina's employer was an alchemist," Whittenfield said with completely unruffled calm.

"No wonder he bought a house in the worst part of town," Lord Graveston said. "That's not the sort of thing that you want put into a grand house. Smells, boilings, who knows what sort of flammable substances being used . . . He had a degree of sense, in any case, if he had such a place for his work."

"Exactly my opinion," Whittenfield said at once. "I decided, as did Sabrina, that the Count was a sensible man. He showed her his laboratory and his equipment and warned her that it was not wise for Cesily to come in because there were various substances that might harm her in the laboratory. He showed her where he made his glass vessels by blowing them himself, and the oven where many of the processes were conducted. It was called an athanor, Sabrina says, and was shaped like a very large beehive made of heavy bricks. The Count showed her, since he was not involved in any experiments at the moment, how the various vessels were placed in the athanor and told her how long, and in what manner they were heated to get the results he desired. She watched all this with great fascination and asked very few questions, though she longed to pester him with them. At last he told her he would appreciate her discretion, but if she had any doubts about remaining in his employ, she would have to tell him and he would arrange for her to have passage back to England. She was taken aback by this suggestion, for she believed that the Count wanted to be rid of her now that she had learned his secret. Apparently he discerned something of this in her countenance, and he assured her at once that he did not wish her to leave, but he was aware that there were many who did not view alchemy kindly and wished to have nothing to do with it. If that expressed her own feelings, then he wanted her to tell him at once in order to make proper arrangements for her. He had, he told her, another house in Antwerp, and he would send her there if she felt she could not remain in good conscience so near his laboratory. Sabrina was startled by this consideration, which was a good deal rarer then than it is now. She told the Count that she would inform him in the morning of her decision, but she wrote in her journal that she was determined to stay, and had been since she was shown the laboratory. In the morning the Count sought her out and asked to know her decision, which she told him at once. He, in turn, declared that he was very pleased to have her willing to stay on with him. She then inquired what sorts of experiments he was making, but he did not wish to discuss that with her, not at that time. He did give her his word that he would present her with a few of the results of his labors in due time, which she, perforce, agreed to. She mentions in her journal for the next several days that she saw little of the Count because he was occupied in his secret room working on some new experiment. It isn't precisely easy to tell, but it seems she put some stock in his skill, for she states she suspects the crucifix he gave her might have been made from alchemical gold."

"Absurd!" Hamworthy declared.

"Oh, naturally," Whittenfield said. "And no doubt the Count had his own reasons behind his actions."

"Wanted to put her at her ease," Twilford ventured.

"Still, a crucifix is hardly appropriate to give an Englishwoman. It seems much too Roman." Lord Graveston had paused in his fiddling with his pipe to give his opinion, and having done so, went back to scraping out the burnt tobacco so that he could fill it again.

"Queen Bess herself was known to wear crucifixes," Everard mentioned, his face darkening from embarrassment. "Probably the Count, being a foreigner, and a Roman Catholic—most of them were, weren't they?—wanted to make a friendly gesture. It's a more circumspect gift than any other sort of jewelry would be."

"Everard, your erudition astounds me," Dominick said with a nasty grin at the young man. "Read Classics, did you?"

"History. At Clare." His voice dropped to a mumble and he would not look at Dominick.

"Clever lad," Hamworthy said, as if to take the sting out of Dominick's remark.

"What else did your great-great-etc. aunt have to say for herself?" Twilford inquired with a polite nod away from Dominick.

"She said that her employer continued to treat her well, that her arm healed completely, and aside from twinges when the weather changed, it never troubled her in all her years. She did not have much opportunity to view the laboratory, but she found that the manservant, Roger, was much inclined to be helpful to her, and told her once, in a moment of rare candor, that he liked her boy Herbert, and said that he had once had a son of his own, but the boy had died many years before. Sabrina was shocked to hear this, for she had not thought that he was much used to families. He offered to assist her with Cesily and Herbert when her duties made it awkward for her, and she thanked him for it, but could not bring herself to trust him entirely, so aloof did he hold himself. In the end, she asked Herbert if he would like to go with Roger when he purchased certain items from the great market in the center of town. Herbert, having turned two, was developing an adventurous spirit, and he was eager to explore a greater part of the world. Roger spoke English, albeit with an accent, and told Sabrina that he would be happy to keep the boy talking in his own language, or teach him German or French. He admitted that his Dutch was not very good and his Flemish was stilted, but he would not mind being Herbert's tutor. In a moment of boldness, Sabrina said that she would rather Cesily be taught the languages for the time being, and Herbert could learn in a year or so, when he had a better grasp of speech. She did not think that the man would accept this, but he did, and inquired what languages Sabrina would like her daughter to speak. When Sabrina expressed her surprise, he reminded her that Queen Bess spoke seven languages quite fluently and it did not seem

38

intolerable to him that other females should do likewise. So little Cesily became his student, learning French, German, Spanish, and Italian. He must have been an excellent teacher, for Cesily was noted for her skill in these tongues for all her life."

"Damned silly waste," Twilford said. "If you ask me, it's a mistake to educate females. Look what happens. You start sending them to school and the next thing you know, they want to vote and who knows what else."

"Reprehensible," said the sixth guest with an ironic smile.

"It isn't fitting," Hamworthy declared. "What could your great-aunt be thinking of, to put her daughter forward that way?" He straightened up in his chair. "Charles, you're not serious, are you? The girl didn't try to be a scholar?"

"It seems to have taken her remarkably little effort to be one," Whittenfield answered. "She took to it like a potentate takes to vice. In the next year she showed herself to be a most ready and enthusiastic pupil. She started to read then, so that by five . . ."

"Started to read? So young? Was Sabrina lost to all propriety?" Lord Graveston demanded.

"She must have been. Herbert soon joined his sister in her studies, but lacked her aptitude, though he did well enough. To Sabrina's surprise, and, I think, disappointment, there were no further invitations to enter the laboratory, though on one occasion the Count presented her with a fine silver bracelet set with amber. She says in her journal that there was nothing remarkable about the amber or the silver except that the workmanship was exceedingly good. I wish I knew what became of that bracelet," Whittenfield added in another voice. "We have the mirror, which is an object of considerable speculation, but not the bracelet, which might have had a great deal of value, both for the materials and the antiquity."

"Don't talk like a merchant, Charles. It's unbecoming," Hamworthy interjected.

"You're a fine one to talk about merchants, Peter," Dominick said to him with false good humor. "Didn't your sister marry that merchant from Leeds?"

Peter Hamworthy's face turned an amazing shade of raspberry. He stared at Dominick with such intense anger that the rest fell hopefully silent. "My sister's husband," he said at last, with great care, enunciating each syllable with hard precision, "is not a merchant. His family started the

39

rail-shipping business in Leeds over eighty years ago, which hardly counts as being shop-stained."

"Naturally, naturally, and the money he brought to the family had nothing to do with it, though your father was almost ruined and your sister twenty-six years younger than her husband." Dominick strolled around the room.

"What about Sabrina and the glass?" Lord Graveston asked in awesome accents. He puffed on his pipe and waited.

"Yes, Charles, what about the glass?" Everard echoed.

"That is coming," Whittenfield said, shooting a blurred, hostile look at his cousin. "I've told you that Sabrina had been given a bracelet and that she had been in the employ of the Count well over a year. That is important to remember, because she had a fair familiarity with the man and his habits. She knew that he spent much of the night in his laboratory and a fair amount of his time otherwise in study and reading. He went out fairly often, but irregularly. If he had friends, she knew nothing of them, though she assumed he must occasionally receive them at his other house, wherever it was. She appreciated his kindness and the attention he gave to her and her children. When she had been working for him about eighteen months, her tone changes slightly. She is not more wary or more forthcoming, but she admits once or twice that he is an attractive and compelling man, and that she has had one or two vivid dreams about him. You may all guess the nature of those dreams. At first, she only mentions that she did dream that he came to her in her bed, and later her descriptions become more detailed and—improper. She mentions that after one such dream, she met the Count in the morning room where she and her children were eating, and to her amazement, she found herself blushing as she looked at him. She records in her journal that until that moment she was unaware of the penetrating strength of his eyes, which she describes as being dark and large. The Count, she says, saw her blush and smiled enigmatically, but made no comment to her. He had come to talk to Cesily in Italian as Roger was out of the house on an errand to the docks."

"Perhaps he read her journal. M' mother always said that it was wise to read the diaries of your servants. She always kept records of what her maids said among themselves and in their diaries," Hamworthy announced with portentous confidence.

"And did she allow the maids to read *her* diary?" the sixth guest asked gently, dark eyes turned on Peter Hamworthy.

"What?" Hamworthy protested loudly.

"They probably did, you know," Dominick said bitterly. "My valet reads mine, though I've told him thousands of times that he must not."

"Sabrina doesn't seem to think that he did read it. She considered the possibility, but her attitude is one of disbelief. For more than a week she had no dreams, and then they began again. After three or four months, she began to anticipate them with pleasure, and was disappointed when nights would pass without them. During the day, she continued to be the sensible woman she was, looking after the house and caring for her children and overseeing their meals. Apparently her employer did his cooking in the laboratory, for he never asked Sabrina to serve him at table. She speculated that he must have his banquets and other entertainments at his other house, for never did such an event take place where Sabrina lived. She commented on it once to Roger and he told her that the Count dined in private, as it was a custom with him to take sustenance with no more than one other person. Roger himself ate alone, but he kept his meat in the coldroom below the pantry."

Twilford, who had been drinking heavily, looked up with reddened eyes. "No fit place for an Englishwoman, if you ask me," he remarked. "Shouldn't have stood for it, myself."

"The children enjoyed their lives in that place, though both lacked playmates. In England there were cousins and others who would have been available to them. In that house in Antwerp there were only the poor, ragged urchins of the street nearby, and so Cesily and Herbert learned to entertain themselves. Roger became a sort of uncle to them, alternately teaching them and indulging them. Sabrina says in one of her entries that he had the remarkable knack of obtaining their obedience without beating or berating them. The Count was regarded with more awe but neither child was afraid of him, and he often was willing to spend time with them correcting their accents in various languages and telling them tales that Sabrina comments were unusually vivid. Cesily was particularly fond of the adventures of a woman named Olivia, whom the Count cast in different roles and different times in history. Sabrina

41

once questioned this, telling the Count that she was not sure tales of the corruption in early Rome were proper for children of such tender years. The Count told her then that he was being mild, and reminded her that there is a marked difference between ignorance and innocence, though one is often mistaken for the other."

"Sophistry!" Lord Graveston insisted.

"And patently false," Hamworthy added. "Haven't we all had cause to observe how quickly innocence departs when too much learning is present?"

"Your brother, I believe, is a Don at Kebel in Oxford," the sixth guest said to Hamworthy. "A most learned man, and yet you remarked this evening that he is as naive and innocent as a babe, and it was not entirely complimentary."

Peter Hamworthy glowered at the elegant foreigner. "Not the same thing at all, Count. You're foreign . . . don't understand."

"I doubt I'm as foreign as all that," the sixth guest said mildly.

"When do we get to the glass, Charles?" Twilford asked plaintively. "You've been going on for more than an hour."

"I'm coming to that," Whittenfield said. "You have all come to understand, I trust, that this household was not a usual one, either for this country or any other in Europe. Sabrina had been with the Count for almost three years. She had put aside a fair amount of money and was beginning to hope that she would not have to return to England as a poor relation to hang upon some more resourceful relative. She writes in her journal that it was the greatest pleasure to think of her condition at that time compared to what it had been before she entered the Count's employ. Then Sir James, her husband, was released from gaol, and came searching for her."

"You said he became a mercenary, Charles," Twilford reminded him.

"He did. That was after he saw his family. He came to the house late one evening. Apparently he had been celebrating his liberation, for Sabrina says in her journal that he was half drunk when he pounded on the door, demanding admittance. She had, of course, left word with the warden of the prison where she might be found, and the warden had told Sir James. He was a pugnacious man, of hasty temper and a touchy sense of honor. A lot of men like that, then," he observed reflectively as he turned his glass of port by the stem and squinted at the reddish light passing through it. "He was most unhappy to find his wife serving as a housekeeper to a foreign Count, and in the wrong part of the city, at that. At first Sabrina was somewhat pleased to see him, and commiserated over his thinned and scarred body, but she quickly realized that the reunion was not as happy as she had intended it to be. First he berated her for her scandalous position, and then he shouted at their children, saying they were growing up among ruffians and thieves. When Sabrina tried to convince him that they were being well-cared-for and educated, he became irate, shouted at her, and struck her."

"As you say, a hasty temper," Twilford commented with a slow, judicious nod of his head. "Still, I can't say I'd like to see my wife in such a situation. A man can be forgiven for imagining any number of things, and if Sir James was touchy of his honor, as you say . . ."

"Probably he suspected the worst. Those three years in prison can't have been pleasant for him," Hamworthy observed.

"Poverty wasn't pleasant for Sabrina, either," the sixth guest pointed out.

"A different matter entirely," Hamworthy explained. "A woman needs the firm guidance of a man. Very sad she should have had such misfortune, but it was hardly unexpected." He reached over for a cigar and drew one out, sniffing its length with enthusiasm before reaching for a lucifer to light it.

"I see." The sixth guest sat back in his chair.

"I'm baffled," Everard confessed. "If her husband returned for her, how does it happen that she came back to England and he went into Europe? And what has the glass to do with it?"

"Yes, you keep holding that glass out as a lure, and I can't see any connection between Sabrina and it," Twilford complained.

"Have patience, have patience," Whittenfield reprimanded them gently. "Let me get on with it. You recall that I said that Sir James struck his wife? They were in the receiving hall of that house, which was quite small, about the size of a back parlor, I gather. Cesily and Herbert both cried out, for they were not in the habit of seeing their father discipline their mother. Sir James was preparing to deliver a second blow as Sabrina struggled to break free of his grasp, when the inner door opened and the Count stepped into the room. Sabrina says that she is certain he knew who Sir James was, but he sharply demanded that the man desist and explain why he was assaulting his house-keeper. Sir James, astounded and enraged, turned on this new arrival and bellowed insults at him, calling him a seducer and many another dishonorable name. The Count inquired if Sabrina had said anything that led him to this conclusion, to which Sir James replied that she had in fact denied such accusations, which made her all the more suspect. He demanded to know who the Count was, and why he had dared to take in Sabrina and her children, knowing that she was a woman in a strange country and without benefit of male protectors. The Count gave a wry answer: he would have thought that Sir James should answer that question, not himself. Sir James became more irate and demanded satisfaction, and ordered his wife and children to prepare to leave the Count's house at once, that he would not tolerate this insult to his name one night longer. In vain did the children scream their dismay. Sir James reminded them that he was their father, with rights and obligations to fulfill. The children besought their mother to refuse, but it was the Count who stayed the question."

"Impudent foreigner!" Twilford burst out, straightening up in his chair with indignation.

"How dared he?" Lord Graveston demanded.

"What did he do?" Dominick asked in a low, harsh tone.

"He said that he would not allow any man to hurt a servant in his employ. At first Sabrina was greatly shocked to hear this, for in the time she had been the Count's housekeeper, he had been most respectful and rarely mentioned her subservient position in the household. But what he said again stayed Sir James' hand. Sir James was furious at the Count for making his wife a servant and explained to him that well-born Englishwomen were not to be hired as common servants. He insisted that he had endured unbearable insults from the Count and would demand satisfaction of him. Now, in Sabrina's journal, she says that the Count laughed sadly and asked her whether or not she wanted her husband to die, but I doubt he was so audacious. Whatever it was, the Count promised to meet him at midnight, in the great hall of his other house. Sabrina, in turmoil from this, begged both men not to embark on anything so foolish, but her husband insisted and the Count told her that if this were not settled now, she would have to leave his employ and go with her husband, and in her journal Sabrina admits that that prospect was

44

no longer a happy one. She turned to her husband and asked that he rescind the challenge, but her husband chose to interpret this request as proof of an illicit relationship between his wife and the Count, and only confirmed his belief that Sabrina was the mistress of the Count. He told her as much and asked for directions to the house the Count had mentioned and vowed he would be there. The matter of seconds was a difficult one, as Sir James, being just released from prison, had no one to act for him. The Count suggested that the matter be private and that each fight on his honor. Sir James agreed with alacrity and went off to find a sword to his liking."

"He did not insist that Sabrina accompany him?" Everard asked, quite startled.

"No, he said that if Sabrina had taken a lover, she could remain with him until he avenged her honor, not that any was left to her." Whittenfield gave a little shrug. "Sabrina says in her journal that at the moment she wished she had become the Count's mistress, for the thought of parting from him was a bitter one. Until she saw her husband, she says, she did not realize how she had come to trust and rely on her employer. At last, the night coming on and the hour of the duel approaching, she searched out the Count as he was preparing to leave the house, and told him that she would pray for him, and that she hoped he would not despise her for turning against Sir James. He answered that he was grateful for her prayers and did not fault her for seeking to stay away from Sir James, if not for her own sake, for the sake of her children, who must surely suffer at his hands. She agreed with some fear and told the Count that she wished she had not told the warden where she could be found, so that Sir James might never have found her. The Count did not chide her for this, but reminded her that she had chosen to follow her husband rather than turn to her family when his cast him out. She did not deny this, but said that part of her fears were that she would become a drudge if she appealed to her father or her uncles for maintenance. With two children to care for, she decided it would hurt them, and when she and Sir James had come to the Continent, it was not too bad at first. The Count heard her out and offered to provide her with funds to allow her to return to England and set herself up in reasonable style. He told her that no matter what the outcome of the duel was, he feared it would be most unwise for her to continue living under his roof, for doubtless Sir James would spend part of the time before the meeting in composing damning letters to send to various relatives. Sadly, Sabrina admitted this was true. Shortly before the Count left, she asked him why he had not made her his mistress. He had an equivocal answer for her—that surely her dreams were sweeter."

"Why, that's outrageous!" Lord Graveston burst out. "And she tolerated it? The effrontery of the fellow."

"How could he know?" Everard wondered. "If she never told him, it may be that he was telling her that he did not fancy her in that way."

"Any real man fancies an attractive woman in that way," Hamworthy said with a significant and critical glance at Everard.

"Whatever the case," Whittenfield said sharply, "the Count left her and went to his other house. And after debating with herself for the better part of an hour, Sabrina got her cloak and followed him. She remembered the directions that the Count had given Sir James, and she went quickly, avoiding those streets where taverns still did business and roistering songs rang through the hollow night. It took her some little time to find the house, and once she feared she was lost, but eventually she came upon the place, a great, sprawling manor, three stories high, with an elegant facade. Most of the windows were dark, but there were lights in the area she thought might be the kitchen, and a few candles flickered in one of the other rooms. Now she was faced with the problem of how to enter the building. There was a wrought iron gate, but she was confident she could climb it, but the house itself puzzled her. She hitched up her skirts and grabbed the ornamental scrollwork . . ."

"What a hoyden!" Dominick sniggered.

"I think she's jolly intrepid," Everard said, turning slightly rosier.

"Sounds like just the bubble-headed thing she would do, judging from the rest of your narrative," Twilford sighed.

"Well, no matter what we think, gentlemen, the fact remains that she did it," Whittenfield said with a hint of satisfaction.

"Does she tell whether or not she stopped the duel?" the sixth guest asked. He had been still while Whittenfield talked, giving his host polite attention.

"She was stymied at first, she indicates in her journal. She looked around the house and judged, from the number of rooms she could see that were swathed in covers, that the Count was not much in attendance here. It was by the veriest chance that she found a door at the far side of the house with an improperly closed latch. With great care she opened the door and entered a small salon with elegant muraled walls she could not easily see in the dark. Realizing that if she were caught by a servant she might well be detained as a thief, she hesitated before entering the hall, but recalling what danger her husband and the Count had wished upon themselves, she got up her courage and went in search of them. It was the greatest stroke of luck that she stumbled on the room where Sir James and the Count were met. Apparently they had already exchanged one pass of arms, and Sir James was breathing hard, though the Count, according to Sabrina, seemed to be unaffected by the encounter. At the sound of the opening door, the Count reminded one whom he supposed to be a servant that he was not to be disturbed, at which admonition, Sabrina revealed herself and hastened forward to confront the two men. Then, just as she neared them, Sir James reached out and took hold of her, using her as a shield as he recommenced his attack on the Count, all the while taunting him to fight back. At first the Count retreated, and then he began to fight in a style quite unknown to Sir James. Sabrina does not describe it adequately, but I gather that he would switch his sword from one hand to the other with startling rapidity, and instead of hacking and thrusting with his sword, he began to use it as if it were some sort of lash. Remember, the art of fence was far from developed at that time, and the swords used were not the fine, flexible épée we know now for sport, but sharp-edged lengths of steel. Yet the Count had a flexible blade that did not break, and it terrified Sir James. Finally the Count pressed a fierce attack, and while Sir James retreated, he was able to wrest Sabrina from his grasp and to thrust her away from the fight. Then, in a move that Sabrina did not see clearly and does not describe well, the Count disarmed Sir James. Sabrina states that she *thinks* that the Count leaped forward and passed inside Sir James' guard, clipping his shoulder and knocking his sword from his hand. That's quite a feat, no matter how it was done, but Sabrina's impression is the only information we have, and so it is nearly impossible to guess what the man actually did. The Count held Sir James at swordpoint and politely inquired of Sabrina what she wanted done with him."

"Disgusting!" Twilford said.

"But the Count didn't kill Sir James, did he?" Everard asked eagerly. He had a certain apologetic air, as if he did not entirely want to be against his countryman but liked the gallantry of the situation in spite of the Count's arrogance.

"No, he didn't kill him, though the thrust to his arm could have done so, Sabrina thought, if he had intended it to," Whittenfield said. "Sabrina said that she wanted Sir James out of her life, and at this the Count told Sir James that he had heard the verdict of his wronged spouse. Sir James began to curse roundly, but the Count brought his blade up and warned him that such behavior would not be tolerated. Sir James lapsed into a sullen silence and barely acknowledged his wife's presence. The Count informed him that on his honor—since Sir James was so jealous of it— he must leave within twenty-four hours and take up whatever station he wished with any noble or fighting company east of the Rhine, and he was not to seek out his wife again, either in person or by message. He required Sir James to swear to this, not only by the oaths of the Church but by his sword. Grudgingly, Sir James did this, and then the Count let him go."

"And that's all there was to it? Charles, you disappoint me," Dominick remarked.

"That is not quite all. There is still the matter of the glass," Whittenfield pointed out.

"Ah, yes, the glass," the sixth guest murmured.

"The Count escorted Sabrina back to his house where she had lived for almost three years, and as they walked, he inquired why it was that she had come. She admitted that she feared for him and did not want him to come to hurt. He told her that was highly unlikely, but did not explain further until she asked if it were an alchemical secret that protected him. Again he gave her an equivocal answer, saying that it was something of the sort. Before they entered his house, she confessed to him that she would not refuse him if he wished to pass what remained of the night with her. He told her that he was much moved by this, for women did not often make that request of him, which, in her journal, Sabrina finds amazing, for according to her the Count was a pleasing man, of middle height and compact body, with attractive, slightly irregular features, who was most fastidious about his person and somber in his elegance. Once in the house, the Count led her to the laboratory and

48

lit a branch of candles, then opened a small red-lacquered cabinet which seemed to be of great age, and removed the glass. It was not in the frame it has now, as I believe I mentioned, but it was rimmed with silver. The Count gave this to Sabrina, telling her that when she could see the spider in the glass, he would come for her. She did not believe this, but he assured her there was the image of a jeweled spider set in the very center of the glass, and that when one stood directly in front of it, under special circumstances, it could be seen."

"Very neat," Dominick approved with a jeering toast of his glass. "I must try that myself, one day."

"Did the poor woman believe that?" Lord Graveston demanded with a shake of his head. "And you have kept that worthless piece of glass?"

"There's a bit more to it," Whittenfield remarked. "Apparently that night, the Count did spend some time with Sabrina, and though she does not record what passed between them . . ."

"It's not difficult to guess," Hamworthy said with marked disapproval.

"I gather that it was not precisely what Sabrina expected. She mentions that the glass was put by the bed and lit with the branch of candles . . ."

"Really!" Twilford's expression was livid with disapproval.

"Decadent foreigner!" Hamworthy ejaculated.

"And," Whittenfield went on, giving them little attention, "Sabrina says in her journal that for one joyous, incomprehensible moment, she could see the spider—that it sat in a fine diamond web, a creature of ruby and garnet and tourmaline. And she was elated at the sight, though she says in a later entry that she does not expect to see it again. She left it to Cesily with the admonition that it be kept in the family as a great treasure."

"A woman's whim for a trinket!" Dominick scoffed.

"It may be. But, as you see, it is still in the family, and no one is willing to part with it. Serena had great faith in it, and she was not given to superstition. I remember her standing here, saying that if it had brought such good fortune to Sabrina that we would be fools to be rid of it. My mother wanted to put it away, but it never happened, and I admit that I'm so used to it that I would miss having it. And every now and again I stare at it, hoping to see the spider."

"Oh, Charles," Dominick sneered.

"Did you see anything?" Everard asked.

"Only my face. If there is a spider in it, only a man who casts no reflection could see it." Whittenfield leaned forward and put his glass down.

"Do you mean that after sitting here for well nigh two hours, you have the effrontery to offer us nothing more than a third-rate ghost story?" Hamworthy demanded.

"Well, that *is* the story of the glass, as it's put down in Sabrina's journal. She returned to England and set herself up well, saying that she had been given a legacy that made this possible. And you will admit that whoever her Count was, he was something of an original."

"If you look into it, you'll find he was just another charlatan," Lord Graveston said with confidence. "Generous, it seems, but nonetheless, a charlatan."

"Why do you believe that?" the sixth guest asked him. There was no challenge in the question, just a certain curiosity.

"It's obvious," Lord Graveston said, rising. "Well, if that's all you're giving us, Whittenfield, I'll take myself off to bed. Excellent port and brandy." He made his way through the room and out the door.

Peter Hamworthy groaned as he got to his feet. "The hour is very late and I like to rise early. I had no idea how long this would be. It's what comes of telling stories about females." As he went to the door he made a point not to look in the direction of the Spider Glass.

"I'm for the billiard room, if anyone cares to join me," Dominick said, staring at Everard. "You may come and do your best to . . . beat me, if you like."

Everard was suddenly nervous. "I . . . in a moment, Dominick." He turned toward his host. "I thought it was a good tale. I don't understand about the mirror, but . . ." On that inconclusive note he left the room in Dominick's wake.

"Whittenfield, that was the damnedest farrago you spun us," Twilford admonished him. "Why did you begin it?"

"You asked about the glass, that's all." Whittenfield had got to his feet and stood, a little unsteadily, beside his Queen Anne chair.

"Then I was an ass to do so." He turned on his heel and stalked majestically from the room.

The sixth guest turned his dark, ironic eyes on Whittenfield. "I found your story most . . . salutary. I had no idea . . ." He got up and went toward the old mirror as if compelled to do so. He touched the glass with his small, beautiful hand, smiling faintly.

Glistening in the mirror, the spider hung in its jeweled web. The body was red as rubies or fresh blood. The delicate legs were garnet at the joints and tourmaline elsewhere. It was delicate as a dancer, and though the mirror had faded over the years, the Count could still take pride in his work. Beyond the image of the spider the muted lamps of the Oak Parlor shone like amber in the glass.

For, of course, le Comte de Saint-Germain had no reflection at all.

Text of two letters from le Comte de Saint-Germain to Charles Whittenfield, written 25 years apart.

> Mindre Län
> Nr. Südertälje
> Svensk
> 9 January, 1911

The Honorable Charles K. O. E. Whittenfield
Ninth Earl of Copsehowe
Briarcopse
Nr. Evesham
England

Charles:

Has it really been ten years since we last saw each other? How swiftly the time goes. I have fond memories of Briarcopse and hope that one day I might return there. However, I fear that it will not be possible for some time yet. My stay in Sweden is necessarily short, brought about by the need to expand some of my ventures in Russia. Conditions in that country are unstable enough that it would be most prudent for me to return there as soon as I can arrange transportation. It is not only my financial interests that concern me, but the welfare of those in my employ.

I admit that I share your worries for Europe. Too many diplomatic schemes have become deadlocked. You mention your son, and fear that he may have to fight, should there be a war. The boy, as I calculate, is only twelve. How young that seems to me. Surely no country fights wars with children, not in these times.

Since you asked for my recommendation, I will give it. Doubtless the Germans are more advanced in chemical and electrical research, but that would be of little benefit to you if war breaks out. If you are interested in foreign investment, then I would consider America. Their commerce is expanding and while they do not have the quality of research establishments to be found in Europe and England, their current policies would favor investments of the sort you have in mind. A Canadian company could negotiate for you, if you believe there still exists prejudice toward the British.

Let me thank you again for the hospitality you have so graciously extended to me. Perhaps another time, when the world is more settled.

Saint-Germain
his seal, the eclipse

Avenida de las Lagrimas
Cádiz, España
12 July, 1936

The Honorable Charles K. O. E. Whittenfield
Ninth Earl of Copsehowe
St. Amelia's Hospital
London, England

   My dear Charles:

   *Your grandson told me of your illness last week,
and I am truly sorry to learn of it. While it is true
that you have had a long life, I fully understand your
sense of brevity. Ancient though I am, I share your
feeling.*

   *Unfortunately, I cannot share the enthusiasm of
your Mister Shaw. Your grandson said that he is confident that the changes in Germany are all to the good,
but it does not seem that way to me. There are deep,
abiding wounds left from the Great War, and a gen-
eration is not enough to heal them. Some, I fear, will
never heal. No one touched by that war can forget it,
or the abuses that followed. Let those blind idealists
say what they will, the power of the NSDAP will exact
vengeance for the Versailles Treaty. I know. I have
seen for myself what they can do.*

   *Enough of that. A man attempting to recuperate
from a stroke does not need to be reminded of such
grim matters. Let me only say that I am more distressed than you know that I did not visit you before
now. I had planned to come some years ago, but
events did not permit me to leave the Continent.*

   *Nor will they for a while. My manservant, Roger, is
a native of Cádiz and for that reason, I will remain
here for a little longer. Then I plan to stay for a time
with an old friend in the south of France.*

   Let me hear from you. It is shameful, the way I

have neglected my old friends. Perhaps, though it is late, I may remedy this in part now, by sending you my sincerest wishes for your speedy recovery and the assurance of my gratitude for your continuing good-will, little though I have done to deserve it.

Saint-Germain
his seal, the eclipse

RENEWAL

WITH bloodied hands, James pulled the ornate iron gates open and staggered onto the long drive that led to the château. Although he was dazed, he made sure the gates were properly shut before starting up the tree-lined road. How long ago he had made his first journey here, and how it drew him now. He stared ahead, willing the ancient building to appear out of the night as he kept up his dogged progress toward the one place that might provide him the shelter he so desperately needed.

When at last the stone walls came into view, James was puzzled to hear the sound of a violin, played expertly but fragmentally, as if the music were wholly personal. James stopped and listened, his cognac-colored eyes warming for the first time in three days. Until that moment, the only sound he had remembered was the grind and pound of guns. His bleary thoughts sharpened minimally and he reached up to push his hair from his brow. Vaguely he wondered who was playing, and why, for Montalia had an oddly deserted look to it: the grounds were overgrown and only two of the windows showed lights. This was more than war-time precaution, James realized, and shambled toward the side door he had used so many times in the past, the first twinges of real fear giving him a chill that the weather had not been able to exert.

The stables smelled more of motor oil than horses, but

James recognized the shape of the building, and limped into its shadow with relief. Two lights, he realized, might mean nothing more than most of the servants had retired for the night, or that shortages of fuel and other supplies forced the household to stringent economies. He leaned against the wall of the stable and gathered his courage to try the door. At least, he told himself, it did not appear that the château was full of Germans. He waited until the violin was pouring out long cascades of sound before he reached for the latch, praying that if the hinges squeaked, the music would cover it.

In the small sitting room, Saint-Germain heard the distant whine of an opening door, and his bow hesitated on the strings. He listened, his expanded senses acute, then sat back and continued the *Capriccio* he had been playing, letting the sound guide the solitary intruder. He gave a small part of his attention to the unsteady footfalls in the corridor, but for the most part, he concentrated on the long pattern of descending thirds of the cadenza. Some few minutes later, when he had begun one of the Beethoven *Romanzas,* a ragged figure clutching a kitchen knife appeared in the doorway and emerged uncertainly from the darkness into the warmth of the hearthlight and the single kerosene lantern. Saint-Germain lowered his violin and gave the newcomer an appraising stare. His dark eyes narrowed briefly, then his brows raised a fraction as he recognized the man. "You will not need that knife, Mister Tree."

He had expected many things, but not this lone, elegant man. James shook his head, his expression becoming more dazed than ever. "I . . ." He brought a grimy, bruised hand to his eyes and made a shaky attempt at laughter which did not come off. He coughed once, to clear his voice. "When I got here, and heard music . . . I thought that . . . I don't know what." As he spoke he reached out to steady himself against the back of one of the three overstuffed chairs in the fine stone room, which was chilly in spite of the fire. "Excuse me . . . I'm not . . . myself."

"Yes, I can see that," Saint-Germain said with gentleness, knowing more surely than James how unlike himself he was. He stood to put his violin into its velvet-lined case, then tucked the loosened bow into its holder before closing the top. This done, he set the case on the occasional table beside his chair and turned to James. "Sit down, Mister Tree. Please." It was definitely a command but one so kind-

57

ly given that the other man complied at once, dropping gratefully into the chair which had been supporting him. The knife clattered to the floor, but neither paid any attention to it.

"It's been . . . a while," James said distantly, looking up at the painting over the fireplace. Then his gaze fell on Saint-Germain, and he saw the man properly for the first time.

Le Comte was casually dressed by his own exacting standards: a black hacking jacket, a white shirt and black sweater under it, and black trousers. There were black, ankle-high jodhpur boots on his small feet, the heels and soles unusually thick. Aside from a silver signet ring, he wore no jewelry. "Since you have been here? More than a decade, I would suppose."

"Yes." James shifted in the chair, his movements those of utter exhaustion. "This place . . . I don't know why." Only now that he had actually arrived at his goal did he wonder what had driven him to seek it out. Indistinct images filtered through his mind, most of them senseless, one or two of them frightening.

"On Madelaine's behalf, I'm pleased to welcome you back. I hope you will stay as long as you wish to." He said this sincerely, and watched James for his response.

"Thanks. I don't know what . . . thanks." In this light, and with the abuses of the last few days, it was not possible to see how much the last ten years had favored James Emmerson Tree. His hair had turned from glossy chestnut to silver without loss of abundance; the lines of his face had deepened but had not become lost in fretwork or pouches, so that his character was cleanly incised, delineated in strong, sharp lines. Now, with smudges of dirt and dried blood on him, it was not apparent that while at thirty he had been good looking, at fifty he was superbly handsome. He fingered the tear on his collar where his press tag had been. "I thought . . . Madelaine might have been . . ."

"Been here?" Saint-Germain suggested as he drew one of the other chairs closer to where James sat. "I am sorry, Mister Tree. Madelaine is currently in South America."

"Another expedition?" James asked, more forlorn than he knew.

"Of course. It's more circumspect to stay there than go to Greece or Africa just now, or wouldn't you agree?" He spoke slowly, deliberately, and in English for the first time.

"I would rather be assured of her safety than her nearness, Mister Tree."

James nodded absently, then seemed at last to understand what Saint-Germain had said, for he looked up sharply and said in a different voice, "God, yes. Oh, God, yes."

"I had a letter from her not long ago. Perhaps you would care to read it later this evening?" He did not, in fact, want to share the contents of Madelaine's letter with James; it was too privately loving for any eyes but his, yet he knew that this man loved her with an intensity that was only exceeded by his own.

"No," James said after a brief hesitation. "So long as she's okay, that's all that matters. If anything happened to her, after this, I think I'd walk into the path of a German tank." His mouth turned up at the corners, quivered, and fell again into the harsh downward curve that had become characteristic in the last month. He looked down at his ruined jacket and plucked at one of the frayed tears.

Saint-Germain watched this closely, then asked, "Has the fighting been very bad?"

"What's very bad? Some days we kill more than they do, and some days they kill more. It sickens me." He turned toward the fire and for a little time said nothing; Saint-Germain respected his silence. Finally James sighed. "Is there anyone else here at Montalia?"

"My manservant Roger, but no one other than he." Again Saint-Germain waited, then inquired, "Is there something you require, Mister Tree? I would recommend a bath and rest to begin with."

This time James faltered noticeably. "It's funny; I really don't know what I want." He gave Saint-Germain a quick, baffled look. "I wanted to be here. But now that I am, I'm too tired to care." His eyes met Saint-Germain's once, then fell away. "It doesn't make much sense."

"It makes admirable sense," Saint-Germain told him, shaking his head as he studied James.

"I'm probably hungry and sore, too, but, I don't know . . ." He leaned back in the chair, and after a few minutes while Saint-Germain built up the fire, he began to talk in a quiet, remote ramble. "I went home in thirty-one; Madelaine might have mentioned it."

"Yes," Saint-Germain said as he poked at the pine log; it crackled and its sap ran and popped on the dry bark.

"It was supposed to be earlier, but what with the Crash, they weren't in any hurry to bring one more hungry reporter back to St. Louis. So Crandell—he was my boss then —extended my assignment and when he died, Sonderson, who replaced him, gave me another eighteen months before asking me to come back. It was strange, being back in the States after more than thirteen years in Europe. You think you know how you'll feel, but you don't. You think it will be familiar and cozy, but it isn't. I felt damn-all odd, I can tell you. People on the street looked so—out of place. Of course the Depression was wrecking everything in the cities, but it was not only that. What worried me was hearing the same old platitudes everyone had been using in 1916. I couldn't believe it. With everything that had happened there was no comprehension that the world had changed. It was so different, in a way that was so complete that there was nothing the change did not touch. People kept talking about getting back to the old ways without understanding that they could not do that ever again . . ."

"They never can," Saint-Germain interjected softly. He was seated once again in the high-backed overstuffed chair.

". . . no matter what." He broke off. "Maybe you're right," he concluded lamely, and stared at the fire. "I've been cold."

"In time you will be warm again, Mister Tree," Saint-Germain said, and rose to pick up a silver bell lying on the table beside his violin case. " "Would you like to lie down? You could use rest, Mister Tree." His manner was impeccably polite but James sensed that he would do well to cooperate with the suggestion.

"Sure," was James' quiet response. "Sure, why not."

"Excellent, Mister Tree." He rang the bell, and within two minutes a sandy-haired man of middle height, middle build, and middle age came into the room. "Roger, this is Madelaine's great good friend, James Emmerson Tree. He has gone through an . . . ordeal." One of Saint-Germain's brows rose sharply and Roger recognized it for the signal it was.

"How difficult for him," Roger said in a neutral voice. "Mister Tree, if you will let me attend to you . . ."

James shook his head. "I can manage for myself," he said, not at all sure that he could.

"Nonetheless, you will permit Roger to assist you. And when you have somewhat recovered, we will attend to the rest of it."

"The rest of it?" James echoed as he got out of the chair, feeling horribly grateful for Roger's proffered arm.

"Yes, Mister Tree, the rest of it." He smiled his encouragement but there was little amusement in his countenance.

"Yeah, I guess," James responded vaguely, and allowed himself to be guided into the dark hallway.

The bathroom was as he remembered it—large, white tiled and old fashioned. The tub stood on gilt crocodile feet and featured elaborate fixtures of the sort that had been in vogue eighty years before. James regarded it affectionately while Roger helped to take off his damaged clothing. "I've always liked that tub," he said when he was almost naked.

"It *is* something of a museum piece," Roger said, and James was free to assume he agreed.

The water billowed out of the taps steaming, but James looked at it with an unexpected disquiet. He was filthy, his muscles were stiff and sore, and there were other hurts on his body which he thought would welcome the water, but at the last moment he hesitated, suppressing a kind of vertigo. With care, he steadied himself with one hand and said to Roger, who was leaving the room, "I'm worn out, that's what it is."

"Very likely," the manservant said in a neutral tone before closing the door.

As he stretched out in the tub, the anticipated relaxation did not quite happen. James felt his stiff back relax, but not to the point of letting him doze. He dismissed this as part of the aches and hurts that racked him. When he had washed away the worst of the grime, he looked over the damage he had sustained when he was thrown from the jeep. There was a deep weal down the inside of his arm. "Christ!" James muttered when he saw it, thinking he must have bled more than he had thought. Another deep cut on his thigh was red but healing, and other lacerations showed no sign of infection. "Which is lucky," James remarked to the ceiling, knowing that he could never have come the long miles to Montalia if he had been more badly hurt. The other two reporters had not been so fortunate: one had been shot in the crossfire that wrecked the jeep and the other had been crushed as the jeep overturned.

This was the first time James had been able to remember the incident clearly, and it chilled him. How easy it would have been to have died with them. One random factor different and he would have been the one who was shot or crushed. With an oath he got out of the tub, and stood shaking on the cold tiles as the water drained away.

"I have brought you a robe," Roger said a few minutes later as he returned. "Your other garments are not much use any longer. I believe that there is a change of clothes in the armoire of the room you used to occupy."

"Hope I can still get into them," James said lightly in an attempt to control the fright that had got hold of him.

"You will discover that later, Mister Tree." He helped the American into the bathrobe he held, saying in a steady manner, "It's very late, Mister Tree. The sun will be up soon, in fact. Why don't you rest for now, and my master will see you when you have risen."

"Sounds good," James answered as he tied the sash. He wanted to sleep more than he could admit, more than he ever remembered wanting to. "I . . . I'll probably not get up until, oh, five or six o'clock."

"No matter, Mister Tree," Roger said, and went to hold the door for James.

James woke from fidgety sleep not long after sunset. He looked blankly around the room Madelaine had given him so many years before, and for several minutes could not recall how he had got there, or where he was. Slowly, as if emerging from a drugged stupor he brought back the events of the previous night. There at the foot of the bed was the robe, its soft heavy wool familiar to his touch. Memories returned in a torrent as he sat up in bed: how many times he had held Madelaine beside him through the night and loved her with all his body and all his soul. He felt her absence keenly. At that, he remembered that Saint-Germain was at Montalia, and for the first time, James felt awkward about it. It was not simply that he was jealous, although that was a factor, but that he had never properly understood the man's importance in Madelaine's life.

He got out of bed and began to pace restlessly, feeling very hungry now, but oddly repulsed at the thought of food. "Rations," he said to the walls in a half-joking tone, "that's what's done it." Telling himself that he was becoming morbid, he threw off the robe, letting it lie in a heap in the nearest chair, and dressed in the slightly old-fashioned suit he had left here before returning to America. The trousers, he noticed, were a little loose on him now, and he hitched them up uneasily. He had neither belt nor suspenders for it, and might have to ask for one or the other. The jacket hung on him, and he reflected that he had not gone in for much exercise in the last few years until he had come back to Europe four months ago. He looked in vain for a tie and recollected that he had disdained them for a time. He would have to find something else.

At last he found a roll-top pull-over at the bottom of one of the drawers, and he gratefully stripped off jacket and shirt to put it on. It was of soft tan wool, with one or two small holes on the right sleeve where moths had reached it, and it felt lovely next to his skin. With shirt and jacket once more donned, James felt that he presented a good enough appearance to venture down into the main rooms of the chateau.

He found his way easily enough, although the halls were dark. His eyes adjusted readily to this, and he told himself that after all the nights when he and Madelaine had sought each other in the dim rooms and corridors, he should be able to find his way blindfolded. For the first time in several days, he chuckled.

"Something amuses you, Mister Tree?" said Saint-Germain from behind him, his tone lightly remote as he approached. "I heard you come down the stairs a few minutes ago. I'm pleased you're up. I thought you might be . . . hungry."

"I was. I am," James said, turning to face the other man. "But there's . . ." He could not continue and was not certain why.

"For whatever consolation it may be to you, I do sympathise, Mister Tree," le Comte said slowly, looking up at the tall American. "It may surprise you to learn that it will be a while before you become used to your . . . transition." As he said this, his dark eyes met James' uncompromisingly.

"Transition?" James repeated with a bewildered smile. "I don't understand."

"Don't you?" Le Comte de Saint-Germain gave James another steady look and said cautiously, "Mister Tree, are you aware of what has happened to you?"

James laughed uneasily. "I think I've been hurt. I *know* I have. There are cuts on my arms and legs, a couple pretty serious." He cleared his throat nervously. "There were three of us in the jeep, and there was an ambush. No one bothered to find out if we were press, but I don't blame them for that. I don't know which side did it, really." He shook himself self-consciously. "Someone must have walked over my grave."

"Very astute, Mister Tree," Saint-Germain said compassionately.

"I don't remember much more than that. It *does* sound lame, doesn't it? But I don't."

"You recall being injured." He motioned toward the tall, studded doors that led to the small sitting room where James had found him the night before. "That is a start."

James fell into step beside the smaller man and was mildly startled to find that he had to walk briskly to keep up with Saint-Germain. "Actually, it's all muddled. I remember the crossfire, and the jeep turning over, and being tossed into the air, but the rest is all . . . jumbled. I must have passed out, and didn't come to until after dark. I can't tell you what made me come here. I guess when you're hurt, you look for a safe place, and I've been here before, so . . ." He heard Saint-Germain close the door behind them and stopped to look about the sitting room.

"It seems eminently reasonable, Mister Tree," Saint-Germain told him as he indicated the chair James had occupied before.

"Good," James responded uneasily.

Saint-Germain drew up his chair; the firelight played on his face, casting sudden shadows along his brow, the line of his straight, aslant nose, the wry, sad curve of his mouth. Though his expression remained attentive, his eyes now had a sad light in them. "Mister Tree, how badly were you hurt?"

James was more disquieted now than ever and he tugged at the cuffs of his jacket before he answered. "It must have been pretty bad. But I walked here, and I figure it's more than forty, maybe fifty miles from . . . where it happened." He ran one large hand through his silver hair. "Those cuts, though. Jesus! And I felt so . . . detached. Bleeding does that, when it's bad, or so the medics told me. But I got up . . ."

"Yes," Saint-Germain agreed. "You got up."

"And I made it here . . ." With a sudden shudder, which embarrassed him, he turned away.

Saint-Germain waited until James was more composed, then said, "Mister Tree, you've had a shock, a very great shock, and you are not yet recovered from it. It will take more than a few minutes and well-chosen words of explanation to make you realize precisely what has occurred, and what it will require of you."

"That sounds ominous," James said, forcing himself to look at Saint-Germain again.

"Not ominous," Saint-Germain corrected him kindly.

64

"Demanding, perhaps, but not ominous." He stretched out his legs and crossed his ankles. "Mister Tree, Madelaine led me to understand that you were told about her true nature. Is this so?" Privately, he knew it was, for Madelaine had confided all her difficulties with James over the years, and Saint-Germain was aware of the American's stubborn disbelief in what he had been told.

"A little. I heard about the aristocratic family, and looked them up." His square chin went up a degree or two. "She made some pretty wild claims . . ."

Saint-Germain cut him short. "Did you bother to investigate her claims?"

"Yes," James admitted, sighing. "I had to. When she told me . . . those things, I had to find out if she had been making it up out of whole cloth." He rubbed his hands together, his nervousness returning.

"And what did you discover?" Saint-Germain's inquiry was polite, almost disinterested, but there was something in his dark eyes that held James' attention as he answered.

"Well, there was a Madelaine de Montalia born here in the eighteenth century. That was true. And she did . . . die in Paris in 1744. She was only twenty, and I read that she was considered pretty." He paused. "The way Madelaine is pretty, in fact."

"Does that surprise you?" Saint-Germain asked.

"Well, the same family . . ." James began weakly, then broke off. "The portrait looked just like her, and she kept saying it was her." These words were spoken quickly and in an undervoice, as if James feared to let them have too much importance.

"But you did not believe her," Saint-Germain prompted him when he could not go on. "Why was that?"

"Well, you should have *heard* what she said!" James burst out, rising from the chair and starting to pace in front of the fireplace. "She told me . . . Look, I know that you were her lover once. She didn't kid me about that. And you might not know the kinds of things she said about herself . . ." He stopped and stared down at the fire, thinking that he was becoming more famished by the minute. If he could eat, then he would not have to speak. Unbidden, the memories of the long evenings with Madelaine returned with full force to his thoughts. He pictured her dining room with its tall, bright windows, Madelaine sitting across from him, or at the corner, watching him with delighted eyes as he ate. She never took a meal with him, and he had not been able to accept her explanation for this. As he tried to recall the taste of the sauce Claude had served with the fish, he nearly gagged.

"I know what she told you," Saint-Germain said calmly, as if from a distance. "She told you almost twenty years ago that she is a vampire. You did not accept this, although you continued to love her. She warned you what would happen when you died, and you did not choose to believe her. Yet she told you the truth, Mister Tree."

James turned around so abruptly that for a moment he swayed on his feet. "Oh, sure! Fangs and capes and grave-yards and all the rest of it. Madelaine isn't any of those things."

"Of course not."

"And," James continued rather breathlessly now that he was started, "she said that you were . . . and that you were the one who changed her!" He had expected some reaction to this announcement, but had not anticipated that it would be a nod and a stern smile. "She said . . ." he began again, as if to explain more to Saint-Germain.

"I'm aware of that. She had my permission, but that was merely a formality." He sat a bit straighter in his chair as the significance of his words began to penetrate James' indignation. "She and I are alike in that way, now. It is correct: I did bring about her change, as she brought about yours." His steady dark eyes were unfaltering as they held James'.

"Come on," James persisted, his voice growing higher with tension. "You can't want her to say that about you. You can't."

"Well, in a general way I prefer to keep that aspect of myself private, yes," Saint-Germain agreed urbanely, "but it is the truth, nonetheless."

James wanted to yell so that he would not have to listen to those sensible words, so that he could shut out the quiet, contained man who spoke so reasonably about such completely irrational things. "Don't joke," he growled, his jaw tightening.

"Mister Tree," Saint-Germain said, and something in the tone of his voice insisted that James hear him out: the American journalist reluctantly fell silent. "Mister Tree, self-deception is not a luxury that we can afford. I realize that you have been ill-prepared for . . . recent events, and so I have restrained my sense of urgency in the hope that you would ask the questions for yourself. But you have not, and it isn't wise or desirable for you to continue in this way. No," he went on, not permitting James to interrupt, "you must listen to me for the time being. When I have done, I will answer any questions you have, as forthrightly as possible; until then, be good enough to remain attentive and resist your understandable inclination to argue."

James was oddly daunted by the air of command that had come over le Comte, but he had many years' experience in concealing any awe he might feel, and so he clasped his hands behind his back and took a few steps away from the fire as if to compensate for the strength he sensed in Saint-Germain. "Okay; okay. Go on."

Saint-Germain's smile was so swift that it might not have occurred at all—there was a lift at the corners of his mouth and his expression was once again somber. "Madelaine took you as her lover sometime around 1920, as I recall, and it was in 1925 that she tried to explain to you what would become of you after you died." He saw James flinch at the last few words, but did not soften them. "Like Madelaine, you would rise from death and walk again, vampiric. As long as your nervous system is intact, you will have a kind of life in you, one that exerts a few unusual demands. You have some experience of them already. You are hungry, are you not? And yet you cannot bring yourself to eat. The notion of food is repulsive. We're very . . . specific in our nourishment, Mister Tree, and you must become accustomed to the new requirements . . ."

"You're as bad as she is," James muttered, looking once toward the door as if he wanted to bolt from the room. He wanted to convince himself that the other man was a dangerous lunatic, or a charlatan enjoying himself at James' expense, but there was undoubted sincerity in Saint-Germain's manner, and a pragmatic attitude that was terribly convincing.

"Oh, I am much worse than Madelaine, Mister Tree. It was I who made her a vampire, back in the autumn of 1743." He frowned as James turned swiftly, violently away. "Your change was assured possibly as early as 1922, but Madelaine was so fearful of your hatred that it took her over two years to gather her courage to explain the hazard to you. You see, she loves you, and the thought of your detestation was agony for her. She could not leave you unprepared, however, and eventually revealed . . ."

67

"This is crazy," James insisted to the ceiling; he could not bring himself to look at Saint-Germain. "Crazy."

"Do you appreciate the depth of her love?" Saint-Germain went on as if he had not heard James' outburst. "Your protection was more important to her than your good opinion. She risked being loathed so that you would not have to face your change in ignorance." He folded his arms. "And you make a paltry thing of her gift by refusing to admit that the change has happened."

James threw up his hands and strode away from the fireplace toward the farthest corner of the room. "This doesn't make any sense. Not any of it. You're talking like a madman." He could hear the unsteadiness of his voice and with an effort of will lowered and calmed it. "I remember what she told me about being a vampire. I didn't believe it then, you're right. I don't believe it now. And you keep talking as if something has happened to me. True enough. My jeep was shot out from under me, I've lost a lot of blood and I've been wandering without food for over three days. No wonder I feel so . . . peculiar."

Slowly Saint-Germain got out of the chair and crossed the room toward James. His compelling eyes never left James' face, and the quiet command of his well-modulated voice was the more authoritative for its lack of emotion. "Mister Tree, stop deluding yourself. When that jeep turned over, when you were thrown through the air, you suffered fatal injuries. You lay on the ground and bled to death. But death is a disease to which we are, in part, immune. When the sun set, you woke into . . . Madelaine's life, if you will." He stopped less than two strides from James. "Whether you wish to believe it or not, you are a vampire, Mister Tree."

"Hey, no . . ." James began, taking an awkward step back from Saint-Germain.

"And you must learn to . . . survive."

"NO!" He flung himself away from le Comte, bringing his arms up to shield his face as if from blows.

"Mister Tree . . ."

"It's *crazy!*" With an inarticulate cry, he rushed toward the door.

Before he could reach it, Saint-Germain had moved with remarkable speed and blocked James' path. "Sit down, Mister Tree."

"I . . ." James said, raising one hand to threaten the smaller man.

68

"I would advise against it, Mister Tree," Saint-Germain warned him gently, with a trace of humor in his expression that baffled James anew. "Sit down."

The impetus which had driven James to action left him as quickly as it had possessed him, and he permitted himself to be pointed in the direction of the chair he had just vacated. He told himself that he was in the presence of a lunatic, and that he ought to go along with him; but deeper in his mind was the gnawing fear that against all reason, Saint-Germain might be right. He moved stiffly, and as he sat down, he drew back into the chair, as if to protect himself. "You're . . ."

"I'm not going to hurt you, if that is what concerns you," Saint-Germain sighed. When James did not deny his fear, Saint-Germain crossed the room away from him, and regarded him for two intolerably long minutes. "Madelaine loves you, Mister Tree, and for that alone, I would offer you my assistance."

"You were her lover once, if you're who I think you are." He had summoned a little defiance into his accusation.

"I have told you so. Yes, she and I were lovers, as you and she were." There was an eighteenth century lowboy against the wall, and Saint-Germain braced himself against it, studying James as he did.

"And you're not jealous?" James fairly pounced on the words.

"In time, we learn to bow to the inevitable. My love for Madelaine has not diminished, Mister Tree, but for those of our nature, such contact is . . . shall we say nonproductive?" His tone was sardonic; his face was sad. "No, I am not jealous."

James heard this out in disbelief. "You want me to believe that?"

"I would prefer that you did," Saint-Germain said, then shrugged. "You will discover it for yourself, in time."

"Because I'm a vampire, like you two, right?" The sarcasm James had intended to convey was not entirely successful.

"Yes."

"Christ." James scowled, then looked up. "I said Christ. If I'm a vampire, how come I can do that? I thought all vampires were supposed to blanch and cringe at holy words and symbols." He was not enjoying himself, but asking this question made him feel more comfortable, as if the world were sane again.

"You will find that there are a great many misconceptions about us, Mister Tree. One of them is that we are diabolic. Would you be reassured if I could not say God, or Jesus, or Holy Mary, Mother of God? Give me a crucifix and I will kiss it, or a rosary and I will recite the prayers. I will read from the Torah, the Koran, the Vedas, or any other sacred literature you prefer. There is a Bible in the library—shall I fetch it, so that you may put your mind at rest?" He did not conceal his exasperation, but he mitigated his outburst with a brief crack of laughter.

"This is absurd," James said uncertainly.

Saint-Germain came a few steps closer. "Mister Tree, when you accepted Madelaine as your mistress, you knew that she was not entirely like other women. At the time, I would imagine that lent a thrill to what you did. No, don't bristle at me. I'm not implying that your passion was not genuine: if it was not, you would not have been given her love as you have." He fingered the lapel of his jacket. "This is rather awkward for me."

"I can see why," James said, feeling a greater degree of confidence. "If you keep telling me about . . ."

"It's awkward because I know how you love Madelaine, and she you. And how I love her, and she me." He read the puzzled look that James banished swiftly. "You will not want to relinquish what you have had, but . . ."

"Because you're back, is that it?" James challenged, sitting straight in the overstuffed chair.

"No. After all, Madelaine is on a dig, so her choice, if one were possible, is a moot point at best. I am afraid that it is more far-reaching than that." He came back to his chair, but though he rested one arm across the back, he did not sit. "For the sake of argument, Mister Tree, accept for the moment that you have been killed and are now a vampire."

James chuckled. "All right: I'm a vampire. But according to you, so is Madelaine, as well as you."

"Among vampires," Saint-Germain went on, not responding to James' provocation, "there is a most abiding love. Think of how the change was accomplished, and you will perceive why this is so. But once we come into our life, the expression of that love . . . changes, as well. We hunger for life, Mister Tree. And that is the one thing we cannot offer one another."

"Oh, shit," James burst out. "I don't know how much of this I can listen to."

70

Saint-Germain's manner became more steely. "You will listen to it all, Mister Tree, or you will come to regret it." He waited until James settled back into the chair once again. "As I have told you," he resumed in the same even tone, "you will have to learn to seek out those who will respond to . . . what you can offer. For we do offer a great deal to those we love, Mister Tree. You know how profoundly intimate your love is for Madelaine. That is what you will have to learn to give to others if you are to survive."

"Life through sex?" James scoffed feebly. "Freud would love it."

Though Saint-Germain's fine brows flicked together in annoyance, he went on with hardly a pause. "Yes, through, if you take that to mean a route. Sex is not what you must strive for, but true intimacy. Sex is often a means to avoid intimacy—hardly more than the scratching of an itch. But when the act is truly intimate, there is no more intense experience, and that, Mister Tree, is what you must achieve." He cocked his head to the side. "Tell me: when you were with Madelaine, how did you feel?"

The skepticism went out of James' eyes and his face softened. "I wish I could tell you. I can't begin to express it. No one else ever . . ."

"Yes," Saint-Germain agreed rather sadly. "You will do well to remember it, in future."

On the hearth one of the logs crackled and burst, filling the room with the heavy scent of pine resin. A cascade of sparks flew onto the stone flooring and died as they landed.

James swallowed and turned away from Saint-Germain. He wanted to find a rational, logical objection to throw back at the black-clad man, to dispel the dread that was filling him, the gnawing certainty that he was being told the truth. "I don't believe it," he whispered.

Saint-Germain had seen this shock so many times that he was no longer distressed by it, but merely saddened. He approached James and looked down at him. "You will have to accept it, Mister Tree, or you will have to die the true death. Madelaine would mourn for you terribly, if you did that."

" 'Die the true death.' " James bit his lower lip. "How . . ."

"Anything that destroys the nervous system destroys us: fire, crushing, beheading, or the traditional stake through the heart, for that matter, which breaks the spine. If you choose to die, there are many ways to do it." He said it matter-of-factly enough, but there was something at the back of his eyes that made James wonder how many times Saint-Germain had found himself regretting losses of those who had not learned to live as he claimed they must.

"And drowning? Isn't water supposed to . . ." James was amazed to hear this question. He had tried to keep from giving the man any credence, and now he was reacting as if everything he heard was sensible.

"You will learn to line the heels and soles of your shoes with your native earth, and will cross water, walk in sunlight, in fact live fairly normal lives. We are creatures of the earth, Mister Tree. That which interrupts our contact with it is debilitating. Water is the worst, of course, but flying in an airplane is . . . unnerving." He had traveled by air several times, but had not been able to forget the huge distance between him and the treasured earth. "It will be more and more the way we travel—Madelaine says that she had got used to it but does not enjoy it—but I must be old-fashioned; I don't like it. Although it is preferable to sailing, for brevity if nothing else."

"You make it sound so mundane," James said in the silence that fell. That alone was persuading him, and for that reason, he tried to mock it.

"Most of life is mundane, even our life." He smiled, and for the first time there was warmth in it. "We are not excused from the obligations of living, unless we live as total outcasts. Some of us have, but such tactics are . . . unrewarding."

"Maybe not death, but taxes?" James suggested with an unhappy chuckle.

Saint-Germain gave James a sharp look. "If you wish to think of it in that way, it will answer fairly well," he said after a second or two. "If you live in the world, there are accommodations that must be made."

"This is bizarre," James said, convincing himself that he was amused while the unsettling apprehension grew in him steadily.

"When you came here," Saint-Germain continued, taking another line of argument, "when did you travel?"

"What?" James made an abrupt gesture with his hand, as if to push something away. "I didn't look about for public transportation, so I can't tell you what time . . ."

"Day or night will do," Saint-Germain said.

"Why, it was da . . ." His face paled. "No. I . . . passed

72

out during the day. I decided it was safer at night, in any case. There are fewer patrols, and . . ."

"When did you decide this? Before or after you had walked the better part of one night?" He let James have all the time he wanted to answer the question.

"I walked at night," James said in a strange tone. "The first night it was . . . easier. And I was so exhausted that I wasn't able to move until sundown. That night, with the moon so full, and seeing so well, I figured I might as well take advantage of it . . ."

"Mister Tree, the moon is not full, nor was it two nights ago. It is in its first quarter." He was prepared to defend this, but he read James' troubled face, and did not press his argument. "Those who have changed see very well at night. You may, in fact, want to avoid bright sunlight, for our eyes are sensitive. We also gain strength and stamina. How else do you suppose you covered the distance you did with the sorts of wounds you sustained to slow you down?"

"I . . . I didn't think about it," he answered softly. "It was . . . natural."

"For those . . ."

". . . who have changed, don't tell me!" James burst out, and lurched out of the chair. "If you keep this up, you'll have me believing it, and then I'll start lookng for a padded cell and the latest thing in straight jackets." He paced the length of the room once, coming back to stand near Saint-Germain. "You're a smooth-tongued bastard, I'll give you that, Saint-Germain. You *are* Saint-Germain, aren't you?"

"Of course. I thought you remembered me from that banquet in Paris," came the unperturbed answer.

"I did. But I thought you'd look . . ."

"Older?" Saint-Germain suggested. "When has Madelaine looked older than twenty? True, you have not seen her for more than six years, but when she came to America, did she strike you as being older than the day you met her?"

"No," James admitted.

"And she looks very little older now than she did the day I met her in 1743. You are fortunate that age has been kind to you, Mister Tree. That is one of the few things the change cannot alter." Abruptly he crossed the room and opened the door. "I trust you will give me an hour of your time later this evening. Roger should be back by then, and then you will have a chance to . . ."

"Has he gone for food?" James demanded, not wanting to admit he was famished.

"Something like that," le Comte answered, then stepped into the hall and pulled the door closed behind him.

The Bugatti pulled into the court behind the stables and in a moment, Roger had turned off the foglights and the ignition. He motioned to the woman beside him, saying, "I wil get your bag, Madame, and then assist you."

"Thank you," the woman answered distantly. She was not French, though she spoke the language well. Her clothes, which were excellent quality, hung on her shapelessly, and the heavy circles under her eyes and the hollows at her throat showed that she had recently suffered more than the usual privations of war. Automatically she put her hand to her forehead, as if to still an ache there.

"Are you all right, Madame?" Roger asked as he opened the passenger door for her. In his left hand he held a single worn leather valise.

"I will be in a short time," she responded, unable to smile, but knowing that good manners required something of the sort from her.

Roger offered her his arm. "You need not feel compelled, Madame. If, on reflection, the matter we discussed is distasteful to you, tell me at once, and I . . ." He turned in relief as he saw Saint-Germain approaching through the night.

"You're back sooner than I expected," Saint-Germain said, with an inquiring lift to his brows.

"I had an unexpected opportunity," was the answer. "Just as well, too, because there are Resistance fighters gathering further down the mountain, and they do not take kindly to travelers."

"I see," Saint-Germain responded.

"A number of them wished to . . . detain Madame Kunst, hearing her speak . . . and . . ." Roger chose his words carefully.

"I am Austrian," the woman announced, a bit too loudly. "I *am*. I fled." Without warning, she started to cry with the hopelessness of an abandoned child. "They took my mother and my father and shot them," she said through her tears. "And then they killed my uncle and his three children. They wanted me, but I was shopping. A neighbor warned me. It wasn't enough that Gunther died for defending his friends, oh, no."

74

Saint-Germain motioned Roger aside, then held out his small, beautiful hand to Madame Kunst. "Come inside, Madame Kunst. There is a fire and food."

She sat passively while her tears stopped, then obediently took his hand, and for the first time looked into Saint-Germain's penetrating eyes. "Danke, Mein Herr."

"It would be wiser to say 'merci,' here," Saint-Germain reminded her kindly. "My experience with the Resistance in this area says they are not very forgiving."

"Yes. I was stupid," she said as she got out of the Bugatti and allowed Saint-Germain to close the door. In an effort to recapture her poise, she said, "Your manservant made a request of me as he brought me here."

Roger and Saint-Germain exchanged quick glances, and Saint-Germain hesitated before saying, "You must understand, this is not precisely the situation I had anticipated. Did my manservant explain the situation to you clearly? I do not want to ask you to do anything you think you would not wish to do."

She shrugged, shaking her head once or twice. "It doesn't matter to me. Or it does, but it makes no sense."

"How do you mean?" Saint-Germain had seen this lethargic shock many times in the past, but long familiarity did not make it easier to bear. He would have to make other arrangements for James, he thought: this woman clearly needed quiet and time to restore herself. She had had more than enough impositions on her.

"It's all so . . ." She sighed as Saint-Germain opened the side door for her and indicated the way into the chateau. "No man has touched me since Gunther, and I was content to be in my father's house, where the worst seemed so far away. When I thought those men might force me, I screamed, but there was no reason for it any more."

"You have nothing to fear from anyone at Montalia," Saint-Germain told her quietly.

She nodded and let Roger escort her into the breakfast room off the kitchen. There was a low fire in the grate and though the striped wallpaper was faded, in the flickering light it was pleasant and cozy. As Saint-Germain closed the door, she sat in the chair Roger held for her and folded her hands in her lap. Her age was no more than thirty, but the gesture was that of a much younger person. "Gunther died six months ago. I didn't find out about it at first. They don't tell you what's happened. The SS comes and people go out with them and don't come home again, and no one dares ask where they have gone, or when they will return, for then the SS might return. It was the local judge who told me, and he was drunk when he did."

Roger bowed and excused himself to prepare a simple meal for Madame Kunst.

"When did you leave Austria, Madame?" Saint-Germain asked her as he added another log to the fire.

"Not many days ago. Eight or nine, I think. It could be ten." She yawned and apologized.

"There is no need," Saint-Germain assured her. "The fare here is adequate but not luxurious. If you are able to wait half an hour, there will be soup and cheese and sausage. Perhaps you would like to nap in the meantime?"

She thought about this, then shook her head. "I would sleep like the dead. I must stay awake. There are too many dead already." She fiddled with the fold of her skirt across her lap, but her mind was most certainly drifting. "I ate yesterday."

Saint-Germain said nothing but he could not repress an ironic smile, and was relieved that he had attended to his own hunger a few days before. The matter of nourishment, he thought, was becoming ridiculously complex.

"You did *what?*" James exclaimed, outraged. He had come back to the sitting room some ten minutes before and had tried to listen in reserved silence to what Saint-Germain was telling him.

"I saw that she was fed and given a room. I'm sorry that this adds so many complications. Had Roger been able to reach Mirelle, the problem would not have arisen." He was unruffled by James' outburst.

"*First,* you send your valet out to get a cooperative widow for me, and when that doesn't work because he can't get through to the village, he brings a half-starved Austrian refugee here as a weird kind of substitute, never mind what the poor woman thinks, being half kidnapped. *Second,* you think I'll go along with this impossible scheme. *Third,* you're telling me that you bring women here the way some cooks rustle up a half a dozen eggs, and I'm supposed to be grateful?" His voice had risen to a shout, as much to conceal the guilty pleasure he felt at the prospect of so tantalizing a meeting.

"Mister Tree, if there were not a war going on, all this would be handled differently. It may surprise you to know that I am not in the habit of 'rustling up,' as you say, coop-

76

erative widows or anyone else, for that matter. However, your situation will be critical soon, if something is not done, and I had hoped to find as undisruptive a solution as possible."

"Well, you sure as hell botched it," James said, taking secret pleasure in seeing this elegant stranger at a loss.

"Lamentably, I must concur." He thrust his hands into his pockets and started toward the door.

James could not resist a parting shot. "You mean you were going to lay out a woman for me, like a smorgasbord, so I could . . ."

Saint-Germain's mobile lips turned down in disgust. "What do you take me for, Mister Tree? Mirelle knows what I am and finds it most satisfying. She would enjoy the . . . variety you would offer her. Good God, you don't believe that I would expose a woman like Madame Kunst to what we are, do you? She understands there is a man here suffering from battle fatigue, and is prepared to make allowances. It is dangerous and unwise to spend time with those who are repelled by us. If you are to survive in this life, you must learn to be circumspect." He reached for the door, then added, "Roger found the two boxes of earth from Denver, and that will afford you some relief, but not, I fear, a great deal."

"Earth from Denver?" James echoed.

"Of course. When Madelaine knew that you would walk after death, she arranged to have two cartons of your native earth shipped here, in case it was needed." It was said lightly, but the significance did not escape James. "She had stored it in the stables, and Roger did not find it until late afternoon."

"Earth from Denver. I can't believe it." There would have been comfort and denial in laughter, but James could not summon any.

"She cares what happens to you, Mister Tree. It was not whim but concern for your welfare that made her get those two boxes." He opened the door wide and stepped into the hall. His face was clouded with thought and he made his way slowly to the kitchen.

Roger looked up as Saint-Germain came quietly through the door. "She's bathed and gone to bed."

"Good. Did you learn anything more?" He was frowning slightly; there was an indefinable restlessness about him.

"Nothing significant. She's twenty-nine, comes from Salzburg. She used to teach school, her husband . . ."

77

"Gunther?"

"Yes. He was an attorney, I gather." He finished tidying the clutter in the kitchen and turned to bank the coals in the huge, wood-burning stove.

"Do you believe her?" Saint-Germain asked quietly.

"That she was a teacher and her husband an attorney, yes. The rest, I don't know." Roger closed the fuelbox and wiped his hands on a rag, leaving blackened smudges on the worn cloth.

"Nor do I," Saint-Germain admitted. "It may only be shock, but. But."

Roger blew out one of the kerosene lanterns. "Is she what she seems?"

"Superficially, no doubt," Saint-Germain said measuredly. "And everything she has told us may be true. If that's the case, she might be blackmailed. If she has children, and they are held by the SS, she might undertake almost anything to save them. Because if she is what she claims to be, and wants to be out of Austria and away from the war, why didn't she stop in Switzerland? That's a neutral country."

"She might not feel safe there," Roger suggested.

"And instead she feels safe in France?" Saint-Germain countered in disbelief. "You know what the French want to do to the Germans these days. Why should she leave the comparative haven Switzerland offers for this?"

"It is espionage?" Roger asked, taking the other lantern and starting toward the door.

"We will doubtless soon find out. But we must be very cautious. All the Resistance would need is an excuse to come here hunting German spies and matters might suddenly become unpleasant for us." He accompanied Roger out of the kitchen and toward the tower, the oldest part of the chateau. "I'm afraid I've scandalized Mister Tree again," Saint-Germain remarked as the reverberations of their footsteps clattered away into the eerie darkness. "He's accused me of pimping."

Roger gave a snort of amusement. "How charming. Did he say it directly?"

"Not quite. That would mean he would have to see too clearly what has become of him. It is unfortunate that you did not reach Mirelle. She would have put an end to all this nonsense, and the worst of his anxiety would be over by now. He's badly frightened; the thing that could not possibly happen to him has happened. Mirelle would tease him out of it. It's a pity she does not want to be one of my blood in the end. She would do well." They reached a narrow, uneven stairway that led into the upper rooms of the tower, and Saint-Germain stood aside for Roger so that he could light his way. The lantern was unnecessary for Saint-Germain, but his manservant required more illumination.

"It's best that she should know her mind now," Roger said, picking his way up the hazardous stairs. "Later, it might be inconvenient."

"True enough," Saint-Germain murmured. "Which room are the boxes in?"

"The second, where the trunks are stored. I stumbled on them by chance." They were halfway up the stairs now, and Roger paid particular attention to this stretch, for he knew that the one short trip stair was located here.

"To hide a box, put it with other boxes," Saint-Germain said, paraphrasing the maxim. "I have always applauded Madelaine's cleverness."

Roger got past the trip stair and moved faster. "Both boxes are unmarked, but there is the stencil design of an oak on both of them, which was what alerted me."

"How very like her," le Comte chuckled. They were almost at the landing, and he smiled his anticipation. "He'll be more at ease with this."

"Perhaps, perhaps not," Roger responded with a shrug. On the landing, he pointed to the door. "That one. There's a stack of boxes in the north corner. They're on the top of it."

As he opened the door and stepped into the room, Saint-Germain said over his shoulder, "You know, it is inconvenient that our scars can't be altered. Plastic surgery might change any number of things. Mister Tree is going to have some distinctive marks on his arms and thighs which will make identification simple. If there were a way to remove them, it might be easier to go from alias to alias. Well, that time may come." He looked around for the stack Roger had described. "Ah. There. If you'll give me a hand getting them down, I will take them to Mister Tree's room."

James woke at sunset feeling more restored than he had since his accident. He stretched slowly, oddly pleased that there were no aches to hamper his movements. He was healing, he insisted to himself. When he rose from the bed, there was the first hint of an energetic spring in his step.

He dressed carefully, noticing that his clothes had been pressed some time during the day. The only things that he could not find were his shoes. After a brief hunt for them, he shrugged and settled for a pair of heavy boots he had worn years before when he and Madelaine had gone tramping over the rough hillsides together. As he laced them up, he thought how comfortable they were, and hoped that le Comte would not be too offended by them.

When at last he ventured down to the sitting room, he found Madame Kunst finishing the last of her tea, a few crumbs left on the Limoges plate beside her cup and saucer. He hesitated, then came into the room. "Good afternoon."

She looked up suddenly, guiltily, then smiled as best she could. "Good afternoon, though it is more evening, I think. You are . . ."

"The American suffering from battle fatigue, yes," he said with the same directness he had used to disarm politicians and industrialists for more than two decades. "You needn't worry, Madame. I am not precisely out of control, as you can see." To demonstrate this, he took a chair and arranged himself casually in it.

"I'm glad you're feeling . . . better?" This last change of inflection caught his attention and he leaned forward to speak to her.

"Yes. I'm much revived, thanks." He had deliberately chosen a chair that was far enough away from her that she would not be too much disturbed by his presence.

"You're an officer?" she asked when she had poured herself another cup of tea. She pointed to the pot in mute invitation, saying, "If you like, I could ring for another cup."

"That would be . . ." He broke off, finding the thought of tea distasteful. "Very good of you, but it would be wasted on me," he finished, frowning a bit.

"Is anything the matter?" she inquired apprehensively.

"No, not really." He decided to answer her question. "I'm not an officer, or a soldier, I'm afraid. I'm a journalist. I've been covering the action toward Lyon, but it hasn't been what I expected."

Madame Kunst smiled politely. "I'd think not." She sipped her tea. "What is your impression? Or would you rather not discuss it?"

"You must know the answer to that better than I," James suggested blandly, the habits of caution exerting themselves.

"Only what we are told," she said with a degree of sadness.

"But there must be raids and . . ." he said, hoping she would take up his drift.

"We hear about them, naturally, but Salzburg is not as important as other places. It is not important to shipping or the offensive, so we do not know how the rest of the country is going on." She finished the tea and reluctantly set the cup aside. "They have real butter here, and the milk is fresh."

The mention of food made James queasy, but he was able to nod. "Yes. There are shortages everywhere. Back home, there are ration cards used for meat and other necessary items. The government encourages everyone to grow their own vegetables." He knew it was safe to mention this, because it was common knowledge and there were articles in the newspapers which any enemy spy who wished to could read.

"There isn't much opportunity to grow vegetables in a city flat," she said.

"True enough. I have a cousin who always sends me canned goods at Christmas. She has quite a garden and thinks I need her food." He wanted to get off the subject, but did not quite know how.

Madame Kunst spared him the trouble. "How long have you been in France, Herr . . . I believe I was not told your name."

This time he could not avoid giving his name. "Tree, Madame Kunst. You see, I have been told who you are. I'm James Emmerson Tree. I've been in France a little more than a year."

"So long, with the war and all." She waited patiently for him to answer.

"Reporters go where the story is, and this is the biggest story around," he said with a shrug that did not completely conceal his disillusion with his work. "I'd been in France before, in the Twenties, and it made me the logical candidate to come back to cover this." He ran his hand through his hair. "You'll have to forgive me, Madame Kunst. I must be disconcerting company. These clothes aren't the latest, I haven't done anything much about my hair or shaving, but don't be alarmed." He touched his chin tentatively and felt a slight roughness, as if he had shaved the evening before.

"We do what we can in these times," she said, trying to

appear at her best. "I have two dresses, and the other is worse than this one."

There was a tap at the door, and then Roger entered. "Excuse me, Madame Kunst, but if you are finished with your tea, I will remove the tray for you."

"Yes, I am, thank you," she replied, a trifle more grandly than she had addressed James. "It was very good."

"There will be a supper in two or three hours. Served in the breakfast room, as it is easiest to heat." He picked up the tray and started toward the door. "Mister Tree, le Comte would appreciate it if you could spare him a moment of your time."

James scowled. "When?"

"At your convenience. In the next two hours, perhaps?" He gave a little bow and left the room.

"My aunt had a butler like that, years ago," Madame Kunst said wistfully when Roger had gone.

"He's very efficient," James admitted grudgingly, deciding that Roger was a bit *too* efficient.

"Servants aren't like that any more." She smoothed the skirt of her dress and looked over at James. "How did you find the situation in France? When you arrived?"

"Chaotic," James answered. "It's apparent that this war has taken a dreadful toll on the country."

"On all Europe," Madame Kunst corrected him.

"Sure. But I've been covering France, and this is where I've had to look for the damage, the ruin and the destruction. I've heard about conditions in Russia, and I'm appalled. Italy is supposed to be having very bad troubles, and the Netherlands and Scandinavia are suffering, too, but France, in many ways, is taking the brunt of it. When I was in London, I was shocked, but when I came to France, I was horrified." He sensed that he was talking too much, but was no longer able to stop himself. "The First World War was ruinous, but this is something a lot worse. And the rumors we keep hearing make it all sound more awful than we think it is. There's nothing as bad as trench warfare going on, and no mounted cavalry against tanks, as there was before, but the cities are burning, and the country is laid waste, and there doesn't seem to be any end in sight. What can anyone think? It can't go on endlessly, but there is no way to end it."

"At home, we all pray that it will end," she said softly, her large brown eyes turned appealingly toward him. "Don't you think the Americans could do something? If your President would insist that we stop, all of us, at once, then it could not go on. Without the Americans, the British and the French could not continue this insanity."

"The Americans don't see it that way, Madame Kunst," James said rather stiffly, feeling disturbed by her afresh.

"But what are we to do, if it goes on and on? Everyone in my family is dead but myself, and no one cares that this is the case. Down the street from where my family lived, there is a widow who has lost four sons, all of them flyers, killed in air battles. She is like a ghost in her house. And there are hundreds, thousands like her."

"As there are in France and Italy and England and Holland, Madame Kunst. As there are in Chicago and Montreal and Honolulu." He got up. "Excuse me, but it might be best if I talk to le Comte now, rather than later."

Her face changed. "Have I offended you? Please, don't think me heartless, or uncaring of the sufferings of others. That is why I spoke to you about a resolution to this terrible war, so that there need not be such women ever again."

"I'm not offended," James said, knowing that he was and was uncertain why. As he left the room, he passed near her chair, and for one moment, he was caught and held by the sound of her pulse.

"She gave me a lecture on pacifism," James said at last when Saint-Germain had asked him for a third time what he and Madame Kunst had found to talk about. "She wants me to end the war so no more widows will lose sons. God knows, I don't want to see any more deaths, but what's the alternative?"

"Capitulation?" Saint-Germain suggested.

"Oh, no. You've seen the way the Germans have treated every foot of land they've taken. And they say there's worse things going on. One of the Dutch reporters said that there were cattle cars full of people being taken away. If they're doing that in Germany to Germans, what would they do to the rest of us?" He gestured once. "That could be propaganda about the cattle cars, but if it isn't . . ."

"I do see your point, Mister Tree. I am not convinced that you see mine. Montalia is isolated and splendidly defensible. A person here, or in one of the houses in, shall we say, a ten-kilometer radius, with a radio receiver and a reasonable amount of prudence, might provide the Germans with extremely useful information." He watched James as he said this, expecting an argument.

"But what good would it be?" James objected, taking his favorite role of Devil's advocate. "You said yourself that the château is isolated, and God knows, this part of Provence is damned remote. What could anyone find out here? There's nothing very strategic in your ten-kilometer radius unless you think that they're going to start last-ditch battles for the smaller passes."

"We're very close to Switzerland. As many secrets as gold are brokered through Geneva and Zurich. With a listening post here, a great deal could be learned." Saint-Germain raised one shoulder. "I may be feinting at shadows, but it worries me."

"If they want a listening post for Switzerland, why not *in* Switzerland?" James asked.

"The Swiss take a dim view of the abuse of their neutrality. Certainly there are monitoring posts in Bavaria and Austria, but it is not as easy to watch Geneva and Lausanne. The Resistance have found men and women doing espionage work in these mountains before. Last year, it was a gentleman claiming to be a naturalist hoping to preserve a particular bird; he climbed all over the mountains, and stayed in the old monastery on the next ridge. He might have accomplished his task, whatever it was, if one of the Resistance men did not become suspicious when he saw the supposed naturalist walk by a nest of the bird in question without a second look. It may be that Madame Kunst is nothing more than an Austrian refugee in a panic, but I am not going to assume anything until she has shown me I have no reason to be concerned."

James chuckled. "And where do you fit into this?"

"I don't want to fit into it at all," was Saint-Germain's short rejoinder. "War ceased to amuse me millen . . . years ago." He shook his head. "Apparently you haven't considered our position. We are both foreigners in a country at war. If we are imprisoned, which could happen—it has happened before—our particular needs would make a prolonged stay . . . difficult." He recalled several of the times he had been confined, and each brought its own burden of revulsion. "You would not like prison, Mister Tree."

"I wouldn't like it in any case," James said at once. "I knew a reporter who was shot by the Spanish for trying to file an uncensored story. He'd done it before, and they caught him trying the same thing again."

Saint-Germain lifted his head, and listened. "Ah. That will be Mirelle. We will continue this at a later time, Mister Tree."

"What?" James cried, remembering the woman's name all too clearly. Now he, too, could hear an approaching automobile.

"You do have need of her, Mister Tree," Saint-Germain said quietly. "More than you know now."

James came off the sofa to round on le Comte. "It's monstrous. I've gone along with some of what you've told me, but I draw the line at this!"

"Perhaps you should wait until you have a better idea of what 'this' is," Saint-Germain said, a touch of his wry humor returning. "She is looking forward to this evening. It would be sad if you were to disappoint her."

"Come on," James protested.

This time, when Saint-Germain spoke, his voice was low and his eyes compassionate. "Mister Tree, you will have to learn sometime, and we haven't the luxury of leisure. Mirelle wants to have the pleasure of taking your vampiric virginity, and you would do well to agree. We are rarely so fortunate in our first . . . experiences. You will spare yourself a great deal of unpleasantness if you will set aside your worry and pride long enough to lie with her. Believe this."

"But . . ." James began, then stopped. He could feel his hunger coiled within him, and he knew without doubt that it was hearing the beat of Madame Kunst's heart that had sharpened it. "Okay, I'll try. If nothing else," he went on with a poor attempt at jauntiness, "I'll get a good lay."

Saint-Germain's brows rose. "It is essential that *she* have the . . . good lay. Otherwise you will have nothing, Mister Tree. Males of our blood are like this." He was about to go on when there was a quick, emphatic step in the hall and the door was flung open.

Mirelle Bec was thirty-four, firm-bodied and comfortably voluptuous. She did not so much enter the room as burst into it with profligate vitality. Drab clothes and lack of cosmetics could not disguise her sensuality. Her hair was a dark cloud around a pert face that was more exciting than pretty, and when she spoke, it was in rapid, enthusiastic bursts. "Comte!" she called out and hastened across the room to fling her arms around him. "You've kept away so long, I ought to be annoyed with you, but I could never do that."

Saint-Germain kissed her cheek affectionately. "I have missed seeing you too, Mirelle."

As she disengaged herself from his embrace, she pointed dramatically at James. "Is *this* the baby? Comte, you are a bad, bad man: you did not tell me he was so beautiful." To James' embarrassment, Mirelle gave him a thorough and very appraising looking-over. "Oh, this is very promising," she declared as she approached him. "I do like the white hair. It is distinguished, is it not?" As James tried not to squirm, she laughed aloud and reached for his hand. "You are shy? But how delightful." Over her shoulder she added to Saint-Germain, "How good of you to offer him to me. I am going to enjoy myself tremendously."

"But, Madame, we . . ." James said in confusion, trying to find some way to deal with her.

"Have not been introduced, is that what concerns you? I am Mirelle, and you, I have been told, are James. So. We are introduced now. It remains only for you to show me which room is yours."

James had had experience with many women, but this one took him wholly aback. Yet even as he tried to separate himself from her, he felt the draw of her, and his much-denied hunger responded to her. "Madame . . ."

"No, no, no. Mirelle. You are James. I am Mirelle. It is more friendly that way, is it not?" She drew his arm through hers. "You will tell me how you come to be here as we walk to your room."

"I am not sure that . . ." James began with a look of mute appeal to Saint-Germain which he studiously avoided.

"But I am. Let us go, James." She waved to le Comte and went quickly to the door, taking the ambivalent James with her.

"Christ, I'm sorry," James muttered some time later. They were in a glorious tangle on his bed with the covers in complete disarray. "If you give me a little time, Mirelle. I must be more worn out than I knew."

Mirelle gave a sympathetic laugh. "It is not fatigue, James, it is what you are." She trailed her fingers over his chest. "Weren't you told?"

"I've been told all kinds of things the last couple days," he sighed in disgust.

"But this, this is different," Mirelle said generously. "For a man, this is more important, is it not?" She snuggled closer to him, pressing her body to his. "It is not the same when one changes. But there are compensations."

"For this? I've never been impotent before," James said, a note of distress creeping into his voice.

"It is not impotent," Mirelle assured him. "You are more than ready to make love to me, yes? And you are not repelled by me. So this is another matter."

"You don't know what it is that I . . . almost did." He felt suddenly miserable; he wanted to shut out the drumming of her heart that was loud as heavy machinery in his ears.

Mirelle laughed deeply. "But of course I know what you almost did. You are the same as le Comte. You wanted to put your lips to my neck and taste . . ."

"For God's sake!" James interrupted her, trying to move away from her but not succeeding.

"Well," Mirelle said reasonably, "it is what I expected of you. But you have not entirely got the way of it. You are judging yourself by your earlier standards, and they do not apply, my cabbage."

James rolled onto his side and rested his hand on the rise of Mirelle's hip. "Look, you're being very nice about this, and I appreciate it, but . . ." He wanted to shrug the incident off, to promise her another hour when he was feeling a bit better, but he could not find a gracious way to do so. He loved the feel of her skin under his hand and her nearness was oddly intoxicating, so that he could not bring himself to leave the bed or ask her to leave it.

"You are discouraged, but you need not be, James. You have not got used to your new ways. You don't have to worry. Let me show you. I love showing." Her hazel eyes took on a greenish shine of mischief. "You must learn how to satisfy me. It is not too difficult, ami, and when it is done, you will do well enough for yourself." She wriggled expertly. "Now, your hand *there,* if you please. That is a good beginning."

Dazed, James did as he was told, letting her instruct him as if he were a boy of fourteen. At first he could not get the memory of the long nights with Madelaine out of his thoughts, but then, as his passion grew in answer to Mirelle's, he responded to her, and only to her, and this

87

time, though he did not love her as he had supposed he would, he had no reason to apologize.

Roger escorted Madame Kunst to her room, and listened quietly to her protestations that she was reluctant to remain at Montalia. "I have those I wish to meet. It isn't wise for me to remain here."

"But there is fighting, Madame, and you would not be safe, should you venture out into the world as it is now." Roger had received Saint-Germain's instructions several hours before to be solicitous of the Austrian woman.

"They said that there would be a boat at Nice that would take me to Scotland. I must reach that boat. I must."

"My master will make inquiries on your behalf, Madame. It would not be pleasant for you to suffer any more mishaps." Roger was unfailingly polite and slightly deferent, but gave no indication that he would accommodate her.

"He has some influence, this Comte? Could he help me?" Her voice pleaded but her wary eyes were hard.

"That is for him to decide, Madame Kunst. I will mention what you have told me." The hallway was dark where the glow of the lantern did not shine. "You have enough candles in your room?"

"There are plenty, thank you," she answered abruptly. Again she grasped the handle. "I must leave. I must go to Scotland. Can you explain that?"

"I will tell my master what you have said."

Her hands came up to her chin in fists. "Oh, you stupid man!" she shouted in her frustration, and then was at once quiet and restrained. "Forgive me. I must be more . . . tired than I realize."

"Of course, Madame Kunst." He lifted the lantern higher. "You can see your way?"

She did not entirely take the hint. "That woman," she said as she paused on the threshold. "I suppose she is necessary?"

Roger gave her no response whatever and there was a subtle sternness about his mouth that indicated he would not indulge in speculation about his master or Mirelle Bec.

"Well, such things happen, I suppose." She gave a polite shrug to show it made no difference to her if those in the house wanted to be immoral. "The highborn live by their own rules, do they not?"

"Good night, Madame Kunst," Roger said, and stepped

back from her doorway. When he was satisfied that the door was firmly closed, he turned away from it and made his way back toward the sitting room where he knew that Saint-Germain waited for him. His sandy head was bent in thought and his face was not readable.

Shortly before sunrise, Saint-Germain found James walking in the overgrown garden. He came up to the American silently and fell into step beside him, letting James choose the path they were to take.

"She showed me," James said after a long while.

"Ah."

Their feet as they walked crunched on the unraked gravel that led between the abandoned flower beds. James reached out and pulled a cluster of dried, faded blossoms off a trailing branch as it brushed his shoulder. "It wasn't what I expected." The paper-crisp husks of the flowers ran between his fingers and fell.

"But tolerable?" Saint-Germain inquired as if they were discussing nothing more important than the temperature of bath water.

"Oh, yeah. Tolerable." He laughed once, self-consciously. "Tolerable."

Saint-Germain continued his unhurried stroll, but pointed out that the sun would be up in half an hour. "You are not used to the sun yet, Mister Tree. Until you are, it might be wisest to spend the day indoors, if not asleep."

"Unhuh." He turned back toward the chateau, saying with some awkwardness, "Mirelle told me she'd be back in three or four days. But she didn't . . . Oh, Christ! this is difficult."

"She will be here for you, Mister Tree. My need is not great just now." He answered the unasked question easily, and sensed James' relief.

"That's what she hinted." James looked sharply at the shorter man. "Why? Is it because you're after that Austrian woman?"

"What an appalling notion! No, of course I'm not." He expressed his indignation lightly, but decided that he had better explain. "Oh, if I were determined to . . . use her, I could wait until she was asleep and visit her then, and she would remember little more than a very pleasant dream. It is something we all learn to do in time, and it has its advantages upon occasion. But Madame Kunst is a bit of a puzzle. Her purpose for being here is not known to me, and

89

it would not be sensible or wise to . . . be close to her. If she learned or guessed what I am, and wished me ill, she would have me at a distinct disadvantage. The Resistance might not mind taking off time from hunting Nazis and Nazi sympathizers to hunt a more old-fashioned menace. You must not forget that is how most of the world sees us —as menaces. I would not like to have to leave Montalia precipitately just now." There had been many times in the past when he had had to take sudden flight in order to save himself: it was not a thing he wished to do again. "We must be circumspect, James."

This was the first time Saint-Germain had addressed him by his Christian name, and it startled him. "Why do you call me James? Is it because of Mirelle?"

"Don't be absurd." Saint-Germain's wry smile was clear in the advancing light.

"You've been calling me Mister Tree since I arrived here." The tone of his statement was stubborn and James was plainly waiting for an answer.

"And you have not been calling me anything at all," was Saint-Germain's mild reply.

James faltered. "It's that . . . I don't know what to call you."

"Is it." Saint-Germain gestured toward the side door that led into the pantry. "This is the quickest way."

As James was about to go in, there came the drone of planes overhead. He looked up, searching the sky, and at last, off to the north, saw a formation of shapes headed west. "I can't tell whose they are," he said quietly.

"American or British bombers back from their night-time raids. They keep to the south of Paris for reasons of caution." He held the door for James.

"This far south?" James wondered aloud, already stepping into the shadow of the doorway.

"It is possible, James. They have done it before. You have been here very little time and until last night, you were not paying much attention to the world around you." There was no rebuke in what he said, and he felt none.

"True enough," James allowed, and waited while Saint-Germain closed the door behind them and latched it. "Why bother?"

"The crofters around here are very insular, careful folk, like all French peasants. They respect and admire Madelaine because she is the Seigneur. Don't look so surprised, Mister Tree. Surely you can understand this. The peasants

90

are proud of their estate and they are protective of Montalia. Most of them think it is a great misfortune that the lines have passed through females for so long, but that makes them all the more determined to guard Madelaine. They know what she does—or part of it. They would beat their daughters senseless for taking lovers, but the Seigneurs are different, and her adventures provide them endless entertainment."

They had come into the kitchen where Roger was cutting up a freshly-killed chicken. He looked up from his task and regarded the two men quizzically. "I didn't know you were outside."

"James was taking the air, and I was coming back from checking the gatehouse," Saint-Germain said. "You might want to purchase some eggs from the Widow Saejean. Her boy told Mirelle that times are hard for them just now."

Roger nodded. "This afternoon." He bent and sniffed the chicken. "They're not able to feed them as well as they did."

"We could purchase a few of our own, if that would help," Saint-Germain suggested, but Roger shook his head.

"Better to buy them. If we bring chickens here, we won't be able to feed them much better than the rest do, and they would resent it. We are still the foreigners, and it would not take much to have them remember it." He began to cut up the bird with a long chef's knife, letting the weight of the blade do much of the work.

"About Madame Kunst . . ." Saint-Germain prompted.

"Nothing more, my master. I have not been able to touch her valise, which is locked in any case. But I do know that it is heavy, heavier than it ought to be, considering her story." Roger looked down at the chicken parts and smiled.

"Very good." Saint-Germain motioned to the American. "Come, James. Let's permit Roger to enjoy his breakfast in peace." He indicated the passage toward the main hall and waited for James to accompany him.

Once they were out of the kitchen, James said, "I don't mean to sound stupid, but I thought Roger was . . ."

"A vampire?" Saint-Germain finished for him. "No."

Apparently needing to explain himself, James went on. "It's only that you seem to be so . . . used to each other."

Saint-Germain turned toward the front reception room where tall windows gave a view of the rising mountains behind the promontory where Montalia sat. "I did not say that he is . . . unchanged, simply that he is not a vampire.

91

Do sit down, if you wish, and be at ease. No," Saint-Germain said, resuming his topic, "Roger is not like us, but he has died and recovered from it. You were right; we are old friends. We met some time ago in Rome."

"If he's died and . . . what is he?" James knew that he ought to be bothered by these revelations, or to admit he was in the company of madmen, but after his night with Mirelle, he could not bring himself to accuse Saint-Germain of anything.

"He is a ghoul," Saint-Germain responded matter-of-factly. He saw James blink. "Don't imagine him back there tearing that poor fowl's carcass to bits with his teeth. There is no reason for it. He eats neatly because it is easier and more pleasant. The only restriction his state imposes on him is that the meat—for he only eats meat—be fresh-killed and raw."

James shuddered and looked away. "I see."

"I'm not certain of that," Saint-Germain said quietly.

Eager to change the subject, James asked, "Why was he trying to look at Madame Kunst's valise?"

"Because she guards it so zealously," he answered at once. "I am curious about a woman who says that she avoided arrest by being out shopping when the rest of her family were taken, and yet carries a large valise. Did she take it shopping with her? Then for what was she shopping? If she picked it up later, why that bag, rather than another? She says that she has three changes of clothes. Good. But where did they come from? Did she buy a dress while shopping, and take it with her when she fled? Did she buy it later? If Roger says that the valise is heavy, then you may believe him. In that case, what is in it?"

"Maybe she went back to her house and grabbed the only valise she could find, stuffed clothes into it, and something of value, say, silver candlesticks, so that she could pay for her passage. She wants to go to Scotland, and I don't know if it would be safe to pay for her trip in marks." James turned the questions over in his mind as he answered, enjoying the process. "What if she got as far as Zurich, had to buy some clothes, but could only afford to buy a cheap valise? If she'd gone to the train . . ."

"And where did she get her travel permit?" Saint-Germain inquired evenly. "Whether she is going to Scotland or Poland, she would have to have the proper papers, or she would not be able to get a ticket, let alone come this far."

"But if she didn't come by train? If she had a car . . ."

He thought this over. "She would require proper documents to get over the border, that's true, and if her family was arrested, her name would probably be on a detain list."

"Yes. And where does that leave Madame Kunst?" With a shake of his head, Saint-Germain drew up a chair. "You are a journalist, James, and you are used to examining persons and facts. If the occasion should arise, and you are able to draw out Madame Kunst, I would appreciate your evaluation. Don't force the issue, of course, because I don't want her alarmed. If she is truly nothing more than a refugee determined, for reasons best known to herself, to get to Scotland, it would be a shame to cause her any more anguish. If she is not that, it would be foolish to put her on her guard."

"Are you always such a suspicious bastard?" James asked with increased respect.

"I am not suspicious at all. If I were, I should not have allowed her to come here. But I have seen enough treachery in my . . . life to wish to avoid it." He studied the tall American. "You would do well to develop a similar attitude, James. It spares us much inconvenience."

James gave this a reserved acceptance, then inquired, "What if she is an agent? What will you do then?"

"Inform the Resistance leaders. Yes, there are ways I can do this, and I will if it is necessary. I hope that it is not; I do not want to live under constant surveillance, as I have told you before." He got up. "I have a few tasks to attend to. If you will excuse me?"

As he started toward the door, James called after him. "What tasks?"

Saint-Germain paused. "I like to spend some time in my laboratory each day. It's a bit makeshift, but better than nothing."

"Laboratory? What do you do there?" James was somewhat intrigued, for although he had no great interest in scientific experimentation, he was curious about how Saint-Germain occupied his time.

"I make gold, of course." With James' indulgent laughter ringing in his ears, Saint-Germain left the reception room.

That afternoon James discovered Madame Kunst to be a fairly good, if impatient, card player. They had begun with cribbage and had graduated to whist. As Madame Kunst put down her cards, she said, "After I have my supper, let us play another rubber. You have some skill, it seems."

James, who was used to thinking of himself as a very good card player, was piqued by her comment. "Perhaps, after you have your meal, I will have forgotten my good manners, Madame."

She smiled widely and insincerely. "I do not believe that you have been deliberately allowing me to win—you aren't that shrewd in your bidding, for one thing." She looked around the room. "It is getting dark. How unfortunate that there are no electric lights here."

"But there are," James said impulsively, remembering Madelaine's pride at having them. "There is not enough gas to run the generator to power them. If the cars are going to be driven, it must be kerosene and candles here."

"But there is a generator? Curious." She smiled at James. "Have you seen this château when it is alight?"

"Yes," James said, not entirely sure now that he should have told her about the generator. But where was the harm, he asked himself, when a quick inspection of the old stables would reveal the generator, and the allotted fuel for Montalia?

"It must be quite impressive," Madame Kunst said quietly. She was wearing one of her two dresses, an elegantly-knitted creation of salmon pink with a scalloped hem and long full sleeves. There were travel stains on the skirt and it would have been the better for cleaning and blocking. Madame Kunst fidgeted with the belt, putting her fingers through the two loops at either side of the waist. It was much more a nervous than a provocative gesture, but James could comprehend that in a lanky, high-strung way she might be attractive.

"It is," he said, taking the deck and shuffling it methodically. "After your meal, we can try again."

"Are you not going to join me?" she asked him.

"No, thank you." Then he recalled what Madelaine had said to him the first time he had dined at Montalia, and he paraphrased her words. "I have a condition which severely restricts my diet. It's simpler for me to make private arrangements for my meals."

"This is the oddest household. Roger tells me that le Comte dines privately in his rooms; you have a . . . condition. If it were fitting, I would suggest to Roger that we both eat in the kitchen, but he won't hear of it." She gave a tittery laugh, then left the room.

James shuffled the cards two more times, taking time and

care, then put them back in their ivory box. That done, he rose and sauntered out into the hallway, pleased to see that no one was about. Five careful minutes later, he was in Madame Kunst's room, tugging the valise from under her bed. He knelt on the floor, holding the leather case between his knees while he inspected the lock that held it closed. The valise was not unlike a large briefcase, with accordion sides and a metal re-enforced opening. The lock most certainly required a special key, but James thought he might be able to make some progress against it with a bent hairpin, if he could find one. He was so preoccupied that he did not hear the door open.

"You arrant fool," Saint-Germain said quietly but with intense feeling.

James started up, and the valise fell heavily onto its side. "You said . . ."

"I said that you might try to draw her out when talking with her: I did not recommend you do this." He shook his head. "I might as well scribble all over the walls that we have our doubts about her. Good God, if I had wanted the lock picked, I could do that myself. Use a little *sense*, James."

James' indignation was all the greater for the disquieting suspicion that Saint-Germain was right. "I thought I was taking your hint."

"After all I told you about prudence? Truly?" He bent down and very carefully put the valise back under the bed. "If it reassures you, James, I have examined the lock already, but under less questionable circumstances. It is not as simple as it looks. Not only is there the lock you see, there is a second lock under it, and it is a good deal more complex."

"How complex?" James inquired acidly.

"It takes two keys. I am not sure why, but it does give me pause." He was already crossing the room. "We should leave. Madame Kunst sat down to her supper not long ago, but there is no reason for her to linger over the food. She may come back here shortly, and I doubt either of us could adequately explain what we are doing here."

Grudgingly, James permitted Saint-Germain to take him from the room, but as they started down the long stairs, he made one protest. "Why don't you just break into the valise and tell her that you were required to do it?"

"James, for an intelligent man, you suffer from curious

95

lapses. Why would I do that? What excuse would she believe? And where would be the benefit?" His brows arched and he let James take whatever time he needed to answer the questions.

"Well," James said lamely as they reached the main floor again, "you would know what is in the valise."

"True enough. But do you know, I would rather find out some less compromising way." He frowned, then the frown faded. "I don't fault you for wanting the question resolved: so do I."

James accepted this with ill grace. "You aren't willing to do the obvious, so . . ."

"Do the obvious? It is not quite my style," he said sardonically. "James, play cards with the woman, listen to her, and make note of what she asks you. Tomorrow morning, I will tell her I have arranged for her transportation down the mountain so that she can reach Nice and the boat she says she wishes to take to Scotland. That should precipitate matters."

"And what if that is what she wants, and all she wants?" James asked.

"Then Roger will do it. He has arranged with the authorities in Saint-Jacques-sur-Crete to have a travel pass when it is necessary. In these matters the local officials are strangely flexible." He put one hand on James' arm. "Try to restrain your impulses until then, if you will. Should it turn out that we come through this with nothing more than a touch of war-time paranoia, we may count ourselves fortunate."

James had nothing to say in response, and knew that he was not very much looking forward to another round of losing at whist, but he offered no protest as he went back into the room to wait for Madame Kunst.

"Oh, thank you, Herr Comte," Madame Kunst said listlessly over a cup of weak tea the following morning.

"It was nothing, Madame. You told me that this was your wish. I only regret that it took so long to arrange the details. But surely you understand."

"Yes, of course I do." She paused to cough delicately. "I am surprised that you were able to accomplish this so quickly. After what I have been through, I expected I would have to intrude on your hospitality"—again a quiet, emphatic cough—"for a much longer time."

"It is best to act quickly in cases such as yours," Saint-Germain said ambiguously.

"How kind," she murmured, and achieved another cough.

"Is something the matter, Madame Kunst?" le Comte inquired politely, giving in.

"A slight indisposition, nothing more, I am sure." She smiled apologetically.

"Good. I would not like to think that you were ill." He rose from the chair he had taken across from her.

"Oh, I don't believe I'm that. My throat, you know. And it has been chilly." She said this last in a tone a bit more hoarse than when she had begun.

"It is often the case in the mountains," Saint-Germain said by way of courteous commiseration. "I believe there is aspirin in the chateau, but little else. If you like, I will ask Roger to bring you some."

Her hand fluttered up to her throat, lingered there artistically, then dropped once more. "I don't think it will be necessary. If I am troubled by it still this afternoon, then I might ask for one or two tablets."

"Very good. You may want to rest an hour or so. The drive to the coast is long and fatiguing." He left the room to the dry sound of her cough.

"She claims to be feeling poorly," Roger explained to Saint-Germain later that morning. "I brought her the tea she asked for and said that I was looking forward to taking her down to Nice. She claimed to be enthusiastic, but said she did not think she was entirely well, and did not know how easily she would travel."

"She coughed for me," Saint-Germain said. "Apparently she is not as eager as she claimed to be."

"Give her a break," James protested, watching the other two. "Maybe she's got a cold. She's been through enough."

"No matter what she has done, it's possible, of course, that she has caught a cold," Saint-Germain allowed. "But if you were as anxious as she has claimed to be to be out of this country and on your way to Scotland, would you permit a cold to keep you from completing your journey?"

"She might be worn out," James said, determined to discount anything Saint-Germain suggested. "If she's tired enough, she might not be able to fight off a cold or any other bug that happens to be around."

Saint-Germain's dark eyes were wryly amused. "Is that

what you thought when you tried to search her valise? Never mind, James. We'll find out shortly what the case truly is."

"How're you planning to do that?" He was a little belligerent, and huffy.

"Why, I want to find out if she is really ill. I will offer her a remedy. If she takes it, I'll give her the benefit of the doubt. If she doesn't, then I will be extremely careful with her. As you should be." He turned away toward the old wing where he had set up his laboratory. "And James, if you would not mind, I would like to begin this myself. You may talk to her later, if you choose, but just at first, let me."

"You sound like you think I'd warn her . . ." James shot back. "I didn't get to be good at my job by shooting off my mouth."

"I am aware of that," Saint-Germain said. "But you have gallantry, my American friend, and there are those who have a way of turning that virtue to their advantage. All I ask is that you remember that."

Roger intervened before James could say anything more. "Should I get the Bugatti ready?"

"Yes. Whether Madame Kunst uses it, or one of us, it doesn't matter: the car should be fueled, and ready."

"You're anticipating some difficulty other than this?" James asked, looking about him involuntarily.

"Nothing specific, but in as unsettled a situation as we are in, it might be best." Saint-Germain gave James a penetrating, amused glance. "Do you wish to visit our patient in half an hour or so, to wish her godspeed?"

"Do you want me to?" James sounded irritable, but it was more from frustration at his own inactivity than genuine anger.

"Let us see how she responds to Roger." He motioned toward his manservant. "And to me."

James accepted this with a shrug, and went off to the old library to pass the better part of the morning in trying to decipher the Medieval French of the oldest volumes there. He found it intriguing and it kept him from pacing the halls like a stalking tiger.

"How are you doing, Madame Kunst?" Saint-Germain inquired of his guest as he went into her room twenty minutes after his conversation with Roger and James.

"Very well," she said listlessly.

"I trust so; the travel permit I have been able to secure for you is dated only for the next twenty-four hours. It would not be easy to get another one." He came to stand at the foot of her bed. "I can arrange for you to stop at the physician's, perhaps, but you might not wish to be subjected to the questions he is required to ask."

Madame Kunst turned blush rather than pale. "I want to keep away from officials."

"And so you shall. It is better for me, as well, to come as little to their attention as possible. Then, if it is satisfactory to you, I will make sure you have aspirin and brandy and plenty of lap rugs in the Bugatti. It will not make you entirely comfortable, but you probably will not be so until you are in Scotland." He gave her a sympathetic half-smile, and watched her face.

"Yes," Madame Kunst said, her brows twitching into an expression of impatience and dissatisfaction.

Saint-Germain assumed an expression of diffidence. "My manservant has reminded me that there is another medication in the château. It is . . . an herbal remedy, and very efficacious, or so I have been told. I would be pleased to bring some to you." He had made that particular elixir for more than three thousand years: it was a clear distillate that began with a solution prepared from mouldy bread. The recent discovery of penicillin had amused him.

Madame Kunst looked flustered. "A peasant remedy? I don't know . . . peasants are so superstitious and some of their practices are . . . well, unpleasant."

Very gently, Saint-Germain said, "In your position, Madame Kunst, I would think you would take that chance, if only to make your ship. Brandy is a help, but you will not be clearheaded. With the herbal remedy, you need not be fuddled."

She slapped her hands down on the comforter. "But what if the remedy is worse? Some of those remedies the monks made were mostly pure spirits with a little herbal additive. This is probably more of the same thing."

"I assure you, it is not," Saint-Germain said.

"Oh, I don't know. I will have to think about it." She remembered to cough. "I have to have time to recruit my strength, Herr Comte. I will tell you in an hour or so what

99

I have decided." With a degree of quiet malice, she added, "It was so good of you to offer this to me."

Saint-Germain bowed and left the room.

Slightly less than an hour after this, James came bursting out of Madame Kunst's room, running down the corridor, calling for Saint-Germain.

The response was almost immediate. Saint-Germain hastened from his laboratory as he tugged his lab coat off, wishing there were a way he could curb some of James' impetuosity. "A moment!" he cried as he reached the foot of the main staircase.

"We don't have a moment!" James shouted as he came into view on the upper floor. "It's urgent."

"So I gather," Saint-Germain said as he flung his wadded-up lab coat away from him. "But if it is, it might be best not to announce it to the world."

"Jesus! I forgot." He paused at the top of the stairs, then raced down them. "I don't know why it didn't occur to me. It should have."

"We will discuss it later," Saint-Germain said. "Now, what has you so up in arms?"

"Madame Kunst." He opened up his hands. "She's not in her room and her valise is gone."

"Indeed." Saint-Germain's brows rose and he nodded grimly.

"I went to her room, as you instructed, and it was empty. The bed was still a bit warm, so she can't have gone far, or have left too long ago. If we hurry, we can find her." Now that he had forced himself to be calm, all his old journalistic habits came back. "If she's carrying that thing, she'll have to stay on the road, and that means someone will see her, if only a farmer or a shepherd."

"You're assuming she's left Montalia," Saint-Germain said. "I doubt that she has."

"Why?" James demanded.

"Because Roger is down at the gatehouse and he has not signaled me that he has seen her. Not that that makes it simpler," he added dryly. "This place is a rabbit warren and it is not easily searched."

"Especially since we don't know what we're looking for, right?" James said, running one hand through his silver hair.

"That is a factor." Saint-Germain looked up toward the ceiling. "But we also know what we are *not* looking for, which is a minor advantage." He turned away from James, his eyes on the heavy, metal-banded door to the old wing of the chateau. "I think she may be armed, James. Be cautious with her. Bullet wounds are painful, and if they damage the spine or skull, they are as fatal to us as anyone else. No heroics, if you please. Madelaine would never forgive me."

James did not quite know how to take this, but he shrugged. "If that's how you want it, that's how I'll do it."

"Very good," Saint-Germain said crisply. "And we might as well begin now. First the kitchens and pantry, and then the old wing. With this precaution." He went and dropped the heavy bolt into place on the iron-banded door, effectively locking that part of the chateau.

"Why the kitchens first?" James asked.

"Because of the weapons it offers." Saint-Germain answered. "Knives, cleavers, forks, skewers, pokers. A kitchen is an armory on a smaller scale. If she has gone there, it will be touchy for us."

They completed their search in fifteen minutes and were satisfied that wherever Madame Kunst was, she had not been there.

"This might not bode well. If she has panicked—which isn't likely—it is merely a matter of finding her. But if she is acting with deliberation, it means she is already prepared and we must keep that in mind."

"Does she know we're looking for her, do you think?"

"Quite possibly. That is something else to keep in mind." He was walking back toward the main hall and the barred door. "This may be somewhat more difficult. We can close off the wing, but it provides endless places to hide, to ambush."

"Great," James said with hearty sarcasm.

"Although some of the same advantages apply to us. I wish I knew what it was she is trying to do. If I did, then I could counteract it more effectively." His hand was resting on the heavy bolt.

"And you won't call the authorities," James said.

"We've had this discussion already. You know the answer. We must settle this for ourselves. And for Madelaine, since she is the one who will have to live here when this is over." He let James consider this. "You and I are transient. This is her native earth."

"Okay, okay," James said, then waved a hand at the door. "What do we do, once we get in there?"

101

"To begin with, we move very quietly. And we make every effort not to frighten her. Frightened people do foolish and dangerous things." He lifted the bolt and drew back the door. "For the moment, keep behind me, James. If you see or hear anything, tap my shoulder. Don't speak."

"Right," James said, feeling a bit silly. He had seen war and knew how great the risks were for those caught up in the deadly game, but skulking around the halls of an old château after a woman with a worn leather valise seemed like acting out a Grade B movie from Universal. When the door was pulled closed behind him, he was disturbed by it. The hall was very dark, with five narrow shafts of light coming from the high notched windows. James watched Saint-Germain start toward the muniment room, and for the first time noticed the power and grace of his movements—he was controlled and feral at once, beautiful and awesome.

At the entrance to the muniment room, Saint-Germain held up his hand to motion James to stillness. He slipped through the narrow opening, then returned several long moments later. "She is not here, but has been here," Saint-Germain told James in a whisper that was so quiet it was almost wholly inaudible. "One of the old plans of Montalia is missing."

The two rooms below the muniment room were empty and apparently untouched. James was becoming strangely nervous, as if unknown wings had brushed the back of his neck. He found it difficult to be self-contained and was all for hurrying up the search so that he could bring his restlessness back under control. "She's in the upper rooms if she's anywhere in this part of the château," James murmured, wanting to speak at a more normal level.

"Patience, James. You and I have much more time than she does." He made a last check around the small salon, then gestured to James to follow him. "We'll try the tower rooms next. Be careful of the steps."

The narrow, circular stairwell was dark at all times, but Saint-Germain carried no light. James was growing accustomed to his improved dark vision, but was still not entirely confident of this to climb without watching his feet. For once, he was the one who lagged.

The first storeroom proved empty, but Saint-Germain indicated that he wanted to make a warning trap. "Nothing complicated; a few things that will make noise if knocked over. Should she be behind us, we will have a little time," he whispered, and set about his work.

James stood on the landing, experiencing the same unpleasant sensation he had had in the lower room. On impulse, he decided to investigate the next room himself, thereby saving them time as well as giving himself the satisfaction of doing something worthwhile. He moved close to the door, as he had seen Saint-Germain do, and then opened the door just wide enough to be able to slip inside. He was dumbfounded at the sight of the valise sitting on the floor amid the other trunks and broken chairs that were stored there, and was about to call out when he sensed more than felt another presence in the room.

"Not a sound, Herr Tree," Madame Kunst said softly as she brought up a Smith & Wesson .38 pistol. Her hands were expertly steady as she took aim at his head. "I will use this if I must."

Saint-Germain's warning flashed through James' mind— if his nervous system were damaged, if his spine or skull were broken, he would die the true death, and his resurrection would have lasted merely a week—and he stood without moving. He began to dread what might happen if Saint-Germain should come into the room.

"You have been curious about the valise, haven't you? You have all been curious." She no longer looked highstrung and helpless; that part of her had been peeled away, leaving a determined woman of well-honed ruthlessness. "I have promised to see that it is left in working order, and you will not interfere." She nodded toward the valise, her aim never wavering. "Open the valise, Herr Tree."

Slowly, James did as she ordered. He dropped to his knees and pulled open the top of the old leather bag. He stared down at the contraption in it.

"It is a *beacon*, Herr Tree. Take it out, very, very gently, and put it on that brass trunk by the wall, the one under the window. If you trip or jolt the beacon, I will shoot you. Do you understand?"

With more care than he had ever known he possessed, James lifted the beacon. As he carried it toward the trunk she had indicated, he thought to himself that she had told him. Neither of those things was possible, he guessed from put the beacon in place and hoped it was well-balanced.

"Turn around, Herr Tree," she said, softly, venomously.

James obeyed, hoping that she would not shoot in this little narrow room. "I'm not alone."

"Herr Comte?" she asked quickly.

"Yes."

She walked up to him, just far enough to be out of reach. "And the servant?"

"I don't know," James lied, praying she would believe him. "He . . . he was told to get the car ready." He forced himself to speak in an undervoice though he wanted to shout.

"How helpful," she muttered. She glared at him, apparently wanting to make up her mind, and finally, she cocked her head toward the door. "You will have to come with me, I think. You and I."

James all but ground his teeth. He wanted to rush at her, to yell so loudly that she would drop the .38 and flee from him. Neither of those things was possible, he guessed from the hint of a smile she wore. "Where are we going?" he forced himself to ask.

"Out. After that, we'll see." She was wearing her salmon-colored knit dress which in the muted light of the room looked more the shade of diseased roses. "Walk past me, Herr Tree. Hands joined behind your head." She came nearer to him. "What you feel at the base of your skull is the barrel of my pistol. If you move suddenly or try to grapple with me in any way, I will shoot. If you move your hands, I will shoot. Do I make myself clear?"

"Very."

"You will reach with your left hand, slowly and deliberately, for the door. You will open it as wide as possible and you will release it."

James did as she ordered, and when she told him to walk out onto the landing, he did that, too, as the muzzle of the .38 lay like a cold kiss on the nape of his neck.

"Now, down the stairs. One at a time. Carefully." She was speaking softly still, but the sound of her voice rang down the stones. mocking her.

On the fourth step down, James heard a sound behind him that did not come from Madame Kunst's steps. Apparently she was unaware of it,—for she never faltered nor turned. He wondered if she were so confident of her mastery of the situation that she paid no attention to such things. He moved a little faster, trying to remember where the trip stair was.

"Not so fast," Madame Kunst insisted. "It's dark in here."

Obediently, James slowed. He heard the whisper-light tread behind her, and wished he dared to turn. The trip stair was only a few treads below him. He made his way carefully.

Then, just as he passed the trip stair, something tremendously strong swept by him on the narrow curving stair, knocking him to the side and catching Madame Kunst on the most unstable footing in the tower.

She screamed, twisted. She fired once, twice, and the bullets ricocheted off the stone walls, singing and striking sparks where they touched. One of the bullets struck her in the shoulder and she fell, slid and slid, screaming at first and then whimpering. Her descent stopped only when Saint-Germain reached her.

"You may get up, James," he said as he lifted Madame Kunst into his arms.

Moving as if he were tenanted in a body that was unfamiliar to him, James rose, testing his legs like an invalid. When he was shakily on his feet again, he looked down at the other man. "Thank you."

"Thank *you*, James. Your methods were reckless but your motive laudable." He looked down at Madame Kunst, who was half conscious and moaning. "I should bandage her and get her to a physician. There must be a plausible story we can tell him."

James had not the strength to laugh at this as he came down the stairs.

"But it will arrange itself," Mirelle said confidently with a nonchalant French shrug. "A refugee woman, she says, came to my farmhouse, and I, what could I do but take her in? I did not know that she was carrying valuables, and when there was a commotion, I investigated." Her minx's eyes danced as she looked up at James. "It was very nice of you to give me the pistol, Mister Tree. I would not have been able to defend her if you had not been so generous." She held out her hand for the pistol.

"How do you explain the rest? The beacon and her wound?" Saint-Germain asked, not quite smiling, but with the corners of his mouth starting to lift.

Mirelle gave this her consideration. "I don't think I will explain the beacon. I think I will present it to a few of my

105

friends in the Resistance and they will see what kind of game it attracts. For the rest, the thief was holding Madame . . . Kunst, isn't it? so tightly that I was not in a position to get a clean shot." She sat back in the high-backed chair that was the best in her parlor. "The physician in Saint-Jacques-sur-Crete will not ask me too many questions, because he likes me and he hates the Germans and the war. Beyond that—who knows? The Germans may take her back, the Resistance may kill her. It does not matter so much, does it?" She folded her hands.

"Mirelle," Saint-Germain said, with more sadness than she had ever heard in his voice, "you cannot simply abandon her like so much refuse."

"You say that, after she tried to kill James and would have killed you?" Mirelle shot back at him. "You defend her?"

"Yes," was the quiet answer.

Mirelle got out of her chair and turned her helpless eyes on James, then looked away from them both. "Perhaps you can afford to feel this way, you who live so long and so closely with others. But I am not going to live long, and I have very few years to do all that I must. Extend her your charity, if you must, but do not expect it of me. My time is too brief for that." She folded her arms and stared defiantly at Saint-Germain.

"You have chosen it," Saint-Germain reminded her compassionately; he took her hand and kissed it.

"So I have," she agreed with her impish smile returning. "For the time, I have the best of both, and when that is done, well, we shall see." She turned toward James. "Would you like to remain here for the evening, James?"

"Thank you, Mirelle, but no." He glanced out the window to the parked Bugatti.

"Another time then. I will be at Montalia tomorrow night?" Her eyes went flirtatiously from Saint-Germain's to James' face. "You would like that, yes?"

"Of course," Saint-Germain said, answering for James.

"Then, good afternoon, gentlemen, and I will see you later. I have a few old friends who will want to hear from me, and the physician to mollify." Without any lack of courtesy, she escorted them to the door, and stood waving as the Bugatti pulled away.

James returned the wave, then looked at Saint-Germain. "What *will* happen to Madame Kunst?"

"I don't know," he said quietly.

"Does it concern you at all?" James was beginning to feel a twinge of guilt.

"Yes. But it is out of my hands now." He drove in silence.

"Just that easy, is it?" James demanded some minutes later when he had been alone with his thoughts.

Saint-Germain's small hands tightened on the steering wheel. "No, James—and it never becomes easy."

Text of a letter from the Count of Saint-Germain to his manservant Roger.

7 Grovesnor Mews
London, England
22 April, 1950

Sassevert Parc
Lausanne, Switzerland

Roger;

Your report arrived this morning and I am most grateful for it. The succinct compilation is admirable, as always, and tells me a great deal.

It will probably be best to remove the athanor; its design is somewhat outmoded in any case. You may dispose of it in the usual manner, but take care to sell the components in more than one city or one country. I am not eager to sustain another investigation. Doubtless I need not remind you of this precaution, but in such times as these—and when have there been other times?—we must be circumspect.

When you return, we will make arrangements to expand my laboratories here and in Italy. It might also be wise to continue work with that young American on his ceramic experiments. What would he think, I wonder, if he knew that those "revolutionary techniques" he and I discussed were as old as the Great Art itself? Or, for that matter, that he was not dealing with a chemical physicist but an alchemist? Do proceed with the licensing of the process, but let me review the terms of the agreements before the contracts are signed.

Be safe, old friend, and accept my sincere thanks.

Saint-Germain
his seal, the eclipse

108

Text of a letter from le Comte de Saint-Germain to Henry McMillian of Columbia University.

43 Corso Solitudine
Roma, Italia
15 May, 1952

Professor Henry McMillian
Department of Chemistry
Columbia University
New York City, New York, U. S. A.

Dear Doctor McMillian:

I am somewhat baffled by your letter, but I will do what I can to answer your questions. Yes, it is true that I have conducted some of the experiments you inquire about, but I am not now associated with the activities of any government, anywhere in the world. Those of us whose countries are lost through the predations of politics and war are often reluctant to engage in such projects.

It may be that in the future I will visit your country, but at the moment I have no such plans. My business interests there are being handled with great ability by American attorneys and there is no reason I can determine why I should change so worthwhile an arrangement.

As to the equipment you have purchased through the agency of my company in Switzerland, I assure you I have no objection whatsoever to your proposed adaptation of it to your uses. My own experiments have been concluded and I have no specific interest in the metallic shell you mention. However, I should warn you that I made no provision to shield it for radiation, and you may wish to take precautions if you still intend to pursue atomic research with it. In candor, I must add that I am not sure that it is pos-

*sible to make an adequate shield with the shell you
have. Let me urge caution in that respect.*

*With cordial good wishes to you and your col-
leagues, I am*

> **Saint-Germain**
> *his seal, the eclipse*

ART SONGS

O danke nicht für diese Lieder
mir ziemt es, dankbar Dir zu sein;
Du gabst sie mir, ich gebe wieder,
was jetzt und einst und ewig Dein.

IT was a small concert hall, holding less than eight hundred people; what it lacked in size it made up for in sumptuousness. The seats were red velvet plush, the carpets had been made to order in France, the murals on the ceiling, showing the whole court of Apollo, were the beautifully restored work of Giorgione. All the railings on the high-stacked balconies were the finest baroque carved wood covered with gold leaf. The orchestra pit was not large, accommodating thirty musicians in a pinch, and for that reason the hall was rarely used for anything other than baroque music.

Tonight was an exception: a concert of art songs with two singers and a piano accompaniment, and the hall was filled, for although the program was fairly unexciting, the baritone and the mezzo-soprano had a large and enthusiastic following, and the charity which the concert benefitted was socially popular.

Baronessa Alexis dalla Piaggia occupied the box immediately to the left of what was still designated the Royal

Box. She was a self-possessed forty-four years old, of sleek and lean New England good looks which contrasted oddly but not unattractively with the soft Roman extravagance of her silken peach-colored gown. The Barone was away for a month in Britain, and so for the evening, her escort was Francesco Ragoczy, who sat beside her in evening dress and with the Order of Saint Stephan of Hungary on his formal sash.

"I have to tell you this," Alexis whispered to him at the first break in the music. She spoke in English, hardly above a whisper. "They are investigating you."

"They?" Ragoczy murmured as he joined in the applause.

"You know, the government. You have dealings with Americans, don't you?" She turned her head toward the stage as the mezzo came forward. He was reminded of the line from *Don Giovanni: Nella grande maestosa,* oh, the big ones—so majestic, and had to stop himself from mentioning it to Alexis. The mezzo's voice was warm and creamy and rich, like an exotic sauce. "Francesco, are you listening to me?"

"Yes, Alexis. The government. Of course I have dealings with Americans. I have business holdings there and ventures here," he whispered. "My taxes are paid and my attorneys are respectable. What is the difficulty with the government?"

Alexis sighed. "In a bit," she said, listening again to the music. If only, she thought bitterly, her brother had not let drop that question about Ragoczy. She would not be in this awkward position. She sat back and listened to the delicious sounds of Hugo Wolf. When the song was finished, she leaned forward again. "You know how things are in the States right now; investigations and security checks and all the rest of it. That senator, the one from Michigan or Wisconsin or one of those states, is looking for communists everywhere, and those idiots in Congress are helping him. They've got people fired for being in support of the Spanish Civil War. Can you imagine!" She had let her voice rise, and was shocked to hear it over the dying clapping. Chagrined, she slipped back in her chair, and watched while the mezzo continued.

"I am aware of these problems," Ragoczy said at the next break, his face still toward the stage. "But what bearing does it have on me?"

"Well, if I'm not being indelicate, I understand there is a great deal of money involved, Francesco. Your money." Her gown was quite low in front, so that whenever she moved closer to him than required by decorum, she brought her hand up to her décolletage, not realizing that her attempts at modesty only served to emphasize what she intended to conceal.

"Well, that is how most of us do business these days," Ragoczy said with a slight smile.

"But that's just the *point!*" Alexis protested. "Don't you see, if there weren't so much money involved, they would probably leave you alone. But there you are, a very wealthy foreigner with fingers in all kinds of pies . . ." She broke off and leaned forward. "My Lord! That man's as handsome as an Italian Gregory Peck."

"Actually, he's Greek," Ragoczy corrected her mildly.

"A Greek Peck then. Where has he been all my life?" She laughed briefly, in the hope that the handsome man might turn toward her and show some interest. But this did not happen. "Do you know him, Francesco?"

"Slightly. I'll introduce you at intermission, if you wish."

"I do wish, if you please." She folded her hands in her lap, and added, "Chester said that all of Capitol Hill is coming down with security worries. They're all trying to prove they're not going to help the country go to hell, or sell out to communism." She was about to go on, but the music began again, and she was glad of it, because it afforded her four minutes to stare at the back of the handsome man's head. He was tall, she decided, and that pleased her, because at five foot eight she often felt she dwarfed the men around her. With tall men, she was less reserved and could play at being girlish now and again. At the end of the song, she touched Ragoczy's sleeve. "You've got to be careful. I mean it, Francesco. They're going through one of their crazy phases in the States, and it might be hard on you and the people who work for you."

"I thank you for the warning," he said sincerely, not entirely sure yet what he could do about it.

"It's not as if you could be asked to take a loyalty oath, but your employees probably will be. And they'll want to go into your background." She applauded more loudly as the mezzo bowed a third time before relinquishing the stage to her baritone partner.

113

There is a lady sweet and kind
Was never face so pleased my mind
I did but see her passing by
And yet I love her till I die.

"What could they do?" Ragoczy asked when the baritone had finished his first song. "I'm in Europe, and, as you say, a foreigner. I have papers as a displaced person they might check out for themselves."

"Oh, they're all cooperating: Italy, France, that Interpol network. At first they thought they wanted escaping Nazis, but now it's communists. Chester told me that anything that smacks of social reform has only got to be called communist, or the people who support it, communist sympathizers, and that's the end of it." Her eyes were on the handsome Greek again, fixed with all the intensity of a searchlight.

Per la gloria d'avorarvi
   voglio amarvi, o luci care.
Amando peneró,
   ma sempre v'ameró, si, si
Nel mio penare.
Peneró, v'ameró, luci care.

"He's pushing on top, don't you think?" Alexis said when the baritone had finished.

"It's not easy to do those upper phrases pianissimo," Ragoczy answered neutrally.

"I suppose not." She looked at her program. "Intermission isn't for almost twenty minutes," she sighed.

"But he will not escape before then," Ragoczy told her with an amused smile.

"No." She closed the program abruptly. "They'll have photographs and fingerprints and all the tax information, I guess, and they'll probably find a way to get a look at everything but your Swiss records. You must have Swiss records, since half the world seems to." She reached down for her beaded handbag and opened it. When she had found her lipstick, she opened her compact and began to apply it with a great deal of care. "I know this is probably rude, but . . ."

"Go right ahead," Ragoczy said, and crossed one leg over the other.

"It's just that he's so handsome. Well, you are, too, Francesco, in your way, but I'm at least two inches taller than you are, and in heels, it's simply impossible." She flashed a freshly-encarmined smile at him.

"I am desolated to be such a disappointment," Ragoczy told her, and turned toward the stage once again, where the mezzo and baritone were about to do a duet.

"Um," Alexis murmured, bending forward to stare at the Greek again.

"Why should your investigators bother over me?" Ragoczy asked when the two on stage had stopped singing.

"Because you're foreign and rich. They can point to you as another example of questionable foreigners preying off hard-working Americans. There's a lot of that, with inflation going up. Everyone thinks that Eisenhower should do something, but what?" She checked the low V of her neckline, not entirely sure now that it was wise to wear nothing more than the diamond choker Italo had given her for her birthday.

"How long is this likely to last?"

"Oh, who knows? As long as the Congress can get the papers to cover it, I guess. Most of them are using it to get votes, naturally. They like their jobs. What would Speaker Sam do if they ever made him go back to Texas?"

"Your brother told you this?" Ragoczy asked again, wanting to be sure.

"Poor Chester, yes. He's flown over for a couple of weeks, and he's been telling me about some of the things that have been going on. It's shocking!" Her dress, of flowing layers of silk chiffon, slid and drifted as she changed her position in her chair.

> *Mes vers fuiraient, doux et frêles*
> *Vers votre jardin si beau,*
> *Si mes vers avaient des ailes*
> *Comme l'oiseau.*

"What's he like, the Greek?" Alexis asked.

"I don't know; we're not well acquainted. I know him through the woman with him." Ragoczy did not allow his glance to linger on the beautifully coiffured head, nor the angle of her bared shoulder.

"What's *she* like?" The question was sharper than the previous one had been.

115

"She is an old and cherished friend of mine, Alexis," Ragoczy answered with just enough warning implied that the American woman with the Italian title looked up, startled, and knew that in some way, she had overstepped the bounds.

"I didn't mean . . ." She could not unsay the words, so she shrugged and went back to safer ground. "Is there anything they might find out about you or your relatives that they could use against you?"

"My relatives?" Ragoczy repeated. "What significance are they? Or are they still playing that 'you have relatives in the Old Country' record?"

"Something of that nature, I'm afraid. If you know someone who knows someone who knows someone who might think communists are all right, if they find it useful, it might come back to you. In your case, you are an unknown quantity, and they can imply any number of unpleasant things."

"No, infer. I would have to imply," Ragoczy corrected her gently. "It makes little difference."

"They can get a political tempest in a teapot." Alexis lowered her voice as the long musical introduction began, and whispered the last. "You ought to be careful. I've promised Chester to present him to you, but I don't think he'll want to talk about any of this."

"Probably not," Ragoczy agreed.

After the song, there was intermission at last. The singers bowed, the pianist bowed, and they left the stage as the house lights came up and the audience sighed and rustled and moved like a waking dragon.

"Where will the Greek go?" Alexis asked Ragoczy.

"I don't know. I presume he will have a drink," was the answer as he held her chair for her to rise, and then parted the heavy curtain of sculptured velvet at the back of the box.

"I wish it weren't so crowded," Alexis complained as she put her hand through Ragoczy's proffered arm. In three-inch heels, she was quite noticeably taller than he.

"We will find him, never fear." He took her down the plushly-carpeted stairs to the inner lobby where a portable bar was set up. "Does Italo know of your little . . . adventures?"

"Not exactly. He knows that I have them, but prefers to

116

know nothing more." She could feel her pulse against the choker, as if the diamonds had grown tight.

"And does that trouble you?" He guided her toward the bar. "If nothing else, this is an excellent vantage point."

"I hope so," she said, and ordered champagne. As the cork was popped, she thought over what he had asked her. "At the moment it pleases me. When I am fifteen years older than I am now, I might change my mind. Italo knows that there are advantages in a wife like me, and since I am from New Hampshire and not Rome or Naples or Venice, I'm not a blot on the escutcheon of Italian womanhood. It makes a kind of sense." She took the glass held out to her. "Aren't you having any?"

As Ragoczy paid the ridiculously high price for the champagne, he said, "Alexis, you know I do not drink wine."

"That's right," she agreed a little vaguely. "Well, cheers."

"Good fortune, my dear." His dark eyes wandered over the rest of the people in the lobby. "Which may have just come to you," he said, nodding toward the tall Greek making his way through the crowd with a short, curvaceous Frenchwoman on his arm. He stepped forward. "Signor Athanasios," he said, pitching his voice a bit louder than usual so that it would carry over the drone of conversation.

The Greek looked around, then, at the prompting of the woman beside him, nodded toward Ragoczy. "Yes. My Hungarian friend. I did not see you at first." He came through the crowd, tall and imperious, his smile showing fine white teeth.

"Good evening," Ragoczy said as they shook hands. "Have you met Baronessa dalla Piaggia, Signor Athanasios?"

"Baronessa?" Athanasios repeated, taking Alexis' hand and kissing it. "But you must forgive me—you must be an American."

"I am," Alexis said, pleased that he had already paid her so much attention. "It is my husband who is the Barone."

"That would be Italo dalla Piaggia?" Athanasios ventured. "I know something of his reputation, which is formidable." The smile, this time, was predatory, but Alexis did not mind. "Oh, and my companion. This is Professor de Montalia," he said in an off-handed way. "She has been

117

doing explorations in my country and has helped much in preserving our national treasures."

"Professor?" Alexis said, surprised at the title for a woman who looked little more than twenty.

"Of archeology, Baronessa," was the answer as Madelaine de Montalia put out her hand. "I enjoy my work a great deal, but it is most pleasant to spend an evening listening to music instead of the sounds of bugs."

"I must imagine," Alexis said, recalling the dreadful days she had spent at camp in the summer, when miserable heat and the bites of mosquitoes and can't-see-'ems had made the whole experience torture.

"It takes a particular sort of woman to live as the Professor does," Yiannis Athanasios said with an arch look at Alexis which told her that such a woman was not the kind he preferred.

"How do you come to be aware of the Professor's work?" Alexis asked the tall Greek, meeting his eyes recklessly.

"I have some mining interests which now and again turn up artifacts. Of late, the King has said he wishes all Greek subjects to report such finds." He made a gesture to indicate that he would comply with anything the Greek King requested. "I see your glass is empty, Baronessa. Would you permit me to refill it for you?"

"Why, thank you," Alexis said, dropping her eyes and then lifting them to Athanasios' face.

As the two were talking, Ragoczy put his hand through Madelaine's arm and drew her aside. "How do you come to be in his company again?" There was no trace of jealousy or annoyance. "I thought you did not like him?"

"He has half an eleventh century B.C. village buried where he wants to put a mine shaft. I have been trying to explain to him how he can have his mine and I the village without either of us losing anything." Her violet eyes flashed. "All compliance to the Crown, is he? That's the first I've heard of it."

"Then why this gallantry?" The crowd was growing denser around the portable bar, and the bartenders were becoming more harried. Ragoczy moved a bit further away.

"Because he wants to reduce me to a mere woman. If he wines me and dines me, you see . . ."

"Not an easy thing to do," Ragoczy interrupted with a gentle smile.

"So he has found out. As to bedding me, I'm not having anything like that between my sheets, thank you." Her gown was of a very pale lilac silk, designed by Jacques Fath with a long waist and full elaborately pleated skirts. She touched the lowered waistband. "I haven't felt this girded into a dress in years. I should be grateful we're not back to the whalebone of my youth."

Ragoczy's dark eyes lingered on her, warm with his affection for her. "I have missed you, my heart."

"Yes. And I have missed you. But unless there are . . . it is not so painful when I am busy with my work, or I have a new lover, or . . . any number of things." She could not go on, and it took her a little time to recover. "Why can't we try?"

"Because it's not possible." He was speaking very carefully now, and in French. "We do not have . . ."

"Life? Must we have life?" She sighed. "Tell me what is happening with you. Or I will go on asking you fruitless questions."

He nodded, at once relieved and saddened to be free of the demand. "I have been told that the Americans want to find out about me, as part of their new concern for security. They are afraid, apparently, that the grapes at my vinyard may be sympathetic to communists. At least, that is the excuse. And the Baronessa has, I think, been charged with the task of the initial drawing out. I am considering telling her that one Franchot Ragoczy escaped from Russia by the skin of his teeth—what an apt expression—in 1917. That may give them an idea that the Ragoczy family is not likely to admire Stalin. As Austro-Hungarian nobility, it is not typical to favor Spartacists. If she hears that, she will probably filter it back to her brother, Chester, and he to his superiors in America, and perhaps my vintners will be left alone." He shook his head. "Oh, Madelaine, how complex it has become. I keep a waxwork of myself so that I may provide them with photographs for passports and visas and all the rest of those documents they love so. How do you manage?"

"I go many places where they care little for such things, but occasionally I have difficulty with photographs. They are always blurred, no matter what is done." She laughed and shook her head. "You are well known and wealthy. That creates demands, as I need not remind you." There

119

were amethyst drops in her ears which he had sent her as a gift many years ago.

"I suppose I can disguise some of my holdings, but creating new identities is getting trickier." He smiled ruefully. "But if I am to live in this world, I will learn to accommodate it." He looked up. "Your Signor Athanasios . . ."

"He is not *my* Signor Athanasios," she put in with disgust.

". . . appears to be making headway with the Baronessa. She likes tall men, or so she tells me." He looked around as the five well-mannered, unobtrusive bells sounded to recall the audience to the hall. "Are you staying with Bianca? May I call on you tomorrow?"

"Yes, to both. I wish we did not have to . . ." Madelaine's wish was interrupted by the return of Alexis dalla Piaggia who signaled to Ragoczy in a hurried way.

"Francesco," she said urgently as he approached her. "This is very difficult, but I don't know any other way to . . ." She gave him a flustered smile and touched her honey-brown hair where one of the carefully ordered waves was beginning to droop. "I have had the most . . . Mister Athanasios has asked me to go off to dinner with him. Now. Of course, I am with you, and I told him that I must not behave so badly to you, nor should he leave the Professor." She cast a quick, inquisitive glance at Madelaine, and then hurried on. "I don't know how she would feel, but do you think . . . You *do* seem to know her, and . . ."

"Italo isn't often so conveniently away, Alexis?" Ragoczy said easily. "It would be boorish to ruin a rare opportunity."

"You've got every right to be sarcastic, but, honestly, Francesco," she protested as the returning crowd jostled them. "You aren't *that* set on me, are you? And if the Professor is your friend . . . Look, come to dinner next Wednesday night, and meet Chester. It's awful of me, I know . . ." She looked up sharply as the second warning sounded. *"Please,* Francesco."

"Very well. If that is what you want, what can I be but honored to comply?" Ragoczy said, and kissed her hand. "I look forward to seeing you Wednesday evening. Shall we say nine? At your villa?" He watched the color come back into her face. "I hope that your evening lives up to your expectations, my dear. And I mean that most sincerely."

She studied his dark eyes for a moment. "I think you really do," she said slowly, then spun away from him, saying as she did, "You *will* explain it to the Professor, won't you?"

"It will be my pleasure." He had been attempting to resist the pull of the crush of people returning to the concert hall, but now he let them carry him to the alcove which formed a kind of eddy out of the flood where Madelaine waited.

"What was that about?" Madelaine asked, laughter in her violet eyes.

Ragoczy reached down and took her hand in his. It was a familiar intimate gesture, more loving than the kiss he had bestowed on Alexis' hand. "I think this is what the Americans call being stood up, or something of that nature."

"What?" The lights in the lobby were dimming as a last, unsubtle hint to those few who remained there.

"We have use of the Baronessa's box, if you like. She has gone off for the evening with your handsome Greek, and hopes that we will understand." As he spoke, he led her toward the mirrored-and-gilt hallway at the back of the boxes.

"And what of the investigation?" Madelaine asked, her concern genuine.

"I've arranged for it to continue next Wednesday night. She can meet that brother of hers with a clear conscience. At least on my account," he added, shaking his head. "What is it about women like her?" he asked Madelaine as they stepped into the box and dropped the curtain behind him. "She hungers, and gorges on that which leaves her the more famished."

"Perhaps she doesn't know the difference between appetite and nourishment," Madelaine suggested, only to be firmly hushed by one of the unseen persons in the adjoining box.

Ragoczy put his finger to his lips as he sat down. "Perhaps," he whispered, and then began to applaud as the mezzo-soprano sailed magnificently onto the stage.

Auf Flügeln des Gesanges
Herz leibchen trag' ich dich fort,

Fort nach den Fluren des Ganges
Dort weiss ish den schönsten Ort.

As the lovely, languid melody filled the concert hall,
Ragoczy once again took Madelaine's hand in his: their
touch was so much more than most of the world knew, and
so much less than he wished they had.

Text of a letter from le Comte de Saint-Germain to James
Emmerson Tree.

191 Via San Gregorio
Milano, Italia
17 February, 1965

639 Okanagan Road
Ewings Landing, British Columbia, Canada

Dear James:

*First, yes, I have had word from Madelaine. She
sent a telegram from Omdurman, saying that her work
had gone well and that she would be returning to
France at the end of the month. She has promised to
call from Cairo when she has completed her travel
arrangements.*

*How remarkable that seems to me: a hundred years
ago she might have been able to telegraph from Cairo
that she had returned, and then there would be a train
or a ship to carry her home. A hundred years before
that, there would have been the ship but not the telegraph and her message would have moved as slowly
or as rapidly as she herself. With telephones and satel-
lites, it seems the world is quite transformed, and
shrunk to the size of a child's marble. Most of what is
commonplace today would have dazzled the world a
century ago and stunned it into shock before that.
There are times I am tempted to believe that this
heralds that promised new age that will unite the entire human race in brotherhood. But then, on the
television I see the same brutality and want and ne-
glect and rapacity that has plagued humanity from the
beginning and I fear we are not changed at all, but
have only acquired new and more sophisticated toys to
titillate and exhaust us. You see that I say "us", for
in this, we are much the same as the rest of mankind,*

and while our particular needs keep us from being seduced entirely by the marvels around us, still we are none of us entirely immune from them.

And what toys they are! Think how the Gallic Wars might have gone if there had been television coverage. Or what crimes would have been revealed with current forensic skills. Or what the Inquisition might have accomplished with a computer and data bank at its disposal: mixed blessings indeed.

While I am on the subject of detection, let me recommend that you establish a few more aliases if you can. With the spread of dossiers and police records and tax files the world over, it is becoming increasingly difficult to move about in privacy. Passports, fingerprints, and all the rest of it, are making matters awkward at best. Your New Zealand sheeprun should stand you in good stead, and the house you've bought in Mexico is helpful. Tempting though it is, avoid settling in countries where the government is too oppressive, for it may be that foreigners will be singled out with little warning for more investigation than you would like to have. I have been through several such experiences and I do not recommend them. You are an intelligent man and have learned a great deal. With a little reasonable care, you should do very well.

It was easier once; at most you carried a letter of authorization and perhaps knew a code phrase which would indicate that you were genuine. Certainly there were hazards, and often travelers would drop out of sight without anyone learning for certain what had become of them. There were abuses of strangers which were grim at best. But is this obsessive identification so great an improvement? Those of us who have changed have sufficient difficulties hampering our movements without these added inconveniences. In time we will become accustomed to them, and it may be that you will accomplish this adaptation more easily than I. No matter, so long as it is done.

You may be interested to know that I have been doing spectrographic analyses of earth, in the hope that I might be able to isolate those elements that make native earth, wherever it is, unique, and provide a concentrated chemical compound that would provide the same protection and strength that we now require of the earth itself. Should I have success, I will let you know at once. How much more convenient to carry a few bottles of powder and solution instead of sacks and crates of earth. But that is for later. For now, my most cordial regards.

> Saint-Germain
> *his seal, the eclipse*

Text of a letter from le Comte de Saint-Germain to his manservant Roger.

Villa Veneto
Ragusa, Jugoslavia
8 March, 1969

Mr. Rogers
Adams Hotel
Phoenix, Arizona
U. S. A.

Roger;

I have your letter of December 10th at last, and from what you describe, the location is near perfect. Proceed with the purchase plans, using the American bank accounts for most of the monies. Offer them seventy percent in cash and the rest financed for a reasonable time—no more than twenty years. It would be best, I think, to use the name Balletti for this one. Italian names are not as conspicuous as others might be, such as Ragoczy.

My travel plans have not changed. I will be back in Italy before May and will leave for the United States toward the end of summer. I will let you know the precise date shortly.

Apparently we will have little or no chance to re-claim any of the losses incurred in the Balkans. Those holdings must count as lost. How the losses add up— buildings, lands, possessions, all gone, faded in rubble and dust; the rest, the people who are vanished, that is a greater emptiness for which I know no remedy.

As always, you have my gratitude, old friend.

Saint-Germain
his seal, the eclipse

SEAT PARTNER

JILLIAN had lucked out. TWA had too many passengers in coach, and so she—she almost giggled as she came down the aisle of the huge plane—had to ride in first class, jeans, muslin shirt and all. She found her seat by the window and shoved her camera bag that doubled as a purse under the seat, then dropped gratefully into the wide, padded chair. This was great, she thought as she fastened her seat belt, and reached down to pull a couple of paperback books out of her bag, then settled back to read.

She had just got into the story when a voice spoke beside her. "Excuse me."

Marking her place with her finger, she looked up and smiled a little at what she saw. The man was short, dark-haired, and dark-eyed, with the look of early middle age about him. His clothes were very simple and obviously expensive. His black three-piece suit was a wool and silk blend, superbly tailored to his trim but stocky figure. His shirt was lustrous white silk against a black silk tie, just the right width, and secured with an unadorned ruby stick-pin. Jillian noticed with amusement that his shoes were thick-soled and slightly heeled. "Excuse me," he said again in his pleasant, melodic voice. "I believe that is my seat."

Jillian's face sank. This couldn't happen, not after she had been so lucky. She fumbled in her pockets for her

127

boarding pass. "This is the pass they gave me," she said, holding it out to him.

A stewardess, attracted by the confusion, approached them. "Good morning. Is there some trouble?"

The man turned an attractive, wry smile on the woman. "A minor confusion. Your excellent computer seems to have assigned us the same seat."

The stewardess reached for boarding passes, frowning as she read them. "Just a moment. I'm sure we can correct this." She turned away as she spoke and went toward the galley.

"I'm sorry," Jillian said apologetically. Now that she had had a moment to watch the man, she found him quite awesome.

"No, no. Don't be foolish. Machines are far from perfect, after all. And first class is not wholly filled. We will be accommodated easily." He looked down at her with steady, compelling eyes. "I have no wish to impose on you."

Jillian waved her hands to show that there was no imposition and almost lost the book she was holding. She blushed and felt abashed—here she was, almost twenty-two, and *blushing* for chrissake. A swift glance upward through her fair lashes showed her that the stranger was amused. She wanted to give him a sharp, sophisticated retort, but there was something daunting in his expression, and she kept quiet.

A moment later the stewardess: "I'm sorry, sir," she said to the man. "Apparently there was some difficulty with the print-out on the card. Yours is seat B, on the aisle. If this is inconvenient . . ."

"No, not in the least." He took the boarding passes from her and handed one to Jillian. "I thank you for your trouble. You were most kind." Again the smile flashed and he bent to put his slim black leather case under the seat, saying to Jillian, "I am, in a way, grateful you have the window."

"Oh," Jillian said, surprised, "don't you like the window?"

"I'm afraid that I am not comfortable flying. It is difficult to be so far from the ground." He seated himself and fastened the seat belt.

Jillian started to open her book again, but said, "I think flying's exciting."

"Have you flown often?" the man asked somewhat absent-mindedly.

"Well, not very often," she confided. "Never this far before. I flew to Denver a couple of times to visit my father, and once to Florida, but I haven't been to Europe before."

"And you've spent the summer in Italy? What did you think of it?" He seemed to enjoy her excitement.

"Oh, Italy's okay, but I did a lot of traveling. I decided to fly in and out of Milan because it seemed a good place to start from." She folded down the corner of her page and set the book aside for the moment. "I liked Florence a lot. You've been there, I guess."

"Not for some time. But I had friends there, once." He folded small, beautiful hands over the seat belt. "What else did you see? Paris? Vienna? Rome?"

"Not Paris or Rome. I went to Vienna, though, and Prague and Budapest and Belgrade and Bucharest and Sofia, Sarajevo, Zagreb, Trieste, and Venice." She recited the major cities of her itinerary with a glow of enthusiasm. It had been such a wonderful summer, going through those ancient, ancient countries.

The man's fine brows lifted. "Not the usual student trek, is it? Hungary, Rumania, Bulgaria, Yugoslavia . . . hardly countries one associates with American students."

On the loudspeaker, the stewardess said in three languages that cigarettes must be extinguished and seat belts fastened in preparation for take-off.

Jillian frowned. "Is my being an American student that obvious?"

"Certainly," he said kindly. "Students everywhere have a kind of uniform. Jeans and loose shirts and long, straight blond hair—oh, most surely, an American, and from the way you pronounce your *r*'s, I would say from the Midwest."

Grudgingly, Jillian said, "Des Moines."

"That is in Iowa, is it not?"

Their conversation was interrupted by the sound of engines roaring as the jet started to move away from the terminal.

The stewardess reappeared and gave the customary speech about oxygen masks, flotation pads, and exits in English, French, and Italian. Jillian listened to the talk, trying to appear nonchalant and still feeling the stir of pleasure in flying. The man in the seat beside her closed his eyes.

For five minutes or so they taxied, jockeying for a position on the runway, one of three jets preparing for take-off. Then there was the fierce, lunging roll as the plane raced into the air. The ground dropped away below them, there was the ear-popping climb and the hideous sound of landing gear retracting, and then the stewardess reminded the passengers that smoking was permitted in specified sections only, that they were free to move about the cabin, and that headsets for the movie would be available shortly, before lunch was served.

Jillian looked out the window and saw Milan growing distant and small. Without being aware of it, she sighed.

"You are sad?" asked the man beside her.

"In a way. I'm glad to be going home, but it was such a wonderful summer."

"And what will you do when you get home?" was his next question.

"Oh, teach, I guess. I've got a job at the junior high school. It's my first . . ." She looked out the window again.

"You don't seem much pleased with your job." There was no criticism in his tone. "If it is not what you wish to do, why do you do it?"

"Well," Jillian said in what she hoped was her most reasonable tone, "I have to do something. I'm not planning to get married or anything . . ." She broke off, thinking of how disappointed her mother had been when she had changed her mind about Harold. But it wouldn't have worked, she said to herself, as she had almost every day since the tenth of April when she had returned his ring.

"I'm intruding," said the man compassionately. "Forgive me."

"It's nothing," Jillian responded, wanting to make light of it. "I was just thinking how high up we are."

"Were you." His dark, enigmatic eyes rested on her a moment. "Perhaps you would like to tell me of some of the things you saw in eastern Europe."

"Well," she said, glad to have something to occupy her thoughts other than Harold. "I wanted to see all those strange places. They were really interesting. I was really amazed at how different everything is."

"Different? How?"

"It's not just the way they look, and everything being old," Jillian said with sudden intensity. "It *feels* different here, like all the things they pooh-pooh in schools are real. When I went to Castle Bran, I mean, I really understood

130

how there could be legends about the place. It made sense that people would believe them."

The man's interest increased. "Castle Bran?"

"Yes, you know, it's very famous. It's the castle that Bram Stoker used as a model for Castle Dracula, at least that's what most of the experts are saying now. I wanted to go to the ruins of the real Castle Dracula, but the weather was bad, so I didn't."

"Strange. But why are you interested in such places? Surely the resistance to the Turkish invasions is not your area of study."

"Oh, no," she laughed a little embarrassed. "I like vampires. Books, movies, anything."

"Indeed." There was an ironic note in his voice now.

"Well, they might not be great art, but they're wonderful to . . ."

"Fantasize about?" he suggested gently.

Jillian felt herself flush and wished that she hadn't mentioned the subject. "Sometimes." She tilted her chin up. "Lugosi, Lee, all of them, they're just great. I think they're sexy."

The man very nearly chuckled, but managed to preserve a certain gravity that almost infuriated Jillian. "A novel idea," he said after a moment.

"It isn't," she insisted. "I know lots of people who think vampires are sexy."

"American irreverence, do you think?" He shook his head. "There was a time, not so very long ago, when such an avowal would be absolutely heretical."

"That's silly," she said, a little less sure of herself. In her travels, she had come to realize that heresy was not just an obsolete prejudice.

"Hardly silly," the man said in a somber tone. "Men and women and even children died in agony for believing such things. And there are those who think that the practice should be reinstated."

"But it's just superstition," Jillian burst out, inwardly shocked at her reaction. "Nobody today could possibly believe that vampires really exist . . ."

"Are you so certain they do not?" he inquired mildly.

"Well, how could they?" she retorted. "It's absurd."

He favored her with a nod that was more of a bow. "Of course."

Jillian felt the need to pursue the matter a little more.

"If there were such things, they would have been found out by now. There'd be good, solid proof."

"Proof? But how could such a thing be proved? As you said yourself, the idea is absurd."

"There ought to be ways to do it." She hadn't considered the matter before, but she felt challenged by the stranger in the seat beside her. "It wouldn't be the premature burial concerns, because that's a different matter entirely."

"Certainly," he agreed. "If legends are right, burial of a vampire is hardly premature."

She decided to overlook this remark. "The trouble is," she said seriously, "the best way would be to get volunteers, and I don't suppose it would be easy to convince any real vampire that he ought to submit himself to scientific study."

"It would be impossible, I should think," her seat partner interjected.

"And how could it be proven, I mean, without destroying the volunteer? I don't suppose there are any real proofs short of putting a stake through their hearts or severing their heads."

"Burning is also a good method," the man said.

"No one, not even a vampire, is going to agree to that. And it wouldn't demonstrate anything at all. Anyone would die of it, whether or not they were vampires." Suddenly she giggled. "Christ, this is weird, sitting up here talking about experimenting on vampires." Actually, she was becoming uncomfortable with the subject and was anxious to speak of something else.

The man seemed to read her thoughts, for he said, "Hardly what one would call profitable speculation."

Jillian had the odd feeling that she should be polite and decided to ask him a few questions. "Is this your first trip to America? You speak wonderful English, but . . ."

"But you know I am a foreigner. Naturally." He paused. "I have been to America, but that was some time ago, and then it was to the capital of Mexico. A strange place, that city built on swamps."

His description of Mexico City startled Jillian a little, because though it was true enough that the city had been built on swamps long ago, it seemed an odd aspect of its history to mention. "Yes," she said, to indicate she was listening.

"This is my first visit to your country. It is disquieting to go to so vast a land, and be so far from home."

The stewardess appeared at his elbow. "Pardon me,

Count. We're about to serve cocktails, and if you'd like one . . . ?"

"No, thank you, but perhaps"—he turned to Jillian—"you would do me the honor of letting me buy one for you."

Jillian was torn between her delight at the invitation and the strictures of her youth that had warned against such temptations. Pleasure won. "Oh, please; I'd like a gin and tonic. Tanqueray gin, if you have it."

"Tanqueray and tonic," the stewardess repeated, then turned to the man again. "If you don't want a cocktail, we have an excellent selection of wines . . ."

"Thank you, no. I do not drink wine." With a slight, imperious nod, he dismissed the stewardess.

"She called you Count," Jillian accused him, a delicious thrill running through her. This charming man in black was an aristocrat! She was really looking forward to telling her friends about the flight when she got home. It would be wonderful to say, as casually as she could, "Oh, yes, on the way back, I had this lovely conversation with a European Count," and then watch them stare at her.

"A courtesy title, these days," the man said diffidently. "Things have changed much from the time I was born, and now there are few who would respect my claims."

Jillian knew something of the history of Europe and nodded sympathetically. "How unfortunate for you. Does it make you sad to see the changes in your country?" She realized she didn't know which country he was from and wondered how she could ask without seeming rude.

"It is true that my blood is very old, and I have strong ties to my native soil. But there are always changes, and in time, one grows accustomed, one adapts. The alternative is to die."

Never before had Jillian felt the plight of the exiled as she did looking into that civilized, intelligent face. "How terrible! You must get very lonely."

"Occasionally, very lonely," he said in a distant way.

"But surely, you have family . . ." She bit the words off. She had read of some of the bloodier revolutions, where almost every noble house was wiped out. If his was one of them, the mention of it might be inexcusable.

"Oh, yes. I have blood relatives throughout Europe. There are not so many of us as there once were, but a few of us survive." He looked up as the stewardess approached with a small tray with one glass on it. "Ah. Your cocktail, I believe." He leaned back as the stewardess handed the drink to Jillian. "Which currency would you prefer?" he asked.

"How would you prefer to pay, sir?" the stewardess responded with a blinding smile.

"Dollars, pounds, or francs. Choose." He pulled a large black wallet from his inner coat pocket.

"Dollars, then. It's one-fifty." She held out her hand for the bill, and thanked him as she took it away to make change.

Jillian lifted the glass, which was slightly frosted, and looked at the clear liquid that had a faint touch of blue in its color. "Well, thanks. To you." She sipped at the cold, surprisingly strong drink.

"You're very kind," he said, an automatic response. "Tell me," he said in another, lighter tone, "what is it you will teach to your junior high school students?"

"English," she said, and almost added, "of course."

"As a language?" the Count asked, plainly startled.

"Not really. We do some grammar, some literature, some creative writing, a lot of reading." As she said it, it sounded so dull, and a little gloom touched her.

"But surely you don't want to spend your life teaching some grammar, some literature, some creative writing, and a lot of reading to disinterested children." He said this gently, kindly, and watched Jillian very closely as she answered.

"Sometimes I think I don't know what I want," she said and felt alarmed at her own candor.

"I feel you would rather explore castles in Europe than teach English in Des Moines." He regarded her evenly. "Am I correct?"

"I suppose so," she said slowly and took another sip of her cocktail.

"Then why don't you?"

It was a question she had not dared to ask herself and she was angry at him for asking. He had no right, this unnamed former Count in elegant black who watched her with such penetrating dark eyes. He had no right to ask such things of her. She was about to tell him so when he said, "A woman I have long loved very dearly used to think she would not be able to learn everything she wanted to during her life. You must understand, European society has been quite rigid at times. She comes from a distinguished French family, and when I met her, she was nineteen and terrified that she would be forced into the life other women had before she had opportunities to study. Now," he said with a faint, affectionate smile, "she is on a dig, I think it's called, in Iran. She is an accomplished archeologist. You see, she did not allow herself to be limited by the expectations of others."

Jillian listened, ready to fling back sharp answers if he insisted that she turn away from the life she had determined upon. "You changed her mind, I suppose?" She knew she sounded petulant, but she wanted him to know she was displeased.

"Changed her mind, no. It could be said that she changed mine." His eyes glinted with reminiscence. "She is a remarkable woman, my Madelaine." He turned his attention to Jillian once more. "Forgive me. Occasionally I am reminded of . . . our attachment. I did not mean to be rude. Perhaps I meant to suggest that you, like her, should not permit those around you to make decisions for you that are not what you want."

The stewardess returned with headphones for the movie. It was, she explained, a long feature, a French and English venture, shot predominantly in Spain with an international cast. She held out the headsets to Jillian and to the man beside her.

Though Jillian knew it was unmannerly of her to do so, she accepted the headset with a wide smile and said to her seat partner, "I hate to do this, but I've wanted to see this flick all summer long, and I don't know when I'll have the chance again."

She knew by the sardonic light to his smile that he was not fooled, but he said to her, "By all means. I understand that it is most entertaining."

"Headphones for you, Count?" the stewardess asked solicitously.

"I think not, but thank you." He looked toward Jillian. "If you decide that it is truly worthwhile, tell me, and I will call for headsets."

The stewardess nodded and moved away to the next pair of seats.

"You don't mind, do you?" Jillian asked, suddenly conscience-stricken. The Count had bought her a drink and was being very courteous, she thought, but then again, she did not want him to think that she was interested in him.

"No, I don't mind." He glanced down at his leather case

under the seat. "Would it disturb you if I do a little work while the film is running?"

Jillian shook her head and put the thin blue plastic leads to the socket on the arm of her seat. "Go ahead."

He had already pulled the case from under the seat and opened it on his lap. There were three thick, leather-bound notebooks in the case, and he pulled the largest of these out, closed the case, and replaced it. He took a pen from one of his coat pockets and pulled down the table from the seat ahead. He gave Jillian a swift, disturbing smile, then bent his head to his work.

Before the film was half over, Jillian was bored. The plot, which she had thought would be exciting, was tedious, and the filming was unimaginative. Most of the actors looked uncomfortable in their nineteenth-century costumes, and the dialogue was so trite that Jillian could not blame the actors for their poor delivery. She longed to be able to take off the headset and get back to reading, but she was afraid that the Count would engage her in conversation again, and for some reason, this prospect unnerved her. He had a knack for drawing her out. Another half-hour and she would have been telling him about Harold and how he had laughed when she said she wanted to get her Master's before they married. Already he had got her to talk about vampires, and she had never done that before, not with a stranger. So she kept her eyes on the little screen and tried to concentrate on the dull extravaganza. Once she caught the Count looking at her, amusement in his dark eyes, but then he turned back to the notebook, and she could not be certain whether or not he had sensed her dilemma.

When at last the film ground to a messy, predictable finish, Jillian was anxious to take off the headset. She made a point of reaching for a book before handing the plastic tubing to the stewardess, and shot a quick look at her seat partner.

"If you do not wish to speak to me," he said without turning his attention from the page on which he wrote, "please say so. I will not be offended."

Jillian was grateful and annoyed at once. "I'm just tired. I think I want to read a while."

He nodded and said nothing more.

It was not until they were nearing Kennedy Airport that Jillian dared to talk to her seat partner. She had been reading the same paragraph for almost twenty minutes, and it made no more sense now than the first time she had looked at it. With a sigh she closed the book and bent to put it in her bag.

"We're nearing New York," the Count said. He had put his notebook away some minutes before and had sat back in his seat, gazing at nothing in particular.

"Yes," she said, not certain now if she was glad to be coming home.

"I suppose you'll be flying on to Des Moines."

"In the morning," she said, thinking for the first time that she would have to ask about motels near the airport, because she knew she could not go into Manhattan for the night. Between the taxi fare and the hotel bill, she could not afford that one last splurge.

"But it is only . . ."—he consulted his watch and paused to calculate the difference in time—"six-thirty. You can't mean that you want to sit in a sterile little room with a poor television for company all this evening."

That was, in fact, precisely what she had intended to do, but his description made the prospect sound more gloomy than she had thought it could be. "I guess so."

"Would you be offended if I asked you to let me buy you dinner? This is my first time in this city, in this country, and it will feel less strange to me if you'd be kind enough to give me the pleasure of your company."

If this was a line, Jillian thought, it was one of the very smoothest she had ever heard. And she did want to go into Manhattan, and she very much wanted to spend the evening at a nice restaurant. A man like the Count, she thought, wouldn't be the sort to skimp on a night out. He might, of course, impose conditions later.

"I have no designs on your virginity," he said, with that uncanny insight that had bothered her earlier.

"I'm not a virgin," Jillian snapped, without meaning to.

The seat belt sign and no smoking signs flashed on, one after another, and the stewardess announced that they had begun their descent for landing.

The Count smiled, the whole force of his dark eyes on her. "Shall we say your virtue, then? I will allow that you are a very desirable, very young woman, and it would delight me to have you as my guest for the evening. Well?"

"You don't even know my name," she said with a smile, her mind already made up.

"It's Jillian Walker," he answered promptly, and added

137

as she stared at him, "It was on the envelope your boarding pass is in."

For a moment, Jillian had been filled with a certain awe, almost a dread, but at this simple explanation, she smiled. A niggling image had risen in her mind, an image developed from her reading and the films she loved. A foreign, exiled Count, in black, of aristocratic, almost regal bearing, who had refused wine . . . It was an effort not to laugh. "You know my name, but I don't know yours."

"You may call me Franz, if you like. I am Franz Josef Ragoczy, onetime Count, among other things."

"What's that name again?" Something about it was familiar, but she couldn't place it.

"Ragoczy. *Rah*-go-schkee," he repeated. "It's the German version of the Hungarian variant of the name. As I told you, I come from an ancient line." His expression had softened. "It is agreed, then?"

The plane was descending rapidly, and there was that wrenching clunk as the landing gear was lowered. Ahead the sprawl of Kennedy Airport rose up to meet them.

Whatever reservations that were left in Jillian's mind were banished by the warmth in his eyes. If he wanted more than her company, she decided, she would deal with that as it happened. As the plane jounced onto the runway, she grinned at him. "Count, I'd love to have dinner with you."

He took her hand in his and carried it gallantly, ironically, to his lips. "Dinner with me," he echoed her, "dinner with me." There was secret meaning in the soft words that followed, almost lost in the shrieking of the engines. "I will hold you to that, Jillian Walker. Believe this."

Text of a letter from le Comte de Saint-Germain to James Emmerson Tree.

The Mansion Hotel
Santa Fe, New Mexico USA
10 August, 1971

34 New Townsend Road
Hobart, Tasmania

Dear James:

Your letter reached me at last, and I am sorry to be so long in replying, though there is little I can say to you that will comfort you. Sadly, it is one of the burdens shared by those of our blood—that we must say goodbye so very often. I recall a couplet: the poetry is not very good, but the sentiment is genuine.

> *Soon, too soon, comes death to show*
> *We love more deeply than we know.*

You say that there was not time enough for Eina to change. Do not regret this too much. Those who change are lost to us in many ways, some as great as the true death itself. You know my feelings for Madelaine, for you have loved her too. Yet there is no recourse for us. It would have been the same for you with Eina. Do not give way to bitterness or contempt for the brevity of life, James; ultimately it would make your grief even more unbearable.

For what little consolation this may be to you, please accept it, and know that I empathise most sincerely.

Saint-Germain
his seal, the eclipse

Text of a letter from le Comte de Saint-Germain to Edward Whittenfield.

Lost Saints Lodge
Post Office Box 101
Fox Hollow, Colorado USA
29 October, 1978

The Honorable Edward G. C. A. Whittenfield
Eleventh Earl of Copsehowe
Briarcopse
Nr. Evesham
England

My dear Copsehowe:

I thank you very much for your letter of 2 August and only regret that it has taken so long to reach me that my reply is delayed. It was most kind of you to contact me and I appreciate it very much.

Your decision to sell off part of the Copsehowe holdings, while understandable in the economy of the current world, is nonetheless lamentable. Doubtless Briarcopse and the Yorkshire hunting lodge will be an asset to the nation, but the loss to your family must be keenly felt.

Since you mention your great-grandfather's Will, I assume you know that the interest expressed by his friend with my name was genuine, and of course, I will honor whatever offer was made. Certainly my primary concern is with the old mirror described in your letter, and I see no reason to quibble about the price. Name the figure you and your representatives consider reasonable and I will at once authorize my London bankers to transfer the sum. There are a few paintings that I would be happy to add to my collection, but I believe it is in your best interests to offer them for competitive bid. Should there be individual works that you might want to hold back for private sale, by all means let me know of them. In the matter of the Turkish carpets, I would be delighted to negotiate for them, with the understanding that they would be sent to the de Montalia estate in France.

This is a difficult time for you, I am sure, but if it provides you any comfort, let me tell you that I respect your decision and know that given the circumstances, your actions are prudent and farsighted.

Again, accept my gratitude for this opportunity: I trust your efforts will prove worthwhile.

> *Saint-Germain*
> *his seal, the eclipse*

CABIN 33

IN the winter there were the skiers, and in the summer the place was full of well-to-do families escaping to the mountains, but it was in the off-seasons, the spring and the fall, when Lost Saints Lodge was most beautiful.

Mrs. Emmons, who always came in September, sat at her table in the spacious dining room, one hand to her bluish-silver hair as she smiled up at the Lodge's manager. "I do so look forward to my stay here, Mr. Rogers," she said archly, and put one stubby, beringed hand on his.

"It's good of you to say so," Mr. Rogers responded in a voice that managed to be gracious without hinting the least encouragement to the widow.

"I hear that you have a new chef." She looked around the dining room again. "Not a very large crowd tonight."

Mr. Rogers followed her glance and gave a little, eloquent shrug. "It's off-season, Mrs. Emmons. We're a fifth full, which is fine, since it gives us a breather before winter, and allows us a little time to keep the cabins up. We do the Lodge itself in the spring, but you're not here then."

"I'm not fond of crowds," Mrs. Emmons said, lifting her head in a haughty way it had taken her years to perfect.

Nor, thought Mr. Rogers, of the summer and winter prices. He gave her half a smile. "Certainly off-season is less hectic."

She took a nervous sip from the tall stem glass before

142

her. Mrs. Emmons did not like margaritas, and secretly longed for a side-car, but she knew that such drinks were considered old-fashioned and she had reached that point in her life when she dreaded the reality of age. "Tell me," she said as she put the glass down, "is that nice Mr. Franciscus still with you?"

"Of course." Mr. Rogers had started away from the table, but he paused as he said this, a flicker of amusement in his impassive face.

"I've always liked to hear him play. He knows all the old songs." There was more of a sigh in her tone than she knew.

"He does indeed," Mr. Rogers agreed. "He'll be in the lounge after eight, as always."

"Oh, good," Mrs. Emmons said, a trifle too brightly before she turned her attention to the waiter who had appeared at her elbow.

Mr. Rogers was out of the dining room and halfway across the lobby when an inconspicuous door on the mezzanine opened and a familiar voice called his name. Mr. Rogers looked up swiftly, and turned toward the stairs that led to the mezzanine.

The door opened onto a small library comfortably furnished in dark-stained wood and substantial Victorian chairs upholstered in leather. There was one person in the room at the moment, and he smiled as Mr. Rogers closed the door. When he spoke, it was not in English.

"I just saw Mrs. Emmons in the dining room," Mr. Rogers said with a tinge of weariness. "She's looking forward to seeing that 'nice Mr. Franciscus.'"

"Oh, God," said Mr. Franciscus in mock horror. "I suppose that Mrs. Granger will be here soon, too?"

"She's due to arrive on Wednesday." Both men had been standing, Mr. Franciscus by the tall north-facing windows, Mr. Rogers by the door. "I've given them cabins A28 and A52, back to back over the creek."

"And if the water doesn't bother them, they'll have a fine time," Mr. Franciscus said. "I didn't have time to tune the harpsichord, so I'll have to use the piano tonight." He came away from the windows and sank into the nearest chair.

"I don't think anyone will mind." Mr. Rogers turned the chair by the writing table to a new angle as he sat.

"Perhaps not, but I should have done it." He propped his elbows on the arms of the chair and linked his fingers

143

under his chin. His hands were beautifully shaped but surprisingly small for a pianist. "There's part of the ridge trail that's going to need reinforcement before winter or we'll have a big wash-out at the first thaw."

"I'll send Matt out to fix it. Is that where you were this afternoon? Out on the trails?" There was a mild interest but his questions were calmly asked and as calmly answered.

"Part of the time. That ranger . . . Jackson, Baxter, something like that, told me to remind you about the fire watch."

"Backus," Mr. Rogers said automatically. "Ever since that scare in Fox Hollow, he's been jittery about fire. He's the one who put up all the call stations on the major trails."

"It's good that someone is concerned. They lost sixteen cabins at Fox Hollow," Franciscus responded with a touch of severity. "If we had the same problem here, there's a great deal more to lose—and one hundred twenty-four cabins would be a major loss."

Mr. Rogers said nothing, watching Franciscus levelly.

"We're going to need some improvements on the stable. The roof is not in good repair and the tack room could stand some sprucing up. The hay-ride wagon should be repainted. If we can get this done before winter it would be helpful." He brushed his black jeans to rid them of dust. His boots were English, not Western, made to order in fine black leather. There was an elegance about him that had little to do with his black clothing. He stared at Mr. Rogers a moment. "Are there any disturbances that I should know about? You seem apprehensive."

"No," Mr. Rogers said slowly, after giving the matter his consideration. "It's just the usual off-season doldrums, I guess. We're a little fuller than we were last fall. There's a retired couple from Chillicothe, name of Barnes in cabin 12, they're new; a couple from Lansing with a teen-aged daughter in cabin 19. I think the girl is recovering from some sort of disease, at least that's what her mother told me—their name is Harper. There's a jumpy MD in cabin 26, Dr. Muller. Amanda Farnsworth is back again. I've put her in cabin A65."

"It's been—what?—three years since she was here last?" Franciscus asked.

"Three years." Mr. Rogers nodded. "There's also a new fellow up in cabin 33."

"Cabin 33? Isn't that a little remote?" He glanced swiftly toward the window and the wooded slope beyond

144

the badminton courts and swimming pool. A wide, well-marked path led up the hill on the far side of these facilities, winding in easy ascent into the trees. Cabin 33 was the last cabin on the farthest branch of the trail, more than a quarter mile from the lodge and dining room.

"He requested it," Mr. Rogers said with a slight shrug. "I told him he would find it cold and quite lonely. He said that was fine."

"If that's what he wants . . ." Franciscus dismissed the newcomer with a turn of his hand. "What about the regulars? Aside from Mrs. Emmons, God save us, and Mrs. Granger?"

"We'll have the Blakemores for two weeks, starting on the weekend. Myron Shire is coming to finish his new book, as usual. Sally and Elizabeth Jenkins arrive next Tuesday. Sally wrote to say that Elizabeth's been in the sanatorium again and we are not to serve her anything alcoholic. We'll have all four Leilands for ten days, and then they'll go on to the Coast. Harriet Goodman is coming for six weeks, and should arrive sometime today. Sam Potter is coming with his latest young man. The Davies. The Coltraines. The Wylers. The Pastores. Professor Harris. Jim Sutton will be here, but for five days only. His newspaper wants him to cover that murder trial in Denver, so he can't stay as long as usual. The Lindholms. He's looking poorly and Martha said that he has had heart trouble this year. Richard Bachmere and his cousin, whose name I can never remember . . ."

"Samuel," Franciscus supplied.

"That's the one. The Muramotos won't be here until Thanksgiving this year. He's attending a conference in Seattle. The Browns. The Matins. The Luis. Tim Halloran is booked in for the weekend only, but Cynthia is in Mexico and won't be here at all. And that's about it." Mr. Rogers folded his hands over his chest.

"Not bad for fall off-season. What's the average stay?" Franciscus inquired as he patted the dust from his pant-leg, wrinkling his nose as the puffs rose.

"No, not bad for off-season. The average stay is just under two weeks, and if this year is like the last three years, we'll pick up an odd reservation or two between now and the skiers. We'll have a pretty steady flow from now until Thanksgiving. We're underbooked until just before Christmas, when we open the slopes. But those twelve cabins still have to be readied."

Franciscus nodded. "Before the skiers." He stared at his boot where his ankle was propped on his knee. "We'd better hire that band for the winter season, I think. I don't want to be stuck doing four sets a night again. Have you asked around Standing Rock for winter help?"

"Yes. We've got four women and three men on standby." He consulted his watch. "The restaurant linen truck should be here in a few minutes. I'd better get over to the kitchen. What time were you planning to start this evening?"

Franciscus shrugged. "Oh, eight-thirty sounds about right for this small crowd. I don't imagine they'll want music much after midnight. We can let Ross do a couple late sets with his guitar if there's enough of an audience. If not, then Frank can keep the bar open as long as he wants. How does that sound to you?"

"Good for the whole week. Saturday will be busier, and we'll have more guests by then. We'll make whatever arrangements are necessary." He rose. "Kathy's determined to serve chateaubriand in forcemeat on Saturday, and I'm afraid I'm going to have to talk her out of it. I know that the chef's special should live up to its name, but the price of beef today . . ." He rolled his eyes up as if in appeal to heaven.

"Why not indulge her? It's better she make chateaubriand in forcemeat for an off-season crowd than for the skiers. Let her have an occasional extravagance. She's a fine chef, isn't she?" Franciscus leaned back in his chair.

"So they tell me," said Mr. Rogers, switching back to English.

"Then why not?" He reached for his black hat with the silver band. "Just make sure she understands that you can't do this too often. She'll appreciate it." He got to his feet as well. "I want to take one more look through the stable before I get changed for tonight. We've got six guest stalls ready. The Browns always bring those pride-cut geldings they're so proud of. I'll get changed about the time you start serving dinner."

"Fine." Mr. Rogers held the door open and let Franciscus leave ahead of him. "I'll tell Mrs. Emmons."

Franciscus chuckled. "You've no pity, my friend. If she requests 'When the Moon Comes Over the Mountain,' I will expire, I promise you."

The two men were still smiling when they reached the lobby once more. A tall, tweedy woman in her early forties stood at the registration desk and looked around as Mr. Rogers and Franciscus reached the foot of the stairs. "Oh, there you are," she said to the men and gave them her pleasant, horsey grin.

Mr. Rogers said, "Good afternoon, Ms. Goodman" at the same time that Franciscus said, "Hello, Harriet."

"Mr. Rogers. Mr. Franciscus." She extended her hand to them, taking the manager's first. There were three leather bags by her feet and though she wore no makeup beyond lipstick, she now, as always, smelled faintly of *Joy*.

As he slipped behind the registration desk, Mr. Rogers found her reservation card at once and was filling in the two credit lines for her. "Six weeks this time, Ms. Goodman?"

"Yes. I'm giving myself some extra vacation. I'm getting tired. Six years on the lecture circuit is too wearing." She looked over the form. "Cabin 21. My favorite," she remarked as she scribbled her name at the bottom of the form. "Is Scott around to carry my bags?"

"I'm sorry. Scott's off at U.S.C. now," Mr. Rogers said as he took the form back.

"U.S.C.? He got the scholarship? Well, good for him. He's a very bright boy. I thought it was a shame that he might lose that opportunity." She held out her hand for the key.

"He got the scholarship," Mr. Rogers said with a quick glance at Franciscus.

"I'll be happy to carry your bags, Harriet," Franciscus volunteered. "I'm curious to know how your work's been going."

Her hazel eyes were expressive and for a moment they flickered with a pleasant alarm. Then it was gone and her social polish returned. "Thank you very much. I don't know the etiquette for tipping the musician-cum-wrangler, but . . ."

"No tip," Franciscus said rather sharply. "Call it a courtesy for a welcome friend." He had already picked up the smallest bag and was gathering up the other two.

"I must say, I envy the shape you're in. Lugging those things around wears me out. But look at you. And you must be at least my age." She had started toward the door and the broad, old-fashioned porch that led to the path to cabin 21.

Franciscus was a few steps behind her. "I'm probably

147

older than you think," he said easily. He was walking briskly, his heels tapping smartly on the flagging.

They were almost to cabin 21 when a frail-looking teen-ager in an inappropriate shirtwaist dress stepped out onto the path. Franciscus recognized her from Mr. Rogers' description of the new guests in cabin 19.

"Excuse me," she said timorously, "but could you tell me where the nearest path to the lake is?"

Harriet Goodman gave the teen-ager a quick, discerning glance, and Franciscus answered her. "You'll have to go past the lodge and take the widest path. It runs right beside the badminton courts. You can't miss it. There's a sign. But I'm afraid there's no lifeguard, so if you want to swim, you should, perhaps, use the pool. We haven't got the canoes and boats out yet, either. Two more days and they'll be ready."

"It's all right," she said in a quick, shaky voice. "I just want to walk a bit." She clutched her hands nervously, then moved sideways along the path away from them.

"That's one jumpy filly," Harriet Goodman said when the girl was out of earshot. "Who is she?"

"She's new," Franciscus said, resuming the walk to Harriet's cabin. "Mr. Rogers said that she's apparently recovering from an illness of some sort." Having seen the girl, he doubted that was the real problem, but kept his opinion to himself.

Harriet had made a similar assessment. "Recovering from an illness, my ass."

There were five wooden steps down to the door of cabin 21, which was tucked away from the rest on the path, the last one of the twelve on this walk. Harriet Goodman opened the door. "Oh, thank goodness. You people always air out the cabins. I can't tell you how much I hate that musty smell." She tossed her purse on the couch and went to the bedroom beyond. "Everything's fine. Let me check the bathroom." She disappeared and came back. "New paint and fixtures. You're angels."

"The owner doesn't like his property to get run-down," Franciscus said, as he put the bags on the racks in the bedroom.

Harriet Goodman watched him, her hands on her hips. "You know, Franciscus, you puzzle me," she said with her usual directness.

"I do? Why?" He was faintly amused and his fine brows lifted to punctuate his inquiry.

148

"Because you're content to remain here, I guess." There was a puckering of her forehead.

"I like it here. I value my privacy."

"Privacy?" she echoed, not believing him. "In the middle of a resort."

"What better place?" He hesitated, then went on. "I do like privacy, but not isolation. I have time for myself, and though there are many people around me, almost all of them pass through my life like, well, shadows."

"Shadows."

He heard the melancholy in her voice. "I said *almost* all. You're not a candidate for shadow-dom, Harriet. And you know it."

Her laughter was gently self-deriding. "That will teach me to fish for compliments."

Franciscus looked at her kindly before he left the cabin. "You're being unkind to yourself. What am I but, as you call it, a musician-cum-wrangler?" He nodded to her and strolled to the door.

Her eyes narrowed as she stared at the door he had closed behind him. "Yes, Franciscus. What are you?"

He preferred playing the harpsichord to the piano, though the old instrument was cantankerous with age. He had his wrenches laid out on the elaborately painted bench and was busy with tuning forks when the teen-ager found him at work.

"Oh! I didn't mean . . ." She turned a curiously mottled pale pink. "You're busy. I heard music and I thought . . ."

"Hardly music," Franciscus said as he jangled a discordant arpeggio on the worn keys.

"I think it's pretty." Her eyes pleaded with him not to contradict her.

His curiosity was piqued. "That's kind of you to say, but it will sound a great deal better once I get it tuned."

"May I watch? I won't say anything. I promise." Her hands were knotting in the nervous way he had noticed before.

"If you wish. It's boring, so don't feel you have to stay." His penetrating dark eyes rested on her cornflower blue ones, then he gave his attention to the harpsichord again. He used his D tuning fork, struck it and placed it against the raised lid of the instrument for resonance. He worked quickly, twisting the metal tuning pegs quickly. Methodi-

149

cally he repeated the process with all the Ds on the keyboard.

"Is that hard, what you're doing?" she asked when he had worked his way up to F#.

"Hard? No, not when I've got my tuning forks. I can do it without them, but it takes longer because I have difficulty allowing for the resonances, the over and undertones, in my mind." He did not mind the interruption, though he did not stop his task. He selected the G fork and struck it expertly.

"You have perfect pitch?" She found the idea exciting. "I've never known anyone with perfect pitch."

"Yes." Franciscus placed the vibrating fork against the wood, and the note, eerily pure, hummed loudly in the room. "That's the resonant note of this instrument, which is why it's so much louder than the others."

The teen-aged girl looked awed. "That's amazing."

"No, it's physics," he corrected her wryly. What was wrong with that child? Franciscus asked himself. From her height and the shape of her body, she had to be at least sixteen, but she had the manner of a much younger person. Perhaps she had truly been ill. Or perhaps she was recovering from something more harmful than illness. "All instruments have one particular resonant note. In the ancient world, this was attributed to magic," he went on, watching her covertly.

"Did they? That's wonderful." She sounded so forlorn that he worried she might cry.

"Is something the matter, Miss . . ."

"Harper," she said, with an unaccountable blush. "Emillie Harper."

"Hello, Miss Harper. I'm R. G. Franciscus." He offered her his right hand gravely.

She was about to take it when a stranger came into the room. He was a tall, lean man dressed, like Franciscus, predominantly in black, but unlike Franciscus, he wore the color with an air of menace. There was a flamboyance, a theatricality about him: his dark hair was perfectly silvered at the temples and there was a Byronic grandeur in his demeanor. His ruddy mouth curved in a romantic sneer, and though he was certainly no older than Franciscus, he gave the impression of world-weariness that the other, shorter man conspicuously lacked.

"I didn't mean to interrupt," he announced for form's sake, in a fine deep voice that oozed ennui.

"Quite all right," Franciscus assured him. "I'm almost finished tuning, and Miss Harper and I were discussing resonance. Is there anything I can do for you? Dinner service began a quarter hour ago, if you're hungry."

The stranger gave a slight shudder. "Dinner. No. I'm looking for the manager. Have you seen Mr. Rogers?" His soulful brown eyes roved around the lounge as if he suspected the man he sought to be lurking in the shadows.

"He should be with the chef. He usually is at the start of dinner," Franciscus told him with unimpaired good humor. "Give him another ten minutes and he'll be out."

"I need to see Mr. Rogers at once," the stranger stated with great finality. "It's urgent."

Emillie Harper clenched her hands tightly and stared from one man to the other. Her blue eyes were distressed and she moved in quick, fluttery starts, as if attempting to flee invisible shackles.

"Miss Harper," Franciscus said calmly, "I'm going to the kitchen to get Mr. Rogers for this . . . gentleman. Would you like to come with me?" He took his black wool jacket from the bench and began to roll down his shirt sleeves. With a twitch he adjusted the black silk ascot at his neck before shrugging on the jacket.

The depth of gratitude in the girl's eyes was pathetic. "Oh, yes. I would. Please."

Franciscus regarded the tall interloper. "If you'll be good enough to wait at the registration desk, Mr. Rogers will join you shortly. It's the best I can do, Mr. . . . ."

"Lorpicar," was the answer. "I'm in cabin 33."

"Are you." Franciscus had already led Emillie Harper to the door of the lounge. He sensed that Mr. Lorpicar wanted him to look back, and for that reason, he did not, although he felt a deep curiosity possess him as he led the frightened girl away.

Jim Sutton walked into the lounge shortly after ten the next evening, while Franciscus was doing his second set. The reporter was dressed with his usual finicky elegance in contrast to his face which held the comfortable appeal of a rumpled bed. He waved to Franciscus and took a seat at the bar, waiting for the buzzy and unobtrusive sounds of the harpsichord to cease.

"It's good to see you again, Mr. Sutton," the bartender said as he approached. "Cruzan with lime juice, isn't it?"

"Good to see you again, Frank. You're right about the

151

drink." He had often been amused by the tales he had heard of reporters and bourbon: he had never liked the stuff. Rum was another matter. He put a ten dollar bill on the highly polished mahogany of the bar as Frank brought him one of the neat, square glasses used at Lost Saints Lodge with little ice and a fair amount of rum. "When eight of this is gone, you tell me."

"Sure thing, Mr. Sutton," said the bartender in his faded southern accent as he gave the reporter an indulgent smile before answering the imperious summons of Mrs. Emmons at the far end of the bar.

Jim Sutton was into his second drink when Franciscus slipped onto the stool beside him. "I liked what you were playing," he said by way of greeting.

Franciscus shrugged. "Haydn filtered through Duke Ellington."

"Keeps the peasants happy." He had braced his elbows on the bar and was looking over the lounge. It wasn't crowded but it was far from empty. "You're doing well this year. Rogers said that business was up again."

"It is." Franciscus took the ten dollar bill and stuffed it into Jim Sutton's vest pocket. "Frank, Mr. Sutton is my guest tonight. Present me with a tab at the end of the evening."

"Okay, Franciscus," came the answer from the other end of the bar.

"You don't use any nicknames?" Jim Sutton asked.

"I don't encourage them." He looked at the reporter and thought there was more tension in the sardonic, kindly eyes than he had seen before. "How's it going?"

"I wish I had more time off," Sutton muttered as he finished his drink and set the square glass back on the bar. "This last year . . . God! The mass murders in Detroit, and that cult killing in Houston, and the radiation victims in St. Louis, and now this trial in Denver. I thought I was through with that when I came back from Viet Nam. I tell you, it's getting to me."

Franciscus said nothing, but he hooked the rather high heels of his custom-made black shoes over the foot brace of the stool and prepared himself to listen.

It was more than five minutes later that Jim Sutton began to speak again. "I've heard all the crap about reporters being cold sons-of-bitches. It's true of a lot of them. It's easier if you can do it that way. What can you say, though, when you look at fourteen bodies, neatly eviscerated, after two weeks of decomposition in a muddy riverbank? What do you tell the public about the twenty-six victims of a radiation leak at a reactor? Do you know what those poor bastards looked like? And the paper's managers, who know nothing about journalism, talking about finding ways to attract more advertisers! Shit!" Frank had replaced the empty glass with another. Jim Sutton looked at it, and took it with a sigh. "I've been going to a shrink. I used to scoff at the guys who did, but I've had to join them. Lelland University has offered me a post on the faculty. Three years ago I would have laughed at them, but I'm thinking about it."

"Do you want to teach?" It was the first question that Franciscus had asked and it somewhat startled Jim Sutton.

"I don't know. I've never done it. I know that my professors were blithering incompetents, and much of what they told me wasn't worth wiping my ass with. Still, I tell myself that I could make a difference, that if I had had the kind of reporter I am now for a teacher, I would have saved myself a lot of grief. Or maybe I'm just running away, and in a year, I'll be slavering to be back on the job." He tasted the drink and set it aside.

"Why not try teaching for a year, just to find out if you want to do it, and then make up your mind? Your paper will give you leave, won't it?" His suggestion was nonchalant and he said it in such a way that he did not require a response.

Jim Sutton thought about it a moment. "I could do that. It gives me an out. Whether it works or it doesn't, there is a way for me to tell myself I made the right decision." He made a barking sound that was supposed to be a laugh.

"I've got another set coming up," Franciscus said as he got off the stool. "Any requests?"

"Sure." This had become a challenge with them in the last three years. "The ballet music from Tchaikovsky's *Maid of Orleans*." He said it with a straight face, thinking that this was sufficiently obscure, as he himself had only heard it once, and that was a fluke.

Franciscus said, "The court scene dances? All of them?" He was unflustered and the confident, ironic smile returned. "Too easy, Jim; much too easy."

Jim Sutton shook his head. "I should have known. I'll stump you one day." He took another sip of the rum, and added, "Here's a bit of trivia for you—Tchaikovsky collected the music of the Count de Saint-Germain. Do you know who he was?"

"Oh, yes. I know." He had stepped back.

"Yeah, well . . ." Before he could go on, he was interrupted by Mrs. Emmons at the end of the bar who caroled out, "Oh, Mr. Franciscus, would you play 'When the Moon Comes Over the Mountain' for me?"

Emillie Harper was noticeably pale the next day as she sat by the pool in her tunic swimsuit with ruffled neck and hem. She gave a wan smile to Harriet Goodman as the older woman came through the gate onto the wide, mosaiced deck around the pool.

"Good morning," Harriet called as she saw the girl. "I thought I was the first one out."

"No," Emillie said hastily. "I haven't had much sun, so mother said I'd better do my swimming in the morning and evening."

"Good advice," Harriet concurred. "You won't be as likely to burn."

"I was hoping there might be swimming at night," she said wistfully. "I heard that Mr. Rogers has night swimming in the summer."

"Talk to him about it," Harriet suggested as she spread her towel over the depiction of a Roman bireme. She had often been struck with the very Roman feel of the swimming pool here at Lost Saints Lodge. For some reason it did not have that phony feel that so many others had. The mosaics were part of it, but that was not it entirely. Harriet Goodman had a nose for authenticity, and she could smell it here and wondered why. It was cool but she did not deceive herself that her frisson came from the touch of the wind.

"Pardon me," Emillie said a bit later, "but haven't I seen you before? I know that sounds stupid," she added, blushing.

Harriet had cultivated her considerable charm for many years, and she used it now on the distressed girl. "Why, not at all—it's very kind of you. I do occasional television appearances and I lecture all over the country. If I made enough of an impression for you to remember me, I'm flattered."

Emillie's face brightened a little, though on someone as apprehensive and colorless as the teen-ager was, enthusiasm was difficult to perceive. "I did see you. A while ago," she added guiltily.

"Well, I've been around for quite a time." Harriet said as she lay back on the towel. What was bothering the girl? she wondered.

"I'm sorry, but I don't remember what it was you talked about." Emillie was afraid she had insulted the older woman, and was trying to keep from withdrawing entirely.

"Child abuse. I'm a psychiatrist, Miss Harper. But at the moment, I am also on vacation." Her voice was expertly neutral, and she made no move that would suggest disapproval.

"A psychiatrist?" She repeated the word as if it were contaminated.

Harriet had experienced that reaction too many times to be disturbed by it. "Yes, more Jungian than Freudian. I got into child abuse by accident." She had a rich chuckle. "That does sound ominous, doesn't it? What I meant to say, though Freud would have it that my sloppy grammar was hidden truth, is that I became interested in studying child abuse unintentionally. Since I'm a woman, when I first went into practice I had few male patients. A great many men don't feel comfortable with a woman analyst. After a while, I discovered that a fair number of my women patients were either child abusers themselves or were married to men who were." She raised her head and glanced over at the demure girl several feet away. "Now it's you who should forgive me. Here I've told you I'm on vacation and the next thing, I'm starting shop talk."

"It's all right," Emillie said in a politely gelid tone.

They had been there quite the better part of half an hour when the gate opened again. Mrs. Emmons, in a lavish flowered purple bathing suit and outrageous rhinestoned sunglasses, sauntered up to the edge of the pool. "Oh, hello, girls," she called to the others. "Isn't it a beautiful morning?"

"Christ!" Harriet expostulated, and lay back in the sun.

A little bit later, Mrs. Granger arrived, wearing an enormous flowered hat and a beach robe of such voluminous cut that the shrunken body it covered seemed like illicit cargo. By that time Mrs. Emmons was splashing in the shallow end of the pool and hooting with delight.

Pink more with embarrassment than the sun, Emillie Harper gathered up her towel, mumbled a few words that might be construed as excuses, and fled. Harriet propped herself on her elbow and watched Emillie go, scowling, her senses on the alert.

There was a low rock at the tip of the point, and Jim Sutton sat on it, fishing rod at the ready, gazing out over the lake to the steep slope rising on the western bank. A discarded, half-eaten sandwich had already begun to attract ants to the side of the rock.

"Hello, Jim," Harriet said as she came up behind him.

"Hi," he answered, not turning. "There's a spurious rumor that this lake has been stocked with trout."

"But no luck," she inferred.

"No luck." He reeled in the line and cast again. "I got four eighteen-inchers last year."

"Maybe it's the wrong time of day." She had the good sense to stay back from the rock where he sat, though only part of her reason had to do with fishing. "I hear that you'll have to make your stay short this year. There's that trial in Denver . . ."

"There is indeed." He looked down and saw the remains of his sandwich, which he kicked away.

"Mustn't litter," Harriet admonished him lightly.

"Who's littering? I'm supporting the ecological chain by providing a feeding niche," he shot back. "I don't know why I bother. Nothing's going to bite today."

Harriet selected the least-rough part of a fallen log and sat on it, rather gingerly, and was pleased when it held. So much fallen wood was rotten, no matter how sound it appeared. "I'll buy you a drink if you'd like to come back to the Lodge with me."

"A very handsome offer. How can I refuse." He began to reel in his line. "You in cabin 21?"

"As usual. And you?"

"Cabin A42. As usual." He caught up his leader and held it carefully, inspecting his hook and bait before turning to her.

"Then we're almost neighbors." That was a polite fiction: a steep pathway connected the two wider trails on which their cabins were located, and the distance required a good ten minutes after dark.

"Perhaps you'd like to come by." She was careful not to sound too wistful.

"Sounds good." He faced her now, and came up beside her. "Don't worry about me, Harriet. I do take a reason-

156

able amount of care of myself. We're neither of us children, anymore."

She put an arm across his back. "No, we're not children." They were much the same height, so their kiss was almost too easy. "I miss that."

"So do I." They started up the trail together, walking side by side. "Anyone new in your life?"

"No one important," she said with a shrug. "And you?"

"There was one woman, very sensual, but . . . I don't know. Like covering a disaster. Everything afterward is an anticlimax."

They had reached the first turning in the road and were startled to see the strange guest from cabin 33 coming toward them. Mr. Lorpicar nodded to both Harriet and Sutton, but did not speak, continuing down the path with an expression at once determined and abstracted.

"That's one strange duck," Harriet said as they resumed their walk.

"He's the one in cabin 33, isn't he?" Jim Sutton asked, giving the retreating figure a quick look over his shoulder.

"I think so." She dug her hands deep into the pockets of her hiking slacks, watching Jim Sutton with covert concern.

"I saw him after lunch with that Harper girl. I've seen her before, I know I have. I just can't place her . . ." They were at the crest of a gentle rise and through the pines they could see the back of the Lodge. "I hate it when I can't remember faces."

Harriet smiled gently. "You'll think of it. Probably it isn't this girl at all, but another one, equally colorless. Both her parents look like frightened hares." She thought about this as they approached the Lodge. "You'd think one of them would be a tyrant to have the daughter turn out that way. I thought that one of them might be pious or invalidish, but they're as painfully ordinary as the girl is."

"Such language for a psychiatrist," Jim Sutton admonished her, and then they went up the steps into the Lodge, into the lounge, and they did not talk about Emillie Harper or the peculiar Mr. Lorpicar anymore.

Nick Wyler was a hale sort of man, whose body and gestures were always a little too large for his surroundings. He enjoyed his own flamboyance, and was sincerely upset if others did not enjoy it, too. His wife, Eleanore, was a stately woman, given to wearing long skirts and Guatemalan peasant blouses. They had taken cabin A68, right on the lake, one of the largest and most expensive cabins at Lost Saints Lodge.

"Rogers, you're outdoing yourself," Nick Wyler announced as he came into the dining room. "I'm impressed, very impressed."

Mr. Rogers made a polite gesture which was very nearly a bow. "It's good of you to say so."

"That mysterious owner of yours does things right. You may tell him I said so." He gave a sweeping gesture that took in the entire dining room and implied the rest of the building. "Really beautiful restoration. None of the schlock that's turning up all over the place. I'd bet my eye teeth that the lowboy in the foyer is genuine. English, eighteenth century." He beamed and waited for his expertise to be confirmed.

"Actually, it's Dutch," Mr. Rogers said at his most apologetic. "It was built at the Hague in 1761." Before Nick Wyler could take issue with this, or embark on another round of compliments, Mr. Rogers had turned away and was leading Mrs. Emmons and Mrs. Granger to their table by the window.

"The chef's special this evening, ladies, is stuffed pork chops. And in addition to the usual dessert menu, the chef has prepared a custard-filled tart. If you'll simply tell the waiter, he'll see that your selections are brought promptly."

"I like him," Mrs. Granger confided in a loud, gravelly voice. "He knows what service means."

Mr. Rogers had signaled for the waiter and was once again at the door of the dining room. All three Harpers were waiting for him, and smiled ingratiatingly, as if they were the inferiors. Mr. Harper was solicitous of his wife and daughter and respectful to Mr. Rogers.

"Our table there, Doris, Emillie. Mr. Rogers will lead the way." He was so eager to behave properly that he was infuriating.

As Mr. Rogers held the chair for Doris Harper, he saw, with real pleasure, Harriet Goodman and Jim Sutton come in from the lounge. He hastened back to them. "A table together, I assume?"

"Why make more work than's necessary?" Jim asked magnanimously. "Harriet's got the nicer table, anyway." His voice dropped and he stared once more at the Harpers. "I know I've seen that girl. I know it."

"It'll come to you," Harriet told him patiently as they followed Mr. Rogers. She was growing tired of hearing

158

him speculate. They saw each other so rarely that she resented time lost in senseless preoccupation with others.

Franciscus appeared in the door to the lounge and motioned to Mr. Rogers, and when the manager reached him, he said, "Where's Lorpicar? I saw him out on the trails today. Has he come back?"

"I haven't seen him," Mr. Rogers said quietly. "Oh, dear."

"I'll go have a look for him if he hasn't turned up by the end of dinner." He was dressed for playing in the lounge, not for riding at night, but he did not appear to be put out. "I saw the Blakemores come in this afternoon. I think he might be willing to play a while, and he's a good enough pianist for it."

"Last year he did an entire evening for us," Mr. Rogers recalled, not precisely relieved. "I'll make a few inquiries here, in case one of the other guests has seen Lorpicar." He watched Franciscus return to the lounge, and then went to seat the Browns and the Lindholms, who waited for him.

Dinner was almost finished and Mr. Rogers had discovered nothing about the reclusive man in cabin 33. He was about to return with this unpleasant piece of information when he saw the stranger stride through the doors into the foyer.

"Mr. Lorpicar," Mr. Rogers said as he came forward. "You're almost too late for dinner."

The cold stare that Mr. Lorpicar gave the manager was enough to silence a lesser man, but Mr. Rogers gave his blandest smile. "We were concerned when you did not return."

"What I do is my own business," Mr. Lorpicar declared, and stepped hastily into the dining room and went directly to the Harpers' table.

At the approach of Mr. Lorpicar, Emillie looked up and turned even paler than usual. "Gracious," she murmured as the formidable man bore down on her.

"I wonder who this is supposed to impress?" Harriet said very softly to Jim.

"Shush!" was the answer, with a gesture for emphasis. The rest of the dining room buzzed with conversation, and then fell silent as many eyes turned toward the Harper table.

"You did not come," Mr. Lorpicar accused Emillie. "I waited for you and you did not come."

159

"I couldn't," she answered breathlessly.

Mr. Rogers, watching from the door, felt rather than saw Franciscus appear at his elbow.

"Trouble?" Franciscus asked in a low voice.

"Very likely," was the manager's reply.

"See here . . ." Emillie's father began, but the tall, dark-clad man cut him off.

"I am not speaking to you. I am speaking to Emillie and no one else." His burning gaze went back to the girl's face. "I want to see you tonight. I must see you tonight."

The diners were silent, their reactions ranging from shock to cynical amusement to disgust to envy. Jim Sutton watched closely, his face revealing nothing, his eyes narrowed.

"I don't know if I can," she faltered, pushing her fork through the remains of her meal.

"You will." He reached out and tilted her head upward. "You will."

Doris Harper gave a little shriek and stared at her water glass as her husband pressed pleats into his napkin.

"I don't know . . ." Emillie began, but got no further.

"Excuse me," Franciscus said with utmost urbanity. "If Miss Harper wishes to continue what is obviously a private conversation in the lounge, I'll be glad to offer you my company so that her parents need not be concerned. If she would prefer not to talk with you just at present, Mr. Lorpicar, it might be best if you take a seat for the meal or . . ."

Mr. Lorpicar failed to shove Franciscus out of his way, but he did brush past him with a softly spoken curse, followed by a declaration to the room at large. "I'll eat later," and added, in the same breath to Emillie Harper, "We haven't finished yet."

Franciscus left the dining room almost at once, but not before he had bent down to Emillie and said quietly, "If you would rather not be importuned by Mr. Lorpicar, you have only to tell me so." Then he made his way back to the lounge, and if he heard the sudden rush of conversation, there was no indication of it in his manner.

There were five people in the lounge now and Frank was smothering a yawn at the bar.

"I've been meaning to tell you all evening," Harriet said to Franciscus, "that was a masterful stroke you gave in the dining room."

160

Franciscus raised his fine brows in polite disbelief. "It seemed the best way to deal with a very awkward situation." He looked at Jim Sutton on the other side of the small table. "Do you remember where you've seen the girl yet?"

"No." The admission bothered him; he ground out his cigarette in the fine crystal ashtray.

"You know," Harriet went on with professional detachment, "it was most interesting to watch Emillie. Most of the people in the room were looking at Lorpicar, but I found Emillie the more interesting of the two. For all her protestations, she was absolutely rapt. She looked at that man as if he were her salvation, or he a god and she his chosen acolyte. Can you imagine feeling that way for a macho nerd like Lorpicar?"

"Is macho nerd a technical term?" Franciscus asked, favoring her with a delighted, sarcastic smile.

"Of course. All conscientious psychiatrists use it." She was quite unrufflable.

"Acolytes!" Jim Sutton burst out, slapping his hand on the table top and spilling his drink. "That's it!"

"What?" Harriet inquired in her best calming tones.

"That girl. Their last name isn't Harper, it's Matthisen. She was the one who caused all the furor when that religious fake in Nevada brought the suit against her for breach of contract. He makes all his followers sign contracts with him, as a way to stop the kind of prosecution that some of the other cults have run into. She, Emillie, was one of Reverend Masters' converts. She was kidnapped back by one of the professional deprogrammers. A man by the name of Eric Saul. He got himself declared persona non grata in Nevada for his work with Emillie. Reverend Masters brought suit against Emillie for breach of contract and against her parents and Eric Saul for conspiracy." His face was flushed. "I read most of the coverage of the trial. Loren Hapgood defended the Matthisens and Saul. Part of the defense was that not only was the girl under age —she was sixteen then—but that she was socially unsophisticated and particularly vulnerable to that sort of coercion." He took his glass and tossed off the rum with a tight, eager smile.

"Didn't Enid Hume serve as expert witness?" Harriet asked, thinking of her illustrious colleague. "She's been doing a lot of that in similar cases."

"Yes, she and that guy from L.A. I can't remember his

161

name right off. It's something like Dick Smith. You know the one I mean. The psychologist who did the book a couple years back." He leaned toward Harriet, and both were so caught up in what Jim was saying that they were startled when Franciscus put in a question.

"Who won?" He sat back in his chair, hands folded around the uppermost crossed knee.

"The defense," Jim Sutton said promptly. "The argument was that she was under age and that the nature of the agreement had not been explained to her family. There was also a demonstration that she was more gullible to a con of that sort than a great many others might be."

Harriet pursed her lips. "Enid told me about this, or a similar case, and said that she was worried about kids like Emillie. They're always seeking someone stronger than they are, so that they don't have to deal with their own fears of weakness, but can identify with their master. Reverend Masters is fortunate in his name," she added wryly. "I've seen women who feel that way about domineering husbands, kids who feel that way about parents, occasionally, adults who feel that way about religious or industrial or political leaders. It's one of the attitudes that make tyranny possible." Harriet had a glass of port she had been nursing, but now she took a fair amount of the ripe liquid into her mouth.

"Reverend Masters." Jim Sutton repeated the name three or four times to himself. "You know, he's a tall man, like Lorpicar. Not the same type. A blond, fallen-angel face, one of those men who looks thirty-five until he's sixty. He's in Arizona or New Mexico now, I think. Some place where the locals aren't watching him too closely."

"And do you think he'll continue?" Franciscus inquired gently of the two.

"Yes," Harriet said promptly. "There are always people who need a person like Masters in their lives. They invent him if they have to. He's a magnet to them."

"That's damn cynical for a woman in your line of work," Jim Sutton chided her. "You make it sound so hopeless."

For a moment Harriet looked very tired and every one of her forty-two years. "There are times I think it is hopeless. It might be just because I deal with child abuse, but there are times I feel that it's not going to get any better, and all the work and caring and heartbreak will be for nothing. It will go on and on and on."

162

Jim Sutton regarded her with alarm, but Franciscus turned his dark, compassionate eyes on her. "I understand your feeling—far better than you think. Harriet, your caring, your love is never wasted. It may not be used, but it is never wasted."

She stared at Franciscus astonished.

"You know it is true, Harriet," Franciscus said kindly. "You know it or you wouldn't be doing the work you do. And now, if you'll excuse me . . ." he went on in his usual tones, and rose from the table. "I have a few chores I must finish before the bar closes up for the night." He was already moving across the dimly lit room, and stopped only once on his way to speak to the Wylers.

"Well, well, well, what do you know," Jim Sutton observed, a laconic smile curving his mouth. "I'm beginning to see why you have dreams about him. He's got a great line."

"That wasn't a line," Harriet said quietly.

Jim nodded, contrition in his face. "Yeah. I know." He stared into his glass. "Are the dreams like that?"

Her answer was wry but her expression was troubled. "Not exactly. I haven't had one yet this time. I kind of miss it."

"You've got the real thing instead. Your place or mine tonight?" He put his hand on her shoulder. "Look, I didn't mean that the way it sounded. Erotic dreams, who doesn't have them? Franciscus is a good guy."

"I only have the dreams when I'm here," Harriet said, as if to explain to herself. "I wish I knew why." Her laugh was sad. "I wouldn't mind having them elsewhere. Dreams like that . . ."

"It's probably the proximity," Jim Sutton said, and then, sensing her withdrawal, "I'm not jealous of the other men you sleep with, so I sure as hell am not going to be jealous of a dream." He finished his rum and cocked his head in the direction of the door. "Ready?"

"God, yes," she sighed, and followed him out of the lounge into the night.

For the last two days Emillie Harper had wandered about listlessly, oblivious to the stares and whispers that followed her. She had taken to wearing slacks and turtleneck sweaters, claiming she was cold. Her face was wan and her eyes were fever-bright.

"I'm worried about that child," Harriet said to Franciscus as they came back from the stable.

"Victim's syndrome, do you think?" Franciscus asked, his voice carefully neutral.

"More than that. I can't imagine that Lorpicar is a good lay. Men like that almost never are." She was sore from the ride, since she had not been on a horse in eight months, but she walked energetically, doing her best to ignore the protesting muscles, and reminding herself that if she walked normally now, she would be less stiff in the morning.

"Do you think they're sleeping together?" Franciscus asked. They were abreast of the enclosed swimming pool now and could hear Mrs. Emmons' familiar hoots of delight.

"What else? She drags around all day, hardly eats, and meets him somewhere at night. And I've yet to see him up before dusk." She nodded to Myron Shires, who had set a chair out on the lawn in front of the Lodge and had propped a portable typewriter on his knees and was tapping the keys with pianistic intensity. There was a two-beat pause as he waved an off-handed greeting.

"Why do you think that Lorpicar wants her?" Franciscus persisted.

"Because she's the youngest woman here, because she adores him," Harriet said distastefully. "She likes his foreign air, his domination. Poor kid."

"Foreign?" Franciscus asked, reserving his own judgment.

"He does cultivate one," Harriet allowed, glancing up as a large pickup with a two-horse trailer passed by. "Where would you say he comes from?"

Franciscus laughed. "Peoria."

"Do you say that because you're foreign yourself?" She made her inquiry casually, and added, "Your English is almost perfect, but there's something about the rhythm of it, or the word choice. You don't speak it natively, do you?"

"No, not natively." His answer, though terse, was not critical.

Harriet felt herself encouraged. "I've wondered just where you do come from . . ."

They had started up the wide steps of the porch, heading toward the engraved-glass doors that led into the foyer. There was a joyous shout from inside and the doors flew open.

Franciscus' face froze and then lit with a delight Harriet

164

had never seen before. He stopped on the second step and opened his arms to the well-dressed young woman who raced toward him. They stood embraced for some little time; then he kissed her eyelids and murmured to her, "Ah, mon coeur, how good to see you again."

"And you." The young woman was perhaps twenty-two, though her face was a little young in appearance. Her dark hair fell around her shoulders, her violet eyes danced. She was sensibly dressed in a twill pantsuit with cotton shirt and high, serviceable boots. Harriet had seen enough tailor-made garments in her life to know that this young woman wore such clothes.

"You must forgive me," Franciscus said, recalling himself. "Harriet, this is Madelaine de Montalia, though the de is mere courtesy these days, of course." He had stepped back, but he held Madelaine's hand firmly in his.

"A pleasure," Harriet said. She had never before felt herself to be as much an intruder as she did standing there on the steps of the Lodge. The strength of the intimacy between Franciscus and Madelaine was so great that it was a force in the air. Harriet wanted to find a graceful way to excuse herself, but could think of none. She admitted to herself that she was curious about the young woman, and felt an indefinable sort of envy.

"You must not be shocked," Madelaine said to Harriet. "We are blood relatives, Sain . . . Franciscus and I. There are not so many of us left, and he and I have been very close."

You've been close in more ways than blood, Harriet thought to herself, but did not voice this observation. She felt a wistfulness, knowing that few of her old lovers would respond to her now as Franciscus did to Madelaine. "I'm not shocked," she managed to say.

"Harriet is a psychiatrist, my dear," Franciscus explained.

"Indeed?" Madelaine was genuinely pleased. "I am an archeologist."

"You seem fairly young to have . . ." She did not know how to express her feelings, and made a gesture in compensation.

"My face!" Madelaine clapped her free hand to her cheek. "It is very difficult, Harriet, to look so young. I assure you that I am academically qualified. I've done post-doctoral work in Europe and Asia. You mustn't assume

I'm as young as I look." Her dismay was quite genuine and she turned to Franciscus. "You're worse than I am."

"It runs in the family," Harriet suggested, looking from Madelaine to Franciscus.

"Something like that," he agreed. "Harriet, will you forgive me if I leave you here?"

"Certainly. You probably want to catch up on everything." She still felt a twinge of regret, but rigorously overcame it. "I'll see you in the lounge tonight." As she started back down the stairs and along the wooded path toward her cabin, she heard Madelaine say, "I've brought one of my colleagues. I hope that's all right."

"I'm sure Mr. Rogers can work something out with the owner," Franciscus said, and was rewarded with mischievous laughter.

Harriet dug her hands into her pockets and told herself that the hurt she felt was from her unaccustomed riding, and not from loneliness.

The moon was three days past full and one edge was ragged, as if mice had been at it. Soft light illumed the path by the lake where Emillie Harper walked, her face pensive, her heart full of unspoken longing. No one, not even Reverend Masters, had made her feel so necessary as Mr. Lorpicar. A delicious shudder ran through her and she stopped to look at the faint reflection of her form in the water. She could not see the expression of her face—the image was too indistinct for that. Yet she could feel the smile and the lightness of her desires. She had never experienced any feeling before that was as irresistible as what Lorpicar summoned up in her.

A shadow crossed the moon, and she looked up, smiling her welcome and anticipation. In the next instant a change came over her, and her disappointment was almost ludicrous.

"Good evening, Miss Harper," Franciscus said kindly. He was astride his gray mare, saddle and bridle as English as his boots.

"Hello," she said listlessly.

He smiled at her as he dismounted. "I felt you might be here by the lake. Your parents are very worried about you."

"Them!" She had hoped to sound independent and confident, but even to her own ears the word was petulant.

"Yes, them. They asked me if I'd look for you, and I

166

said that I would. I thought you'd prefer talking to me than to your father."

Emillie's chin rose. "I heard that you had a French-woman come to visit you."

"And so I have," Franciscus said with prompt geniality. "She's a very old friend. We're related in a way."

"Oh, are you French?" she asked, interested in spite of herself.

"No, though I've lived there upon occasion." He was leading the gray now, walking beside Emillie with easy strides, not rushing the girl, but in a subtle way not permitting her to dawdle.

"I'd like to go to France. I'd like to go to Europe. I want to be someplace interesting." Her lower lip pouted and she folded her arms.

Franciscus shook his head. "My dear Emillie, interesting is often another word for dangerous. There is an old Chinese curse to that effect."

Emillie tossed her head and her pale brown hair shimmered in the moonlight. She hoped that Mr. Lorpicar was able to see her, for she knew that her pale hair, ordinarily mousy in the daylight, turned a wonderful shade of lunar gold in bright nights. She did not look at the man beside her. "You don't know what it is to be bored."

"I don't?" His chuckle was not quite kind. "I know more of boredom than you could imagine. But I have learned."

"Learned what?" she challenged, staring along the path with ill-concealed expectation.

He did not answer her question, but remarked, "I don't think that Mr. Lorpicar will be joining you tonight." He did not add that he had gone to cabin 33 earlier and made a thorough investigation of the aloof guest. "You know, Emillie, you're letting yourself . . ." He did not go on. When had such advice ever been heeded? he asked himself.

"Get carried away?" she finished for him with as much defiance as she could find within herself. "I want to be carried away. I want something exciting to happen to me before it's too late."

Franciscus stopped and felt his mare nudge his shoulder with her nose. "Too late? You aren't even twenty."

She glared at him, saying darkly, "You don't know what it's like. My father wanted me to marry Ray Gunnerman! Can you imagine?"

Though Franciscus knew nothing of this unfortunate

young man, he said with perfect gravity, "You're hardly at an age to get married, are you?"

"Father thinks I am. He says that I need someone to take care of me, to protect me. He thinks that I can't manage on my own." Her voice had become shrill and she had gone ahead of him on the path.

Privately, Franciscus thought that Mr. Harper might be justified in his conviction, for Emillie Harper was certainly predisposed to harm herself through her desire to be controlled. "You know," he said reminiscently, "I knew a woman, oh, many years ago . . ."

"That Frenchwoman?" Emillie asked so sharply that Franciscus raised his fine brows.

"No, this woman was Italian. She was a very attractive widow, and she wanted new sensations in her life. There always had to be more, and eventually, she ran out of new experiences, which frightened her badly, and she turned to the most rigorous austerity, which was just another form of sensation for her. I'm telling you about her because I think you might want to examine your life now."

"You want me to settle for Ray Gunnerman?" she demanded, flushing in that unbecoming, mottled way.

"No. But you should realize that life is not something that is done to you, but a thing that you experience for yourself. If you always look outside yourself for your definitions, you may never discover what is genuinely your own—your self." He could tell from the set of her jaw that she did not believe him.

"What happened to that Italian woman?" she asked him when he fell silent.

"She died in a fire." Which was no more than the truth. "Come, Emillie. It's time you went back to your cabin. Mr. Lorpicar won't be coming now, I think."

"You just don't want me to see him. That's the second time you said he wasn't coming." She thought he would be impressed with her determination, and was shocked when he smiled gently.

"Of course I don't want you to see him—he's a very dangerous man, Emillie."

"He's not dangerous," she protested, though with little certainty. "He wants to see me."

"I am sure he does," Franciscus agreed dryly. "But you were with him last night and the night before. Surely you can forgo tonight, for your parents' peace of mind, if not your own protection."

"Well, I'll go up to see him tomorrow afternoon," Emillie declared, putting her hands on her hips, alarmed to discover that they were trembling.

"Tomorrow afternoon? That's up to you." There was a sad amusement in his dark eyes, but he did nothing to change her mind.

"I will." She looked across the curve of the lake to the hillside where cabin 33 was located. The path was a little less than a quarter mile around the shore, but from where she stood, the cabin was no more than a hundred fifty yards away. The still water was marked by a moon path that lay like a radiant silver bar between her and the far bank where Mr. Lorpicar waited for her in vain. "He has to see me," she insisted, but turned back on the path.

"That's a matter of opinion," Franciscus said and changed the subject. "Are you going to be at the picnic at the south end of the lake tomorrow? The chef is making Mexican food."

"Oh, picnics are silly," she said with the hauteur that only a woman as young as she could express.

"But Kathy is an excellent chef, isn't she?" he asked playfully, knowing that Lost Saints Lodge had a treasure in her.

"Yes," she allowed. "I liked that stuff she made with asparagus and walnuts. I didn't know it could be a salad."

"I understand her enchiladas and chihuahueños are superb." He was able to speak with complete sincerity.

"I might come for a little while," she said when she had given the matter her consideration. "But that's not a promise."

"Of course not," he agreed gravely as they walked past the bathing beach and pier and turned toward the break in the trees and the path that went from the beach to the badminton courts to the Lodge itself and to cabin 19 beyond, where the Harpers waited for their daughter.

Harriet Goodman was deep in conversation with Madelaine de Montalia, though most of the other guests gathered around the stone fireplace where a large, ruddy-cheeked woman held court while she put the finishing touches on the meal.

"And lots of garlic, comino, and garlic," the chef was instructing the others who stood around her, intoxicated by the smells that rose from the various cooking vessels. "Mexican or Chinese, there's no such thing as too much

169

garlic." She paused. "Most of the time. Now, making Kung-Pao chicken . . ." and she was off on another description.

"I don't know how she does it," Harriet said loudly enough to include Franciscus in her remark.

"She's an artist," Franciscus said simply. He was stretched out under a young pine, his hands propped behind his head, his eyes all but closed.

Mrs. Emmons bustled around the wooden tables setting out the heavy square glasses that were part of the picnic utensils. "I must say, the owner must be quite a surprising man—real glass on a picnic," she enthused.

"He's something of a snob," Mr. Rogers said, raising his voice to call, "Mr. Franciscus, what's your opinion?"

Franciscus smiled. "Oh, I concur, Mr. Rogers."

"Are you going to spend the entire afternoon supine?" Madelaine asked him as Harriet rose to take her place in line for food.

"Probably." He did not look at her but there was a softening to his face that revealed more than any words or touching could.

"Madelaine!" Harriet called from her place in line. "Do you want some of this? Shall I bring you a plate?"

The dark-haired young woman looked up. "Thank you, Harriet, but no. I am still having jet lag, I think."

"Aren't you hungry?" Harriet asked, a solicitous note in her voice.

"Not at present." She paused and added, "My assistant will provide something for me later."
Harriet, but no. I am still having jet lag, I think."
had arrived with Madelaine. "Where's she?"

"Nadia is resting. She will be here later, perhaps." She leaned back against the tree trunk and sighed.

"Nadia is devoted to you, my heart?" Franciscus asked quietly.

"Very." She had picked up a piece of bark and was toying with it, turning it over in her hands, feeling the rough and the smooth of it.

"Good. Are you happy?" There was no anxiety in his question, but a little sadness.

Madelaine's answer was not direct. "You told me many years ago that your life is very lonely. I understand that, for I am lonely, but I would rather be lonely, having my life as it is, than to have succumbed at nineteen and never have known all that I know. When I am with you, I am

170

happy. The rest of the time, I am content, and I am always learning."

"And the work hasn't disappointed you?" His voice was low and lazy, caressing her.

"Not yet. Every time I think that I have truly begun to understand a city or a people, something new comes to light, and I discover that I know almost nothing, and must begin again." She was pulling at the weeds that grew near the base of the tree.

"This doesn't disappoint you?"

"No. Once in a while, I become annoyed, and I suppose if my time were short, I might feel more urgency, but, as it is . . ." She shrugged as only a Frenchwoman can.

A shadow fell across them. "Excuse me," said Mr. Harper, "but have you seen my daughter, Emillie? She went out very early this morning, but I thought surely she'd be back by now." He gave Franciscus an ingratiating smile.

Franciscus opened his eyes. "You mean she isn't here?"

"No. My wife thought that she might have gone swimming, but her suit was in the bathroom, and it's quite chilly in the mornings . . ." He held a plate of enchiladas and chalupas, and he was wearing a plaid shirt and twill slacks that were supposed to make him look the outdoors sort, but only emphasized the slope of his shoulders and the pallor of his skin.

Alert now, Franciscus sat up. "When did you actually see your daughter last?"

"Well, she came in quite late, and Doris waited for her. They had a talk, and Doris left her about two, she says." His face puckered. "You don't think anything has happened to her, do you?"

"You must think so," Franciscus said with an odd combination of kindness and asperity.

"Well, yes," the middle-aged man said apologetically. "After everything the child has been through . . ." He stopped and looked at the food on his plate as if there might be revelations in the sauces.

Franciscus got to his feet. "If it will make you less apprehensive, I'll check out the Lodge and the pool for her, and find out if any of the staff have seen her."

"Would you?" There was a weak, manipulative kind of gratitude in the man's pale eyes, and Franciscus began to understand why it was that Emillie Harper had become the victim of the Reverend Masters.

"I'll go now." He touched Madelaine's hair gently. "You'll forgive me, my heart?"

She smiled up at him, saying cryptically, "The Count to the rescue."

"You're incorrigible," he responded affectionately as he put his black hat on. "I'll be back in a while. Tell Mr. Rogers where I've gone, will you?"

"I'll be happy to." Madelaine patted his leg, then watched as he strode off.

"He seems reliable," Mr. Harper said to Madelaine, asking for reassurance.

"He is," she said shortly, leaned back against the tree and closed her eyes.

Mr. Harper looked at her, baffled, then wandered off toward the tables, looking for his wife.

Kathy had served most of the food and had launched into a highly technical discussion with Jim Sutton about the proper way to cook scallops.

Emillie Harper was not at the Lodge, in the recreation building, at the swimming pool, the badminton courts, or the beach area of the resort. Franciscus had checked all those places and had found no trace of the girl. Those few guests who had not gone on the picnic had not seen her, and the staff could not recall noticing her.

At first Franciscus had assumed that Emillie was giving a show of childish petulance—she clearly resented Franciscus' interference in her tryst the night before. As he walked along the shore trail past the small dock, he wondered if he had been hasty, and his steps faltered. He glanced north, across the bend of the lake toward the hillside where cabin 33 was, and involuntarily his face set in anger. Why, of all the resorts in the Rocky Mountains, did Mr. Milan Lorpicar have to choose Lost Saints Lodge for his stay?

A sound intruded on his thoughts, the persistent clacking of a typewriter. The door to cabin 8 stood ajar, and Franciscus could see Myron Shires hunched over on the couch, his typewriter on the coffee table, his fingers moving like a pair of dancing spiders over the keys. Beside the typewriter there was a neat stack of pages about two inches high. The sound stopped abruptly. "Franciscus," Myron Shires said, looking up quickly.

"Good afternoon, Mr. Shires. I thought you'd be at the

picnic." He liked the big, slightly distracted man, and was pleased to let him intrude on his thoughts.

"Well, I'm planning to go," he said. "What time is it?"

"After one," Franciscus said, smiling now.

"After one?" Shires repeated, amazed. "How on earth . . ."

"There's plenty of food," Franciscus assured him, not quite smiling at Myron Shires' consternation.

Shires laughed and gave a self-deprecating shrug. "I ought to have a keeper. My ex-wife hated it when I forgot things like this, but I get so caught up in . . ." He broke off. "You weren't sent to fetch me, were you?"

"No," Franciscus said, leaning against the door. "As a matter of fact I was looking for the Harper girl. Her parents are worried because she hasn't shown up for lunch."

"The Harper girl?" Shires said. "Is that the skittish teenager who looks like a ghost most of the time?"

"That's her," Franciscus nodded. "Have you seen her?"

Shires was gathering his pages into a neat stack and did not answer at once. "Not today, no. I did see her last night, walking along the trail on the other side of the beach. She stopped under the light and I thought that she was really quite graceful."

Franciscus almost dismissed this, remembering his encounter with Emillie the night before, but his curiosity was slightly piqued: he wanted to know how long the girl had waited for Mr. Lorpicar. "When was that?" he asked.

"Oh, quite late. Three, three-thirty in the morning. You know me—I'm night people." He had put the pages into a box and was putting his typewriter into its case.

"Three?" Franciscus said, dismayed. "Are you sure?"

"Well, it might have been a little earlier," Shires allowed as he closed the lid of the case. "Not much earlier, though, because I had my radio on until two and it had been off for a time." He caught sight of Franciscus' face. "Is anything wrong?"

Franciscus sighed. "I hope not." He looked at the novelist. "Do you think you can find your way to the picnic without me?"

Myron Shires laughed. "I'm absentminded, but not *that* absentminded," he said with real joviality. "Kathy's picnics are one of the best draws this place offers." He had put his typewriter aside and was pulling on a light jacket.

"Would you be kind enough to tell Mr. Rogers what you've told me?" Franciscus added as he went to the door.

"That I saw the Harper girl go out late? Certainly." He was plainly puzzled but too courteous to ask about the matter.

"I'll explain later, I hope. And, if you can, contrive that her parents don't hear what you say." He had the door open.

"I'm not a complete boor, Franciscus." He had picked up his key from the ashtray on the end table and turned to address a further remark to Franciscus, but the man was gone.

The path to cabin 33 was well kept. There were rails on the downhill side of it, and neat white stones on the other, and at night the lanterns were turned on, making a pool of light every fifty feet. Franciscus knew the route well, and he walked it without reading any of the signs that pointed the way to the various clusters of cabins. He moved swiftly, though with such ease that his speed was not apparent. The trail turned and grew steeper, but his pace did not slacken.

Cabin 33 had been built eight years before, when all the cabins at the north end of the lake had been added. It was of medium size, with a front room, a bedroom, bath and kitchenette, with a screened porch which was open in the summer but now had its winter shutters in place.

Franciscus made a quick circle of the place, then waited to see if Mr. Milan Lorpicar would make an appearance. The cabin was silent. Coming back to the front of cabin 33, Franciscus rapped with his knuckles. "Mr. Lorpicar?" A glance at the red tab by the doorframe told him that the maid had not yet come to change the bed and vacuum the rugs, which was not surprising with the small staff that the Lodge kept during the off-season. The more remote cabins were serviced in the late afternoon.

A second knock, somewhat louder, brought no response, and Franciscus reached into his pocket, extracting his passkey. He pounded the door one more time, recalling with certain amusement the time he had burst in on a couple at the most awkward of moments, made even more so because the husband of the woman and wife of the man were waiting for their absent partners in the recreation hall. The tension in his neck told him that this occasion would be different.

The door opened slowly onto a perfectly orderly front room. Nothing there hinted that the cabin was occupied. There were no magazines, no papers, no cameras, no

174

clothes, no fishing tackle, nothing except what Lost Saints Lodge provided.

Emillie was in the bedroom, stretched out with only the spread over her, drawn up to her chin. She was wan, her closed eyes like bruises in her face, her mouth slightly parted.

"Emillie?" Franciscus said quietly, not wanting to alarm her. She did not awaken, so he came nearer after taking a swift look around the room to be sure that they were alone. "Emillie Harper," he said more sharply.

The girl gave a soft moan, but her eyes did not open.

Franciscus lifted the spread and saw, as he suspected, that she was naked. He was startled to see how thin she was, ribs pressing against her skin, her hips rising like promontories at either side of her abdomen. There were dark blotches here and there on her body, and he nodded grimly as he recognized them.

"God, an amateur," he said under his breath, and dropped the spread over Emillie.

A quick search revealed the girl's clothes in a heap on the bathroom floor. There was no sign of Lorpicar there, either—no toothbrush, no razor. Franciscus nodded, picked up the clothes and went back to the bedroom. He pulled the spread aside once more, and then, with deft persistence, he began to dress the unconscious Emillie Harper.

"I don't know what's wrong," Doctor Eric Muller said as he stood back from the bed. He smoothed his graying hair nervously. "This isn't my field, you know. Most of my patients are referred to me. I'm not very good at off-the-cuff diagnoses like this, and without a lab and more tests, I really couldn't say . . ."

Franciscus recalled that Mister Rogers had warned him that the doctor was jumpy, and so he schooled his patience. "Of course. I understand. But you will admit that it isn't usual for a girl, or a young woman, if you prefer, to be in this condition."

"No, not usual," the doctor agreed, refusing to meet Franciscus' eyes. "Her parents ought to get her to an emergency room, somewhere."

"The nearest emergency facility," Franciscus said coolly, "is thirty miles away and is operated by the forest service. They're better suited to handling broken ankles, burns, and snake bites than cases like this."

Doctor Muller tightened his clasped hands. "Well, all I

175

can recommend is that she be taken somewhere. I can't be of much help, I'm afraid."

"Why not?" Franciscus asked. He had hoped that the doctor would be able to tell the Harpers something reassuring when he left this room.

"There aren't lab facilities here, are there? No. And I'm not licensed in this state, and with the way malpractice cases are going, I can't take responsibility. There's obviously something very wrong with the girl, but I don't think it's too serious." Doctor Muller was already edging toward the door. "Do you think Mister Rogers would mind if I checked out early?"

"That's your business, Doctor," Franciscus said with a condemning lift of his fine brows.

"There'll have to be a refund. I paid in advance." There was a whine under the arrogance, and Franciscus resisted the urge to shout at him.

"I don't think Mister Rogers would stop you from going," he said with an elegant inclination of his head.

"Yes. Well." The door opened and closed like a trap being sprung.

Franciscus remained looking down at the girl on the bed. She was in cabin 19 now, in the smaller bedroom, and her parents hovered outside. Harriet Goodman was with them, and occasionally her steady, confident tones penetrated to the darkened room.

There was a knock, and Franciscus turned to see Mr. Harper standing uncertainly near the door. "The doctor said he didn't know what was wrong. He said there would have to be tests . . ."

"A very wise precaution," Franciscus agreed with a reassuring smile. "But it's probably nothing more than overdoing. She's been looking a little washed out the last few days, and all her activity probably caught up with her." It was plausible enough, he knew, and Mr. Harper was searching for an acceptable explanation. "You'll probably want to call the doctor in Fox Hollow. He makes calls. And he will be able to order the right transportation for her if there is anything more than fatigue the matter." He knew that Mr. Harper was wavering, so he added, "Also, it will save Emillie embarrassment if the condition is minor."

Mr. Harper wagged his head quickly. "Yes. Yes, that's important. Emillie hates . . . attention." He came nearer the bed. "Is there any change?"

"Not that I've noticed." It was the truth, he knew, but only a portion of it. "You might like Ms. Goodman or my friend Ms. Montalia to sit with Emillie until she wakes up."

"Oh, her mother and I will do that," Mr. Harper said at once.

Franciscus realized that he had pressed the matter too much. "Of course. But I'm sure that either lady would be pleased to help out while you take dinner, or speak with Dr. Fitzallen, when he comes." It was all Franciscus could do to hold back his sardonic smile. Mr. Harper was so transparently reassured by that very proper name, and would doubtless be horrified when the physician, a forty-two-year-old Kiowa, arrived. That was for later, he thought.

"Did you . . . anyone . . . give her first aid?" Mr. Harper asked in growing distress.

"I know some first aid," Franciscus said kindly. "I checked her pulse, and breathing, and did my best to determine that no bones were broken." It was a facile lie, and not in the strictest sense dishonest. "Mr. Harper," he went on in sterner tones, "your daughter is suffering from some sort of psychological problem, isn't she?" Though he could not force the frightened father to discuss his daughter's involvement with the Reverend Masters, he felt he had to dispel the illusion that all was well.

"Not exactly," he said, watching Franciscus uneasily.

"Because," Franciscus went on relentlessly, "if she is, this may be a form of shock, and in that case, the treatment might be adjusted to her needs." He waited, not moving, standing by Emillie as if guarding her.

"There has been a little difficulty," Mr. Harper said when he could not endure the silence.

"Be sure you tell Dr. Fitzallen all about it. Otherwise he may, inadvertently, do the wrong thing." With a nod, he left the bedside and went to the door to the sitting room. "Harriet," he said crisply as he started across the room, "get Jim and join me for a drink."

Harriet Goodman was wise enough to ask no questions of him, though there were many of them building up in her as she hastened after him.

"I was *horrified!*" Mrs. Emmons announced with delight as she told Mrs. Granger, who had been asleep with a headache, of the excitement she had missed. "The girl was

177

white as a sheet—I can't tell you." She signaled Frank, the bartender, to send over another round of margaritas, though she still longed for a side-car.

At the other end of the lounge, Franciscus sat with Harriet Goodman and Jim Sutton. His face was turned away from the two old women who were now regaling Frank with a catalogue of their feelings on this occasion. "I can't insist, of course," he said to Jim Sutton.

"Let's hear it for the First Amendment," Jim said. "I don't like to sit on good stories, and this one is a beauty." He was drinking coffee and it had grown cold as they talked. Now he made a face as he tasted it. "Christ, this is awful."

Harriet Goodman regarded Franciscus gravely. "That child may be seriously ill."

"She is in danger, I'll concede that," Franciscus responded.

"It's more than that. I helped her mother undress her, and there were some very disturbing . . ." She could not find a word that satisfied her.

"I saw them," Franciscus said calmly, but quietly so that this revelation would not attract the two women at the other end of the lounge.

"Saw them?" Harriet repeated, and Jim Sutton leaned forward.

"What were they like? Harriet hasn't told me anything about this."

Franciscus hesitated a moment. "There were a number of marks on her and . . . scratches."

Jim Sutton shook his head. "That guy Lorpicar must be one hell of a kink in bed."

"That's not funny, Jim," Harriet reprimanded him sharply.

"No, it's not," he agreed. "What . . . how did she get the marks? Was it Lorpicar?"

"Probably," Franciscus said. "She was in his cabin, on his bed, with just the spread over her." He let this information sink in, and then said, "With what Emillie has already been through with that Reverend Masters, she's in no shape for more notoriety. And if this gets a lot of press attention . . ."

"Which it might," Jim allowed.

Franciscus gestured his accord and went on, ". . . then she might not come out of it very well. The family has al-

178

ready changed its name, and that means there was a lot of pressure on them to begin with. If this is added . . ."

"Yes," Harriet said in her calm way. "You're right. Whatever is happening to that girl, it must be dealt with circumspectly. That means you, Jim."

"It means you, too. You can't go putting this in a case-book and getting a big publicity tour for it," Jim shot back, more caustically than he had intended.

"Both of you, stop it," Franciscus said with such assurance and resignation that the other two were silenced at once, like guilty children. "I'm asking that you each suspend your first inclinations and keep quiet about what is going on here. If it gets any worse, then you'll have to do whatever your professions demand. However, Harriet, with your training, I hope that you'll be willing to spend some time with Emillie once she regains consciousness."

"You seem fairly certain that she will regain consciousness," Harriet snapped.

"Oh, I'm certain. I've seen this condition before. Not here. I hadn't expected to encounter this . . . affliction here." He stared toward the window and the long, dense shadows that heralded night. There were patches of yellow sunlight at the ends of dusty bars of light, and the air was still.

"If you know what it is, why didn't you tell the Harpers?" Jim Sutton demanded, sensing a greater mystery.

"Because they wouldn't believe me. They want to talk to a doctor, not to me. Jorry Fitzallen is welcome to talk to me after he's seen Emillie."

Harriet tried to smile. "You're right about her parents. They do need to hear bad news from men with authority." She stood up. "I want to change before dinner, and I've got less than half an hour to do that. I'll look in on the girl on my way back to the cabin."

"Thank you," Franciscus said, then turned his attention to Jim Sutton. "Well? Are you willing to sit on this story for a little while?"

He shrugged. "I'm on vacation. There's a murder trial coming up in Denver that will keep my paper in advertisers for the next six months. I'll pretend that I haven't seen or heard a thing. Unless it gets bigger. That would make a difference." He raised his glass in a toast. "I must be running out of steam—two years ago, maybe even last year, I would have filed the story and be damned. It might be time to be a teacher, after all." He tossed off his drink and looked away.

The dining room was about to open when Franciscus came through the foyer beside the lobby calling out, "Mr. Rogers, may I see you a moment."

The manager looked up from his stand by the entrance to the dining room. "Why, certainly, Mr. Franciscus. In the library?"

"Fine." Franciscus was already climbing the stairs, and he held the door for Mr. Rogers as he came up.

"It's about Lorpicar?" Mr. Rogers said as the door closed.

"Yes. I've been up to his cabin and checked it out. Wherever he's staying, it's not there. No one is staying there. That means that there are almost a hundred other places he could be. I've asked the staff to check their unoccupied cabins for signs of entry, but I doubt he'd be that foolish, though God knows he's bungled enough so far . . ." He pounded the bookcase with his small fist, and the heavy oak sagged. "We don't even know that he's at the resort. He could be camping out beyond the cabins."

"What about Fox Hollow? Do you think he could have gone that far?" Mr. Rogers asked, and only the slightly higher pitch of his voice belied the calm of his demeanor.

"I doubt it. That ranger . . . Backus, he would have seen something if Lorpicar were commuting." He sat down. "The idiot doesn't know enough not to leave bruises!"

"And the girl?" Mr. Rogers said.

"I think we got her in time. If we can keep Lorpicar away from her for a couple of nights, she'll be all right. Certainly no worse than she was in the hands of Reverend Masters." He laughed once, mirthlessly.

"What are you going to do?" Mr. Rogers had not taken a seat, but watched as Franciscus paced the area between the bookcases and the overstuffed Victorian chairs.

"Find him. Before he makes a worse mistake." He halted, his hand to his forehead. "He could have chosen any resort in the Rockies!"

"And what would have happened to that girl if you had not found her?" He expected no answer and got none.

"Harriet thinks that giving Emillie a crucifix would not be a good idea, considering what she's been through. She's probably right, but it makes our job tougher. Because you can be completely confident that Lorpicar believes the

180

myths." Franciscus looked out the window. "I'll see if Kathy can spare some garlic. That will help."

"I'll tell her that you want some," Mr. Rogers promised.

Suddenly Franciscus chuckled. "I'm being an Uncle . . . what? Not Tom, surely. An Uncle Vlad? Uncle Bela? But what else can I do? Either we stop this rash youngster or Madelaine, and you, and I will be exposed to needless risk." He gave Mr. Rogers a steady look and though Franciscus was quite short, he had a kind of majesty in his stance. "We've come through worse, old friend. I'm not blaming you, I'm miffed at myself for being caught napping."

Mr. Rogers allowed himself to smile. "Thank you for that." He took a step toward the door. "I'd better go down and start dinner seating. Oh." He turned in the open door. "There was a call from Fox Hollow. Jorry Fitzallen will be here by eight."

"Good. By then, I'll have a better idea where we stand."

Franciscus' confidence was destined to be short-lived. He had left the library and had not yet reached the glass doors opening onto the porch when he heard an anguished shout from the area of the lounge and Harriet Goodman started toward him.

"Franciscus!" she called in a steadier tone, though by that time, Mrs. Emmons had turned on her barstool and was watching with undisguised enthusiasm while Nick and Eleanore Wyler paused on the threshold of the dining room to listen to the latest. Eleanore Wyler was wearing a long Algerian caftan with elaborate piping embroidery with little mirrors worked into it, and she shimmered in the dusk.

Assuming a levity he did not feel, Franciscus put his small hands on his hips. "Ms. Goodman, if that frog is still living under your bathtub . . ." It had happened the year before and had become a harmless joke. The Wylers had been most amused by it, and Nick Wyler chortled and began in a loud voice to remind Eleanore of the various methods that were used to rout the offending frog.

Under the cover of this hearty basso, Harriet nodded gratefully. "Thanks. I realized as soon as I spoke that I should have remained quiet. You've got your wits about you, which is more than I do." She put her hand up to wipe her brow, saying very softly, "I'm sorry, but Emillie is missing."

"Missing?" Franciscus repeated, genuinely alarmed.

"I heard Mrs. Harper making a fuss, so I went up the path to their cabin and asked what was wrong. She said she'd been out of Emillie's bedroom for a few moments—I gather from her choice of euphemisms that she was in the john—and when she came back the bedroom door was open and Emillie was nowhere to be seen."

Franciscus rubbed his smooth-shaven face. "I see. Thank you. And if you'll excuse me now . . ." He had motioned to Mr. Rogers, but did not approach the manager. Instead he was out the glass doors in a few seconds, walking swiftly on the east-bound path past the parking lot to the trail leading to the Harpers' cabin 19. His thoughts, which had been in turmoil when Harriet had spoken to him, were now focused and untainted by anger. He had let the matter go on too long, he told himself, but without useless condemnation. He had not supposed that any vampire would be as obvious, as flamboyantly inept as Milan Lorpicar. He lengthened his stride and steeled himself to deal with Doris Harper.

Jorry Fitzallen had required little persuasion—he allowed himself to be put up in one of the best cabins and provided with one of Kathy's special late suppers. He was curious about the girl, he said, and would not be needed in Fox Hollow that night unless an emergency arose. He spent the evening listening to the descriptions of the missing girl from her parents, from Harriet Goodman, from all those who had seen Emillie, and all those who had an opinion. From Jim Sutton he got the background of Emillie's disputes with Reverend Masters, and shook his head with distress. He had treated a few of the good Reverend's followers and had some strong words about that cult leader. He was not able to talk to Dr. Eric Muller, for though the physician had examined Emillie Harper, he kept insisting that he was only a dermatologist and had never encountered anything like Emillie's wounds before and did not want to again. At last Jorry Fitzallen abandoned the questions for the pleasure of talking shop with Harriet Goodman.

There was no music in the lounge that night, for Mr. Franciscus was out with half the day staff, searching for Emillie Harper, and for the strange Mr. Lorpicar.

"I *knew* he was not to be trusted," Mrs. Emmons told the Jenkins sisters, Sally and Elizabeth, who had arrived that afternoon shortly before Emillie Harper was reported missing.

"But how could you? What was he like?" Sally asked, watching her sister stare longingly at Mrs. Emmons' margarita.

"Well, *you* know. Men like that—oh, very handsome in a *savage* way. Tall, dark, atrocious manners, and *so* domineering!" Her intended condemnation was wistful. "Anyone could see at once that there would be no discouraging such a man once he made up his mind about a woman."

The Wylers, at the next table, were indulging in more speculation. "If she had bruises all over her, maybe he simply beat her up. Girls like to be treated rough if they're inhibited, and if ever I saw someone who is . . ." Nick Wyler asserted loudly.

"I can't imagine what that poor child must have gone through," Eleanore agreed in a tone that implied she knew what she would want done to her, had Mr. Lorpicar—and everyone was certain that her assailant was Mr. Lorpicar—chosen her instead of Emillie Harper.

The Browns, Ted and Katherine, came in and were instantly seized upon for news. Since they had brought their own horses, they had been out on the trails with Franciscus and two others. Enjoying this moment of attention, they described their meeting with the ranger named Backus who had reluctantly promised to alert his fire patrol to the two missing guests.

"I think," Ted Brown said, his smiling making seams in his face, "that Backus thought those two don't want to be found for a while. He said as much to Franciscus."

There were knowing laughs in answer to this, and listening, Harriet Goodman was glad that the Harpers had remained in their cabin rather than come to the lounge.

"That Backus sure didn't want to help out," Katherine Brown agreed with playful indignation. "He's worried about fire, not a couple of missing people."

Several diverse points of view were heard, and in this confusion, Ted Brown ordered drinks from the bar.

It was more than an hour later, when the noise in the lounge was greater and the talk was much less unguarded, that Franciscus appeared in the doorway. His black clothes were dusty and his face was tired. At the back of his dark eyes there was a cold wrath burning.

183

The conversation faltered and then stopped altogether. Franciscus came across the floor with quick, relentless steps, to where Jorry Fitzallen sat with Harriet Goodman. "I need you," he said to the doctor, and without waiting for a response, he turned and left the lounge.

The Kiowa made no apologies, but followed Franciscus, hearing the talk erupt behind him as he reached the front door.

On the porch, Franciscus stopped him. "We found her. She's dead."

"You're certain?" Jorry asked. "Laymen sometimes think that . . ."

Franciscus cut in sharply. "I've seen enough dead bodies to recognize one, Dr. Fitzallen."

Jorry Fitzallen nodded, chastened, though he was not sure why. "Where is she?"

"In cabin 19. Her parents are . . . distraught. If you have a sedative, a strong one, Mrs. Harper could use it." The words were crisp, and Franciscus' ire was no longer apparent, though Jorry Fitzallen was sure that it had not lessened.

"I'll get my bag. Cabin 19 is on the eastern path, isn't it?"

"Yes. Second from the end on the right." He studied the physician's sharp features. "You will need to be very discreet, Jorry."

Jorry Fitzallen puzzled the meaning of that remark all the way from his car to cabin 19.

Madelaine de Montalia was seated beside Mrs. Harper, her arm around Doris Harper's shoulder, a barrier for the near-hysterical sobs that slammed through her like seismic shocks. Franciscus, who was pouring a third double scotch for the stunned Mr. Harper, gave Jorry Fitzallen a quick glance and cocked his head toward the women on the couch.

With a nod, the doctor put his bag on the coffee table and crouched before Mrs. Harper.

Doris Harper gasped at the newcomer, looking toward her husband in deep distress. "Howard . . ." she wailed.

Franciscus stepped in, letting Mrs. Harper see the full compelling force of his dark eyes. "Yes, you are very fortunate, Mrs. Harper. Dr. Fitzallen came as soon as our message reached him, and he's waiting to have a look at you."

"But Emillie . . ." the woman cried out.

"That will wait," was Franciscus' immediate reply. He laid one beautiful, small hand on her shoulder. "You must be taken care of first." Had that ever happened to this poor, faded, middle-aged woman before in her life? Franciscus thought. He had seen women like her, all his life long. They tried to buy safety and love and protection by putting themselves last, and it had never saved them. He sighed.

"I'm going to give you an injection, Mrs. Harper," Jorry Fitzallen was saying in his most professional tones. "I want you to lie down on the couch afterward. You'll stay with her, will you, Miss . . . ?"

"As long as you think is wise," Madelaine answered at once.

Mrs. Harper gave a little, desperate nod of thanks and gritted her teeth for the injection.

"I think she'll sleep for several hours," the doctor said to Franciscus and Mr. Harper. "But she's already under tension, from what Mr. Franciscus has told me, Mr. Harper, and it would be wise to get her back into familiar surroundings as soon as possible."

"But we sold everything when we moved and changed . . ." He stopped, glancing uneasily from one man to the other.

"Your name, yes," Franciscus said gently. "But now that doesn't matter, and you will have to make certain arrangements. If you have family in another part of the country . . ."

"God help me, the funeral," Mr. Harper said, aghast, and put his hands to his eyes.

Before either Franciscus or Jorry Fitzallen could speak, Madelaine came up beside them. "I think that Mr. Harper would like a little time to himself, gentlemen." With a deft move, she extricated the grieving father from the other two. "Let's see the body," Jorry Fitzallen said quietly, feeling that same disquieting fatigue that the dead always gave him.

Franciscus held the door and the two passed into the smaller bedroom.

Emillie was nude, and her skin was more mottled than before, though this time the marks were pale. The body had a waxy shine and looked greenish in the muted light.

"Jesus H. Christ," Jorry Fitzallen murmured at the sight of her. "Is there *any* post-mortem lividity?"

185

"A little in the buttocks. That's about it." Franciscus kept his voice level and emotionless.

"Exsanguination is your cause of death, then. Not that there could be much doubt, given her color." He bent to touch one of the many wounds, this one on the inside of her elbow. "How many of these on her?"

"Sixteen total. Seven old, nine new. It happened before, which is why you were called. She was unconscious." Franciscus had folded his arms and was looking down at the dead girl.

"If her blood loss was as heavy as I think it might have been, no wonder she was out cold." He bent over the girl and examined the wound at the elbow. "What kind of creature makes bites like this? Or is this one of the new torture cults at work?"

"The wounds were made by a vampire; a very sloppy and greedy one," Franciscus stated surely.

"Oh, for the love of God, don't joke!" Jorry Fitzallen snapped. "I'll have to notify the county about this at once. The sheriff and the medical examiner should be alerted." He was inspecting two more of the bites now, one on the curve of her ribs and one just above her hip. "They're not deep. She shouldn't have bled like this."

Franciscus was silent.

"This is going to take a while," Jorry said, rather remotely. "I'm going to have to be very thorough. Will you give the ambulance service in Red Well a call. Tell them it isn't urgent, but they better bring a cold box."

"Of course," Franciscus said, grateful for the dismissal. There were too many things he had to do for him to spend more time with the Kiowa physician.

The Harpers left the next morning, and so did the Barneses, though they had done little but sit in their cabin and play table tennis in the recreation hall.

"She was so close to us," said Mr. Barnes, who had been in the first cabin on the eastern trail. He looked about nervously, as if he thought that death might be lurking around the registration desk.

"I quite understand," Mr. Rogers assured him, and handed him the accounting of the elderly couple's brief stay.

"How many have checked out this morning?" Madelaine asked when the lobby was empty. She had been standing at the mezzanine, watching Mr. Rogers.

186

"Dr. Muller, the Barneses, the Harpers, Amanda Farnsworth and the Lindholms. As Martha so correctly pointed out, a man with a heart condition does not need to be distressed, and the events of the last two days are distressing." He had closed the huge, leather-bound register.

"But Lorpicar is still here," Madelaine said, her violet eyes brightening with anger.

"Apparently. No one has seen him. He hasn't checked out. He could have decamped without bothering to settle his account, and that would be quite acceptable to me," Mr. Rogers said austerely, but with an understated familiarity.

The lobby doors by the foyer opened and Jim Sutton strode into the room. "Have either of you seen Harriet?" he asked anxiously.

"No, not since breakfast," Mr. Rogers answered. "Miss Montalia?"

"Not this morning."

Jim sighed, tried to look irritated and only succeeded in looking worried. "She was talking some nonsense about that Lorpicar whacko. She said that she could figure out where he was hiding if she could only figure out what his guilt-patterns are. What a time to start thinking like a shrink!" He started toward the door and turned back. "If Franciscus comes in, ask him if he's seen her. It's crazy, I know," he went on in a voice that ached to be reassured. "It's because of that girl. You'd think I'd be used to bizarre deaths by now, wouldn't you? But with Harriet trying to prove a point, damn her . . ." He pushed the door open and was gone.

"Where's the Comte?" Madelaine asked Mr. Rogers quietly.

"Searching the cabins on the north end of the lake. He's already done the southern ones." His face showed no emotion, but he added, "I thank you."

Madelaine tossed her head. "I'll tell him. He likes Harriet." She was down the stairs and almost to the doors. "So do I."

"Next we'll have Mrs. Emmons out skulking in the bushes!" Franciscus burst out when Madelaine had told him about Harriet. "Why couldn't she have waited a bit?"

"For the same reason you didn't, probably," Madelaine said with a sad, amused smile.

He touched her face, a gesture of infinite longing. "I do

187

love you, my heart. The words are nothing. But now, they are all we can share." He took her in his arms briefly, his face pressed against her hair. She was only half a head shorter than he and she was so lonely for him that she gave a little cry, as if in remembered pain.

"Why not you, when I love you best?" she protested.

"You know the answer. It is not possible when you and I are of the same blood. Before, well, since we do not die, we must find our paradise here on earth, and for a time it was ours. My dearest love, believe this. We have had our heaven together. And our hell," he added, thinking back to the desolation of war.

Their kiss was brief and intense, as if each feared to make it longer. It was Madelaine who stood back. "We have not found Harriet," she reminded him.

"And we must do that, if we are to prevent another tragedy." He agreed promptly, taking her hand. "You know what we are looking for. Undoubtedly he will have his box of earth somewhere near."

"And if he has treated Harriet to the same brutality that he gave Emillie?" Madelaine asked gently.

Franciscus tried for humor. "Well, we won't be able to keep Jim Sutton from filing a story on it."

"Don't mock, Saint-Germain."

He sighed. "If he has, we must be very, very cautious. We must be so in any case." He stopped in the open door of the empty cabin. "I don't want to sell this place. I like it here. These mountains remind me of my home, and the life is pleasant. I suppose it is wisest, though."

Madelaine touched his arm. "She may be all right. And a girl like Emillie . . . there will not be too many questions asked. You need not give up Lost Saints Lodge."

"Perhaps." He shook off the despondency. "I'll take the west side of the trail and you take the east. We should be able to do all the cabins in half an hour."

Harriet was on the floor of a tool shed near the stable. There were savage discolorations on her throat and wrists, and one of the rips in her skin still bled sluggishly.

"Good God," Madelaine said in disgust. "Hasn't that man any sense?"

"The evidence is against it," Franciscus said wryly. He bent to pick up Harriet. "She'll come out of it, but I think we'd better hold her in the Lodge. There's a room behind

188

my . . . workshop where I've got a bed. Jorry Fitzallen can check her over."

"And what will he say?" Madelaine asked, not able to conceal her anxiety.

"My dear, Jorry Fitzallen is a Kiowa. He will be very circumspect. Last year there was a shamanistic killing which he attributed to snakebite, which, if you stretch a point, was true." He carried Harriet easily, as if she were little more than a child. "You'd best make sure that there is no one on the trail. I would not like to have any more rumors flying than we already have to contend with."

Jim Sutton had turned first pale, but now his face was flushed and he stammered as he spoke. "If I get m-my hands on that b-bastard . . ."

"You will endanger yourself and Harriet needlessly," Franciscus said sharply. "It won't work, Jim. It's much better that you stay with Harriet—she will be grateful, you know—than that you waste your energy running around the hills looking for this man."

The room off what Franciscus called his workshop was spartanly simple. There was a narrow, hard captain's bed, a simple writing table, and a chair. On the wall were three paintings, two of unremarkable subjects and talents, one, clearly by a more skilled hand, showed a rough-visaged Orpheus lamenting his lost Eurydice.

"This is yours?" Jim Sutton asked as he glanced around. Now that the shock of seeing Harriet had lessened, he was intrigued by his surroundings.

"Yes."

"It's damned austere," he said uncomfortably.

"I prefer it," Franciscus responded.

"That *Orpheus* looks something like a Botticelli," he remarked after staring at it a little while.

"It does, doesn't it?" Franciscus drew the single chair up to the bed where Harriet lay. "Come, sit down. She'll be awake by sunset. I'll have Frank send in an occasional double Cruzan." He waited while Jim Sutton reluctantly sat down. "I would recommend that you open the door only to me and Mr. Rogers. It's true that Lorpicar hasn't been found, but there is a possibility"—he knew it was, in fact, a certainty—"that Lorpicar may try to find Harriet to . . . finish what he started."

Jim Sutton's eyes were too bright. "I'll kill him," he vowed.

"Will you." Franciscus looked at the reporter. "Harriet needs your help. Leave Lorpicar to me."

"You?" There was polite incredulity in his expression.

"I know what I am up against, my friend. You don't. And in this instance, a lack of knowledge might be fatal." He bent over Harriet, his dark eyes keen. "She will recover. I don't think there will be any serious aftereffects."

"God, I hope not," Jim Sutton said quite devoutly.

Franciscus almost smiled. "I'll send you word when we've found Lorpicar. Until then, if you want to stay here, fine. If you'd rather leave, it would be best if you let Mr. Rogers know so that someone else can stay with Harriet."

"Then she isn't safe yet?" he said, catching at Franciscus' sleeve.

"She, herself, is not in any great danger. But Lorpicar is another matter, and he may still try to reach her." He wanted to be certain that Jim Sutton did not underestimate the risk involved. "Harriet is all right now, but if Lorpicar has another go at her . . ."

"Oh, shit." Jim rubbed his face. "The world is full of psychos. I swear it is."

Franciscus said nothing, but before he closed the door, he saw Jim Sutton take Harriet's unresisting hand between his own.

There was little conversation at dinner, though Kathy had outdone herself with the food. Guests drank more heavily than usual, and Nick Wyler had offered to stand guard on the porch with a shotgun, but Mr. Rogers had quickly put an end to that idea, much to the relief of the other guests. By the time the dining room was empty much of the fear had been dispelled, though Mrs. Emmons had declared that she would not sleep a moment for fear she would be the next victim.

Frank kept the bar open until eleven, and Mr. Franciscus sat at the harpsichord in the lounge, playing music no one noticed. But even the most intrepid guests were touched by fear, and the last group bought a bottle of bourbon and left together, taking comfort from the drink and familiar faces.

"You going to bed, Franciscus?" the bartender called as he finished closing out the register for the evening.

"In a while. Don't mind me." He was playing a Scarlatti sonata now. "Turn off the lights when you go."

The bartender shrugged. "Whatever you say."

Half an hour later, Franciscus sat alone in the dark. The harpsichord was silent. The last pan had rattled in the kitchen some time before and the tall clock in the lobby sounded oddly muffled as its St. Michael's chimes tolled the quarter hour.

An errant breeze scampered through the lounge and was gone. Franciscus waited, alert, a grim, sad curve to his lips.

There was a soft tread in the dining room, the whisper of cloth against cloth, the quiet squeak of a floorboard.

The lounge, at an oblique angle to the foyer and separated from the lobby by an arch, was not touched by the single light that glowed at the registration desk, and the soft footfalls turned to the lounge from the dining room, seeking the haven of darkness.

When the steps were halfway across the room, Franciscus snapped on the light over the keyboard. It was soft, dispelling little of the night around it, but to the black-cloaked figure revealed on the edge of its luminescence, it glowed bright as the heart of a star.

"Good evening, Mr. Lorpicar," Franciscus said.

"You!"

Franciscus watched the tall man draw back, one arm raising as if to ward off a blow. "You've seen too many Hammer films," he remonstrated gently.

Milan Lorpicar chose to ignore this remark. "Do not think to stand in my way."

"Far too many," Franciscus sighed.

Mr. Lorpicar had been treated with fear, with hysteria, with abject adoration, with awe, but never with amused tolerance. He straightened to his full, considerable height. "You cannot stop me."

"But I can, you know." He had not moved from the piano bench. His legs were crossed at the ankle and his neat black-and-white clothes were relieved by a single ruby on a fine silver choker revealed by the open collar of his white silk shirt. Short, stocky, compact, he did not appear to be much of a threat, and Mr. Lorpicar sneered.

"You may try, Franciscus." His posture, his tone of voice, the tilt of his head all implied that Franciscus would fail.

The muted sounds of the lobby clock striking the hour caught the attention of both men in the lounge.

"It is time. I cannot stay," Mr. Lorpicar announced.

"Of course you can," Franciscus replied. He had still

191

not risen, and he had maintained an irritatingly civil attitude. "I can't permit you to go. You have been a reckless, irresponsible barbarian since you came here, and were before, I suspect. But you need not compound your mistakes." A steely note had crept into his voice, and his dark eyes regarded the tall man evenly. There was no trace of fear in him.

Mr. Lorpicar folded his arms. "I will not tolerate your interference, Franciscus."

"You have that wrong," Franciscus said with a glittery smile. "I am the one who will not tolerate interference. You've killed one person here already and you are trying to kill another. I will not allow that."

With a terrible laugh, Mr. Lorpicar moved toward the arch to the lobby. "The woman is in the building. I feel it as surely as I felt the power of night at sunset. I will have her. She is mine."

"I think not." Franciscus raised his left hand. He held a beautiful eighteenth-century dueling pistol.

"You think that will stop me?"

"Would you prefer crucifixes and garlic?"

"If you know that, you know that bullets cannot harm me," Mr. Lorpicar announced as he started forward.

"Take one more step and you will learn otherwise." There was sufficient calm command in Franciscus' manner that Mr. Lorpicar did hesitate, regarding the shorter man with icy contempt.

"I died," he announced, "in eighteen-ninety-six."

"Dear me." He shook his head. "No wonder you believe all that nonsense about garlic and crucifixes."

Now Mr. Lorpicar faltered. "It isn't nonsense."

Franciscus got to his feet. He was a full ten inches shorter than Milan Lorpicar, but he dominated the taller, younger man. "And these last—what?—eighty-four years, you have learned nothing?"

"I have learned the power of the night, of fear, of blood." He had said it before and had always found that the reaction was one of horror, but Franciscus merely looked exasperated.

"God save us all," he said, and as Mr. Lorpicar shrank back at his words, he burst out, "Of all the absurdities!"

"We cannot say . . . that name," Mr. Lorpicar insisted.

"Of course you can." He sat down again, though he did not set the pistol aside. "You're a menace. Oh, don't take that as a compliment. It was not intended as one."

192

"You do not know the curse of this life-in-death." He made an effort to gain mastery of the situation, and was baffled when Franciscus laughed outright.

"None better." He looked at Mr. Lorpicar. "You've been so involved with your posturing and pronouncements that you have not stopped to think about what *I* am." He waited while this sunk in.

"You walk in the daylight . . ." Mr. Lorpicar began.

"And I cross running water. I also line the heels and soles of my shoes with my native earth." He saw the surprise on Mr. Lorpicar's features deepen. "I handle crucifixes. And I know that anything that breaks the spine is deadly to us, so I remind you that a bullet, hitting between the shoulderblades, will give you the true death."

"But if you're vampiric . . ." Mr. Lorpicar began, trying to frame an appeal.

"It means nothing. Any obligation I may have to those of my blood doesn't extend to those who do murder." It was said pragmatically, and for that reason alone Mr. Lorpicar believed him. "You're an embarrassment to our kind. It's because of you and those like you that the rest of us have been hunted and hounded and killed. Pray don't give me your excuses." He studied the tall cloaked figure at the edge of the light. "Even when I was young, when I abused the power, this life-in-death as you call it, I did not make excuses. I learned the folly of that quickly."

"You mean you want the women for yourself," Mr. Lorpicar said with cynical contempt.

"No. I don't take those who are unwilling." He heard Mr. Lorpicar's incredulous laugh. "It isn't the power and the blood, Mr. Lorpicar," he said, with such utter loneliness that the tall man was silenced. "It is the touching. Terror, certainly, has a vigor, but it is nothing compared to loving."

"Love!" Mr. Lorpicar spat out the word. "You've grown maudlin, Franciscus." He heard the chimes mark the first quarter hour. "You can't do this to me." There was a desperate note in his voice. "I must have her. You know the hunger. I must have her!"

Franciscus shook his head. "It's impossible."

"I want her!" His voice had grown louder and he moved toward the arch once more.

"Stop where you are!" Franciscus ordered, rising and aiming.

Before he could fire there was the crack of a rifle and

193

Mr. Lorpicar was flung back into the lounge to thrash once or twice on the floor.

Aghast, Franciscus looked toward the lobby, and saw in the dimness that Jim Sutton was standing outside the inconspicuous door to the workshop, a .22 in his hand.

"How long have you been there?" Franciscus asked after he knelt beside Mr. Lorpicar.

"Long enough to know to aim for the neck," was the answer.

"I see."

"I thought vampires were supposed to melt away to dust or something when they got killed," Jim Sutton said between pants as he dragged the body of Milan Lorpicar up the trail toward cabin 33.

Franciscus, who had been further up the trail, said quietly as he came back, "One of many misconceptions, I'm afraid. We can't change shape, either."

"Damn. It would be easier to lug the body of a bat up this hill." He stood aside while Franciscus picked up the dead man. It was awkward because Mr. Lorpicar was so much taller than he, but he managed it well. "I don't think I really accept this," he added.

"There aren't any more occupied cabins from here to 33," Franciscus said, unwilling to rise to Jim Sutton's bait.

"What are you going to do?" he asked, giving in.

"Burn the cabin. Otherwise there would be too many questions to answer." He wished it had not happened. As much as he had disliked Lorpicar himself, and abhorred his behavior, he did not want the man killed.

"Why's that?" The reporter in Jim Sutton was asserting himself.

"Autopsies are . . . inadvisable. There's too much to explain."

Jim considered this and sighed. "I know this could be the biggest story of my career, but I'm throwing it away."

They had reached the last, isolated cabin. "Why do you say that?" He shifted Mr. Lorpicar's body. "The keys are in my left hip pocket."

As Jim retrieved them, he said, "Well, what the hell? Who'd believe me anyway?" Then stood aside and let Franciscus carry Mr. Lorpicar into his cabin.

"How'd that fire get started in the first place—that's what I want to know!" Ranger Backus demanded as he

194

and four volunteers from the Lost Saints Lodge guests stood around the smoking ruin of cabin 33.

"I don't know," Mr. Rogers said. "I thought that Mr. Lorpicar had been out of the cabin for two days."

"You mean this is the fellow you had us looking for?" The ranger was tired and angry and the last thing in the world he wanted on his hands was another mystery.

"Yes. Mr. Franciscus and Mr. Sutton saw him briefly earlier this evening. They suggested that he should avoid the Lodge for a time because of this unpleasant business with the dead Harper girl." He gave a helpless gesture. "The fireplace was inspected last month. The stove was checked out. The . . . remains—" he looked toward the cabin and the mass of charred matter in the center of it— "It appears he was asleep on the couch."

"Yeah," Ranger Backus said disgustedly. "Probably smoking, and fell asleep and the couch caught on fire. It happened in Red Well last year. Damn dumb thing to do!" He rubbed his brow with his forearm. "The county'll probably send Fitzallen out to check the body over. Lucky for you this fellow didn't die like the girl."

"Yes," Mr. Rogers agreed with sincerity.

"You ought to warn your guests about smoking in bed," Ranger Backus persisted.

"Yes." Then Mr. Rogers recalled himself. "Backus, it's almost dawn, and our cook will be up soon. If you'd give the Lodge the chance to thank you for all you've done, I'd be very grateful."

The big man looked somewhat mollified. "Well . . ."

It was Jim Sutton who clinched the matter. "Look, Ranger Backus, I'm a reporter. After what I've seen tonight, I'd like to get your impression of what happened."

Ranger Backus beamed through his fatigue, and admitted, "Breakfast would go good right now, and that's a fact."

Harriet Goodman was pale but otherwise herself when she came to check out the next morning.

"We're sorry you're leaving," Mr. Rogers said as he handed back her credit card.

"So am I, Mr. Rogers," she said in her forthright way, "but since Jim asked me to go to Denver while he covers the trial and there's that conference in Boulder . . ."

"I understand." He paused and asked with great delicacy, "Will you want cabin 21 next year?"

"I . . . I don't think so," she said slowly. "I'm sorry, Mr. Rogers."

"So are we, Ms. Goodman," he replied.

"I'll carry your bags, Harriet," Franciscus said as he stepped out of the library.

"You don't have to," she said bracingly, but with a slight hesitation. "Jim's . . ."

". . . waiting at the car." He came down the stairs toward her. "If nothing else, let me apologize for putting you in danger." He picked up the three pieces of luggage.

"You don't have to," she said, rather remotely. "I never realized that . . ." She stopped, using the opening door as an excuse for her silence.

Franciscus followed her down the steps. "Harriet, you have nothing to fear. This isn't rabies, you know. One touch doesn't . . . condemn you to . . ."

She stopped and turned to him. "And the dreams? What about the dreams?" Her eyes were sad, and though the questions were meant as accusations, they sounded more like pleas.

"Do you know Spanish?" He saw her baffled nod. *"Y los todos están sueños; Y los sueños sueño son.* I think that's right."

" 'And everything is dreams; and the dreams are a dream.' " She stared at him.

"The poet was talking about life, Harriet." He began to walk once more. "You have nothing to fear from me."

She nodded. "But I'm not coming back next year."

He was not surprised. "Nor am I."

She turned to him. "Where will you go?"

"Oh, I don't know. Madelaine wants to see Paris. I haven't lived there regularly for a while." He nodded toward Jim Sutton, who stood by his three-year-old Porsche.

"How long a while?" Harriet inquired.

He paused and waited until she looked him full in the face. "One hundred eighty-six years," he said.

Her eyes flickered and turned away from him. "Goodbye, Franciscus. If that's your name."

"It's as good as another," he said, and they came to the car. "Where do you want the bags?"

"I'll take care of them," Jim Sutton said. "You'll see that her rental car is returned?"

"Of course." He held out his hand to Harriet. "You have meant a lot to me."

She took it without reluctance but without enthusiasm.

"But there's only one Madelaine." There was only disappointment in her words—she was not jealous.

Franciscus shook hands with Jim Sutton, but spoke to Harriet. "That's true. There is only one Madelaine." He held the car door for her as she got in. "But then," he added, "there is only one Harriet."

Then he slammed the door and turned away; and Jim Sutton and Harriet Goodman watched him go, a neat, black-clad figure moving with easy grace through the long slanting bars of sunlight.

Text of a letter from le Comte de Saint-Germain to Madelaine de Montalia.

654 Rue de Janvier
Paris, France
24 December, 1981

c/o the Department of Antiquities
Marsden Expedition
La Paz, Bolivia

Madelaine, my heart:

Very well, very well, I am willing to try—perhaps you are right, after all. There is certainly sufficient love between us if love is enough without life: an ocean and a continent away from you and still I feel your tread, a tremor that speeds along the veins of the earth to me. Nothing will ever diminish it, or could; not disappointment, nor sorrow, nor separation, nor, I think, the true death itself. If our attempt is not successful, nothing will have been lost, and you must not believe that it would be. Whatever comes of this, my love is the same.

That you exist is all my love asks of you; the rest is added riches, and in you, I have a treasure beyond any other.

Saint-Germain
his seal, the eclipse

MY FAVORITE ENIGMA:

The Historical Comte de Saint-Germain
Essay

"IT is not surprising that the English can discover nothing of the true origins of the Count Saint-Germain," wrote the Prime Minister of England in 1749, "for England has no secret police. However, the French can learn nothing of him, either, and they have the most efficient secret police in the world."

The Prime Minister was not alone in his perplexity. His letter echoes statements of many other men and women of his time. There was endless puzzlement about the intelligent, well-traveled, and cultured stranger in all the courts of Europe. It was not as if le Comte de Saint-Germain was inconspicuous or retiring—quite the contrary. He was a prominent figure for about forty years and no one ever unraveled his mystery, which apparently delighted him.

To the Baron von Gleichen, who had mentioned the rumors circulating in France, that le Comte was many centuries old, Saint-Germain gave the following equivocal answer: "It amuses me to allow it to be believed that I have lived in ancient times. The Parisians imagine that I am five hundred years old, and I encourage them in that thought, because it pleases me and them. Of course, I am really far older than I look." Von Gleichen adds in his memoirs that after reflection, he realized that Saint-Germain had given him no useful information at all, and he found himself in sympathy with the bewildered Frenchmen.

Two of those Parisians left descriptions of le Comte. Madame du Hausset recalled him in her memoirs thus: "Le Comte seemed to be forty years old, or perhaps a trifle more; well-made and deep chested, he was neither corpulent nor thin; he had a fine wry countenance and always appeared to advantage. His taste in clothes was extremely simple, restricted for the most part to garments of black and white. Once he appeared at a court gala with shoe-buckles and garters thickly studded with diamonds . . . It is not known by anyone where the extraordinary wealth of this man originated. The King [Louis XV] would not tolerate any condescending or mocking talk about M. le Comte, and was often closeted with him in his laboratory." Madame de Genlis confirms these impressions in *her* memoirs: "He [Saint-Germain] was somewhat below middle size, well-proportioned, and strong, and very active in his movements. His hair was dark, nearly black; his complexion olive. His humorous and intelligent face was expressive of talent. He had the most remarkable eyes, profoundly dark and of a most penetrating character, so that it seemed he could read the very souls of all who met him. He spoke French elegantly with a little accent, and likewise English, Italian, Spanish, German, and Portuguese. He was also said to converse in Latin and Greek. He was an excellent musician and could accompany any song on the harpsichord *extempore,* and with a perfection that astonished Philidor, as much as his style of preluding. He often entertained us with impromptu works played at the keyboard, on the violin, or the guitar."

Casanova met him on at least three occasions, and did not like him at all. When news of Saint-Germain's "death" reached him, he remarked in his memoirs that it was learned that the imposter Saint-Germain was *really* the violinist Giovannini. The composer Rameau concluded that Saint-Germain was *really* the musician Balletti. Astonishingly enough, there is some evidence that suggests both Casanova and Rameau were correct.

Not the least mystifying aspect of the mysterious Comte de Saint-Germain was his long list of aliases. In the Netherlands, for instance, when it was learned that le Comte had invested a large amount of money in a particular firm that owned a foundry as well as making dredging equipment, the government required him to sell off his shares in the business because, being a foreigner, he was not allowed to have so much money invested in an industry that might be militarily critical to the Netherlands. Saint-Germain complied at once, and the government was satisfied, as they never learned that the man who bought Saint-Germain's share of the business was, in fact, another of le Comte's aliases. In his lifetime, he admitted to having more than twenty aliases in a dozen countries. How many he may have had beyond that is impossible to guess.

He was an alchemist, a mystic, a composer, and a patron of the arts. He entertained elegantly, lived conspicuously well, traveled everywhere, and was received by the most august figures eagerly. There are four and possibly five literary works attributed to him, though only one poem, in *Poèmes Philosophiques sur l'homme* (Paris, 1795), is known to have come truly from his pen. The other titles are questionable. He was Anton Mesmer's teacher for three or four years. He hobnobbed with all the major noble, political, artistic, academic, and mystical figures of his day. And he remained a mystery.

He claimed to speak over thirty languages, and though this figure was not put to the test, there is hard evidence that he spoke more than a dozen. He was fluent in all the European languages, including Polish (he served as Polish translator for Frederick the Great) and Czech (he translated dispatches intercepted by French couriers). He most certainly had Russian (translations into Italian), Greek (more translations and conversations), Arabic and Turkish (translations for an Austrian nobleman with whom he stayed as a guest in 1755 or 1756), Swedish (he spoke with the ambassador to the Prussian court), and several Balkan dialects. When writing songs, he preferred to set the music to Italian or English lyrics, claiming that they were more musical languages than French.

In occult circles it is generally accepted that Saint-Germain was the son of the Prince of Transylvania, Francis (or Franz or Ferenc) Ragoczy (or Rakoczi), whose fortune were varied, but who lost his title, lands, rights, and crown before the end of his life. His family was exiled and two of his children were taken into the "protection" of the Hapsburgs. The third child (either the eldest or youngest, depending on which school you favor) was "lost" and therefore assumed to have been Saint-Germain.

Piecing together the few solid bits of information about this man (and there are comparatively few for a man who led so public a life), I have come up with what I think

201

may have been the background of this brilliant, elusive man.

First, as to nationality, I believe he was Czech: his face was occasionally described as Slavic, and his skill with languages suggests an Eastern European background and education. In the western part of Europe there was no particular reason to learn Russian, Polish, Hungarian, Greek, or Turkish; in Eastern Europe there was real necessity for a polyglot fluency. His broad and well-developed knowledge of music, letters, and art makes it unlikely that he was Hungarian because at that time the political situation in Hungary was such that few children and young people received instruction in music and art beyond the most rudimentary levels. Saint-Germain was not only talented, but very well trained; his virtuoso accomplishments were not the result of catch-as-catch-can studies.

Saint-Germain was intimately familiar with the traditions and rituals of the Orthodox Church as well as with those of the Roman Catholic Church, which again suggests Eastern European beginnings. Although he was familiar with the occult disciplines of the Kabbalah, Saint-Germain did not appear to have any deep understanding of Jewish traditions and regular religious practices, which seems to indicate that he was not (as was often suspected during his lifetime) a Jew, Wandering or otherwise. Hebrew was not among those languages which he spoke easily, although he was able to read it, which re-enforces this conclusion.

Because of the ease with which Saint-Germain and his various aliases moved through European financial capitals and institutions, I believe he had a background in commerce. I think he came from a very upper-level merchant's family, and as the most monetarily successful group of merchants dealt in jewels, and Saint-Germain himself was famous for the number and quality of his jewels, it appears possible that he came from a family of Czech jewel merchants. The quality of his education supports this. In the eighteenth century, the children of well-to-do jewel merchants and those dealing in other rare substances (exotic fabrics, woods, and spices, primarily) often received education at least on a par with the nobility, and were generally more highly motivated to expand their studies than those of superior social classes. The son of a merchant would wish to prepare himself to travel extensively on business, to be pleasant company, and to excel at social graces for the benefit of business. Saint-Germain's interest in occult and alchemical studies is consistent with this background, for jewel merchants often sponsored such experimentation in the hope that the means to make artificial but genuine jewels would be discovered.

But why would the son of a wealthy Czech diamond merchant want to baffle most of the European nobility for nearly forty years? Probably for no more complicated reason than simple enjoyment. He often admitted that he took great delight in watching the investigators of various countries and governments try to discover his "true" identity. He threw out tantalizing clues that led nowhere, or contradicted others he had offered at an earlier time. From one or two of his recorded remarks, it is apparent that he knew very well what he was doing, and found the confusion that resulted from these mendacities quite enjoyable.

Assuming that he was in fact not forty but in his mid-twenties when he first came to France in 1743, he would have been in his mid-sixties at the time of his supposed death in 1786. That he was able to disguise his age effectively is not especially surprising, as at that time both men and women used cosmetics, and it was comparatively simple to change one's appearance to seem somewhat older. In a youth-oriented culture it is not easy to understand why he would wish to do so, but the society of the French court, and indeed all European courts, was not enamored with youth for youth's sake. To say that he was in his mid-forties, or to let it be assumed that he was, would make Saint-Germain's position and claims more credible. A Magus of twenty-five is rather silly, but an experienced, well-traveled man of the world, approaching middle-age, is another matter entirely. He was a man to be trusted and confided in. As a merchant's son, he would have had the opportunity for travel that might not be available to the children of noble houses in such troubled times as the first half of the eighteenth century. Assuming he began to go on journeys in his early teens, which was fairly common among rich merchants' heirs, he would have had at least ten years of international travel behind him by the time he arrived in Paris in the spring of 1743.

At one time or another during his years at various European courts, he attended meetings of Kabbalistic, Rosicrucian, and Masonic Lodges. He was well regarded by all those groups, and his studies were taken seriously. He was also interested in all aspects of technology. At one time he advanced quite a good deal of money to a man in Amsterdam who had invented a steam dredge for clearing silted-up canals (that was before he had to sell off his foundry shares). On another occasion he financed a project to develop a more stable spring-and-shock-absorber device for carriages. Both ventures were fairly successful. He was believed during his lifetime to be a partner in at least three importing companies, and the Italians thought the figure was higher than that.

Saint-Germain's "death" occurred under highly suspicious circumstances—he was alone but for servants at a friend's isolated château. When he "died", his body either disappeared mysteriously, or had to be buried at once for fear of infection, depending on which of the two most prevalent stories you wish to believe. Yet he was seen by those who had known him several times after his "death", and in one instance aided a few aristocratic friends to escape from the guillotine in 1793. The noble family he aided said afterward, when they had reached Germany, that they had traveled part of the way with the courier for a firm of jewel merchants.

The last authentic contact with Saint-Germain was in Genoa in 1802, when a French military officer saw him at the palazzo of one of the Genovese noblemen. At the time, Saint-Germain said that he was about to embark to Egypt to further his occult studies. According to the French colonel, Saint-Germain sailed four days later, and that was the last anyone saw of him. However, it is curious to note that there is a persistent oral tradition in some of the higher occult circles in the Near East, that claims a very old and powerful European Magus died near Cairo in 1817. It is my personal conviction that the very old and powerful European Magus was Saint-Germain.

When I first began to develop the idea for the Saint-Germain cycle of novels back in 1972-3, I began researching the eighteenth century for *Hotel Transylvania*. At the time it was not my intention to use Saint-Germain as a vampire, but as a major secondary character, as I used Botticelli and Nero in later books. In the years I have studied occult subjects, I had become familiar with Saint-Germain and thought that he would be a colorful and ambiguous addition to an historical horror story. However, the more I read about him, the more convinced I became that I did not need to invent a vampire and juxtapose him with Saint-Germain: my vampire was already developed and available. He stood five-foot-six; wore black and white almost exclusively; rarely, if ever, ate or drank in public, though he often gave extravagant supper parties; was believed to have uncanny powers; claimed to be anything from two to four thousand years old; was a linguist and widely traveled; was enormously cultured; was a patron of the arts; was a great mystery. I took him at his highly equivocal word and assumed that all the various rumors he encouraged were true and went on from there. In the Saint-Germain cycle of books, the only thing I claim for Saint-Germain/Ragoczy that he did not claim for himself in his lifetime is vampirism, and since he said that he had achieved his great longevity by drinking the Elixir of Life, I doubt vampirism is stretching the point too far.

For those who are interested, I have constructed a biography for my vampiric Saint-Germain. He is about 4,000 years old, taking the most outlandish figure given by the historical man. He was born in the region now called Transylvania of proto-Etruscan stock. Because he was born at the dark of the year (the historical Saint-Germain told King Louis XV that his birthday was December 24th), he was initiated into the priesthood, which was vampiric, but before he died and changed, he was taken captive and made a slave. Some of this information appears in the novel *Path of the Eclipse*, which is fourth in the cycle.

My choice of proto-Etruscan background is not entirely capricious. Those of you who have seen Etruscan sarcophagi know that the Etruscan attitude about death and the afterlife was unique. Instead of lying in supine, shown in sleeping postures, or represented at profound religious rites, most Etruscans are depicted in very lively pursuits—eating, drinking, playing, making love. Since one arm of current academic thought tends to the theory that the Etruscans originated in the Carpathians and on the Hungarian plains, I found them irresistible for this character. The Etruscan representations of the afterlife seem so appropriate for the cycle of novels, and their possible early location so providential that I seized on them without apology.

Should you be interested in delving further into the background of the historical Saint-Germain, here are a few sources that might be of use to you:

Jacques Casanova de Seingalt, *Memoirs*
A. Cockren, *Alchemy Rediscovered and Restored*
Isabel Cooper-Oakley, *The Comte de Saint-Germain*
Madame la Comtesse de Genlis, *Memoirs*
Baron von Gleichen, *Memoirs*
Poèmes Philosophiques sur l'homme
Grove's Dictionary of Music and Musicians

If you are curious about Saint-Germain's music (which is not available in the United States) some of it is still extant and available with effort. A few titles are:

> *Musique Raisonée*
> *Six Sonatas for Two Violins with a Bass for the Harpsichord or Violoncello*
> *Seven Solos for a Violin*

I trust that le Comte de Saint-Germain, whoever he was, would find his affectionate transmogrification at my hands amusing and complimentary. Surely anyone who enjoyed baffling people as much as he did would be pleased to add one more bizzare attribute to his list. Without doubt he has given me six years of joy in his well-loved vampire persona, which is as good a way as any for him to continue his self-proclaimed immortality.

Le Comte de Saint-Germain: it has been an honor and a pleasure to know him.